To John, with love always.

Crowfield Abbey 1348

Eastfield

Westfield

Marshland beyond

Paddock

Shed

West door

Nave

Refectory

Barn

Kitchen

Shed/workshop

N

Abbey wall

Two Penny Copse

Sheep pasture

River

Old burial ground

North transept

Side Chapel

Chancel

Crossing (tower over)

Hazel coppice

New Orchard

Vegetable gardens

North alley

Chapter House

Cloister Garth

Warming room

Brother Snails hut

Dovecot

South alley

Infirmary

Flood meadow

Goats

Hens

Orchard

Store room (cellarium)

Peter's room

Pig pen

Gatehouse

Well

Stables

Wood Shed

Causeway

To Foxwist Wood

Southfield

Chapter One

March 1348

William put the pail of water on the bench beside the workshop door and blew into his cupped hands to warm them. The March morning was cold and a biting wind whipped the grey clouds across the sky. Rain fell steadily, as it had done for weeks past, filling ditches and puddles, and dripping from the reed thatch of Brother Snail's hut.

He heard a rustling in the blackthorn tree beside the hut. A twig dropped onto his head and he peered up through the branches. A long tail with a tuft of red fur on the end curved around the trunk of the tree. It twitched and flexed and suddenly flicked out of sight.

'Brother Walter?' William called. 'What are you doing up there?'

'Watching things,' the hob said softly.

William walked around the tree until he could see the hob sitting in the fork of a branch, his golden-green eyes wide and fierce as he stared out over the sheep pasture beyond the vegetable garden of the abbey. His fox-red fur was sleek with rainwater.

William peered into the misty distance but couldn't see anything to explain the hob's odd behaviour. 'What things?'

'Them,' said the hob, pointing to the far side of the pasture, towards Two Penny Copse, where a huddle of wet ewes and lambs sheltered beneath the low sweeping branches of the oak trees.

'The sheep?'

The hob shook his head impatiently. 'No, no, no. *Them.*'

William squinted through the rain. The hob's eyesight was sharper than his, and it took some moments before he saw what the hob was watching so intently. Crows perched beside twiggy nests, cawing into the wind as the trees swayed and creaked like ships at sea. And far below them, four of the strangest creatures William had ever seen were making their way hurriedly past the sheep. Hunched and wizened and no taller than a small child, they looked like little old men in tattered, dun-coloured clothing. They moved furtively, scurrying between the animals and the tree trunks, clearly anxious to stay hidden.

William caught his breath. 'What are *they?*'

'Mound elves,' the hob said. There was something in the tone of his voice that told William he didn't much like these creatures. 'They live inside grave mounds where humans have buried their dead long ago. Something must have frightened them very badly to make them come above ground in daylight.'

William watched as the creatures darted towards the thorn hedge marking the western boundary of the abbey's lands and disappeared from sight.

Why were they in such a hurry? What were they running away from? William looked uneasily across the sheep pasture towards the misty grey outline of Foxwist Wood. Something in the forest had frightened them.

What if it's him? William thought with a sudden shiver. *What if the Dark King has returned?*

The hob climbed down from the tree. He stood beside William for a few moments, his face sharp with anxiety. 'Something bad is coming,' he whispered.

William crouched down beside him. 'Is it the Dark King?'

'No,' said Brother Walter, edging a little closer to

him, 'not the king. Something much, *much* worse than him.'

'And it's in the forest?'

The hob nodded. 'It's close by, maybe in the forest, maybe here in the brother men's stone place. I don't know for sure, but I can *feel* it.'

With a last fearful glance, the hob hurried to the door of the hut and disappeared inside. William got to his feet. He trusted the hob's instincts. If something evil was stirring, then Brother Walter would sense it long before William did.

But if it wasn't the Dark King, what was it?

William trudged along the path through the abbey garden. The ground was sodden underfoot and water oozed up, soaking his boots. He reached the wattle gate and climbed over. It was easier than fiddling with the bit of wet rope which tied it closed.

Three monks emerged from the passageway between the abbey church and the chapter house. Their cowls were pulled up against the rain, hiding their faces, but William recognised tall, skinny Prior Ardo and plump little Brother Gabriel. The third monk was Brother Snail, small and hunch-backed. He trailed a little way behind his two companions as they walked around the east end of the church.

The prior saw William and called, 'Come here, boy.'

William broke into a run, jumping over puddles, and coming to a skidding halt in front of the monks. The prior frowned at William's muddy boots and hose. His expression was more than usually sour.

'Come with us,' the prior said. He turned and walked along the narrow path around to the north side of the church. Here the ground was rough and overgrown and permanently in the shadow of the huge building. It had been used as a burial ground by the first monks at Crowfield, but the abbey's dead were now buried in the graveyard behind the chapter house.

William walked along beside Brother Snail. 'Where are we going?'

Brother Snail pointed to a corner between two walls where a triangle of deep water reflected the rain clouds.

'Here?' William asked, glancing at the monk. 'Why?'

Brother Snail twisted his head and shoulders sideways so he could look up at the wall of the chancel. 'Because of *that*.'

William followed his gaze. A crack, wide enough to

fit his fist into, had split the stonework from the roof to the edge of one of the windows.

'It's wider than it was yesterday,' Brother Gabriel said anxiously. Raindrops collected on the end of his nose and he wiped them away with his sleeve. 'Perhaps if we drain the water . . .'

'It wouldn't make any difference,' the prior interrupted impatiently. 'It will just flood again. The ground on this side of the church has always been waterlogged.'

'But why has the wall started to crack apart *now*?' Brother Snail said. He spoke calmly but William saw the worried look in his eyes.

'Does it matter? That wall has probably been weakening for years,' the prior said.

'I'm sure it has, but it doesn't look as if the wall is sinking,' Brother Snail said slowly. 'It looks more like something is pushing it up from *under* the ground.'

An uneasy silence fell as William and the monks stared at the base of the wall. Brother Snail was right, William realised. There was a definite upward tilt to the rows of stone.

'But what could possibly be doing that?' Brother Gabriel asked, a quiver of panic in his voice.

'What indeed?' Brother Snail murmured.

'An underground spring?' William suggested.

'Quite possibly,' the prior said. 'But if the crack continues to grow, it could bring the wall down. We should move whatever we can out of the church, just in case. You, boy, go and fetch Shadlok. He can start taking the statues to safety. And then I want you to take a message to Sir Robert at Weforde.'

'Sir Robert?' William asked, mystified.

'He has stonemasons working on the manor house,' Brother Snail said. 'He might be kind enough to spare one to come and advise us.'

The prior's frown deepened. He didn't look pleased that one of his monks was taking time to explain such important matters to a servant boy. 'Don't just stand there,' he snapped. 'Do as you're told.'

William sprinted back around the end of the church, through the monks' graveyard and on past the hazel coppice. Shadlok had spent the last week clearing a patch of rough ground for a new orchard between the coppice and the sheep pasture. The old trees were giving less fruit with each passing year and the prior had decided it was time to start again on new ground.

Shadlok looked surprised to see him. He straightened up and rested his hands on his spade. Rainwater dripped from the ends of his long silver-white hair and soaked the shoulders and back of his dark green tunic. 'You are going the wrong way,' he said, and nodded to the abbey buildings. 'The kitchen is over there. Isn't that where you are supposed to be?'

'The prior sent me to fetch you. He has work for you in the church.'

Shadlok went very still. There was a strange look in his pale blue eyes as he stared at William. 'In the church?'

William nodded. 'He thinks the chancel wall is in danger of falling down and he wants you to move whatever you can out of harm's way.'

Shadlok's long fingers gripped the spade handle tightly. 'It is not a place I care to go near.'

'Why not?'

Shadlok pulled the spade from the ground and turned away. 'I have my reasons.'

William stood for a few moments, not sure what to do. He didn't relish the prospect of telling the prior that Shadlok had refused to come.

'There'll be trouble,' William said with a helpless shrug. 'Prior Ardo expects his orders to be obeyed.'

Shadlok said nothing. He swung the spade into the ground and started to dig. William watched him in silence.

Shadlok glanced over his shoulder with a quick frown. 'Why are you still here?'

'I'm waiting for you to tell me why you won't go into the church. And I know it's not because you're a fay and you *can't*,' he added, 'because the hob goes in there all the time, even though I tell him not to.'

Shadlok straightened up and turned to face him. 'There is something in the building that I have no desire to go near.'

William didn't like the sound of this. 'Oh? What is it?'

'I do not know,' Shadlok said slowly. 'It is hidden from my sight.'

'The hob and I saw some mound elves this morning,' William said. 'They were crossing the sheep pasture, heading westwards. They were running away from something.'

'They are not the first fays to leave the forest in the last few days. I have seen others, all moving westwards. Something is waking . . .' the fay's voice trailed away and he turned to gaze at the rain-misted bulk of the abbey church with a frown. It was several moments before he spoke again. 'They sense a growing threat. I feel it too.'

'The hob said something evil is coming.'

'Perhaps it is already here,' Shadlok said grimly.

Was it a coincidence, William wondered, that Shadlok and the hob sensed the stirring of something evil near the church at the same time that a crack had begun to split apart the chancel wall? *Was* there something beneath the church, as Brother Snail believed, pushing its way up through the waterlogged ground? And if there was, why was it waking now?

Shadlok hefted the spade in his hand and turned away. 'You can tell the prior that I will not step inside the building. If he wants the statues moved, he will have to find someone else to do it.'

Chapter Two

The prior's bony nose was barely a hand's span from William's face.

'He said *what*?'

William swallowed. 'He said . . . no.'

Prior Ardo straightened up. His face was white with anger. William half expected him to turn in a whirl of black-robed fury and march off to find Shadlok, but the prior remained where he was. Perhaps he realised there was nothing he could do or say to force Shadlok to obey him. Shadlok wasn't a monk or a lay brother, so the prior's authority meant very little to him. He might work as a labourer, but he was no man's servant and the prior knew it.

William saw the uncertainty in the monk's eyes and almost felt sorry for him. The prior did not have the faintest idea why Shadlok had chosen to stay at Crowfield after the death of his master Jacobus Bone

– how could he? He didn't know that his taciturn new labourer was a great and noble fay warrior, or that Shadlok's fate was now tied to William's with bonds of deep magic that could only be broken by death.

'Very well,' Prior Ardo said at last. He stared at William for a couple of moments, his eyes cold and hard. 'Take word to Sir Robert of what has happened to the church. Tell him I would consider it a great favour if he would send one of his stonemasons to the abbey to look at the crack in the wall. Be as quick as you can.'

Brother Snail insisted on lending William his old woollen cloak for the journey. They walked to the workshop to fetch it.

'It's good and thick and will keep out the worst of the rain,' Brother Snail said, taking the cloak from a peg near the hut door and handing it to William. It smelled of wood smoke and old dried herbs and William wrapped it around his shoulders gratefully.

'Go quickly, Will, and be back here before dark. You don't need me to tell you it's not safe to be out in the forest by yourself after sunset.'

It probably wasn't much safer *before* sunset, William thought, but he just nodded. He decided not to mention the mound elves, or what the hob and

12

Shadlok had told him earlier. There was no sense in worrying the monk with talk of some nameless threat, when he had no choice but to do as the prior told him. He would keep to the track and hurry as fast as he could, there and back.

William tied the cloak firmly at the neck and arranged the cowl of his hood over his shoulders. The cloak was shorter on him than it was on Brother Snail, and it stopped just below his knees, but it would keep him warm and dry, something he rarely was these days.

'Just be careful, Will,' Brother Snail added, a trace of anxiety in his voice. He was clearly not happy that William was being sent out from the abbey by himself. 'We don't know when the Dark King might decide to come back to the forest, if indeed he ever left.'

There had been no hint or whisper of the Dark King's presence in Foxwist Wood for the last three months, not since the day William and Shadlok had dug up an angel in the Whistling Hollow and released it from the king's spell. But the king was a dangerous enemy. He would never forgive them for freeing the angel, or for rescuing the leper Jacobus Bone from the curse of immortality he had placed on him many years

13

ago. William knew it was just a matter of time before the king reappeared.

'Don't worry,' William said, sounding more confident than he felt, 'I'll be back before dark, if I have to run all the way.'

Brother Snail smiled and patted his shoulder. 'Good lad.'

They left the hut and, with a quick wave, the monk headed back to the abbey. William cut across the vegetable garden and past the goat pens to the abbey gateway. He glanced up at the shuttered windows of the two small chambers above the gate passage. They had been empty for years, apart from spiders' webs and nesting starlings, but the chambers were now Shadlok's quarters. William was sure the fay never used them, though where Shadlok went at night, and whether or not he actually slept, William had never discovered.

He let himself out of the abbey by the small wicket gate and crossed the wooden bridge over the river. He was alarmed to see the water lapping over the edge of the timbers. After weeks of rain the river had broken its banks and flooded the meadows below Foxwist Wood. On the abbey side, the restless brown water had now reached the fence running alongside the vegetable garden. And it was still rising.

The track beyond the bridge was raised up on a causeway built from hard-packed gravel and stone, to lift it above the flood meadow and up to the main Weforde to Yagleah trackway. Nevertheless a stretch of the causeway close to the river was under water. William's boots and the feet of his hose were wet through by the time he splashed his way up to drier ground. He sighed in exasperation as he watched water ooze out from a hole in the toe of one boot. It was going to be a long and uncomfortable walk to Weforde.

The track through the forest was ankle deep in mud, and puddles filled the cart ruts. William kept to the grass along the edge as much as possible. When he reached the rag-hung bushes which warned travellers that they were passing close by the Whistling Hollow, he quickened his pace, as he always did. The memory of searching for the grave of the angel in the Hollow was as vivid as if it had happened yesterday rather than three months ago. He felt a shiver of fear as he peered into the undergrowth. There was nothing to see or hear but William sensed something there, among the tangled branches, watching him. He suddenly felt very alone and vulnerable.

William broke into a run, and didn't slow down until the track dipped down into a wide glade of oaks and dead bracken and he could no longer see the bushes with their straggling wet rags. The rain had eased off for now, though the scudding clouds warned that it would only be a brief respite. He pushed back his hood and took deep breaths to steady the wild thump of his heart. Already he was dreading the return journey.

At the eastern edge of the forest, the track sloped down the side of a hill into a wide valley, in the middle of which lay Weforde, surrounded by its three large fields. The track cut across the West Field. Ruts and holes had been filled in with gravel and the ground here was drier. The field strips were different shades of green and brown, as the wheat sown last autumn grew between strips of fallow ground. Three young village boys charged up and down the grassy humps of the plough headlands, yelling and laughing as they scared the crows and pigeons from the fields with slingshots. William smiled and remembered when he had done the same thing at home in Iwele. It seemed a very long time ago now.

Wednesday was market day in Weforde. It was too early in the year for many traders to be there, and the few who were had been there since dawn or soon after. By now they were getting ready to pack up and start for home. On one edge of the green there were several animal pens made from wattle hurdles, but the buying and selling of livestock was finished and the pens were empty.

William liked Weforde market; he loved the bustle and the friendliness of the place. It was the only time he had the chance to mix with ordinary people and talk about everyday things. Best of all, there was always music. The two le Wyt brothers from Yagleah were usually there, playing the recorder and a pair of small drums, while Adam Shirford, the son of Sir Robert's reeve, would play his hurdy-gurdy and sing. People danced to the faster tunes, especially if they had spent a couple of hours in the alehouse first. They clapped along in time with the music or sang the often bawdy songs. William, keenly aware of Brother Gabriel's disapproval of such revelry, never joined in. Sometimes his body ached with the effort of not clapping or stamping to the beat of a lively tune, but he knew he would be punished by Prior Ardo for such ungodly behaviour if ever he did so.

Today someone was playing a flute, but it wasn't Adam or either of the le Wyt brothers. They were good, but this musician was so much better. William crossed the green to join a small crowd and listen for a few minutes. He didn't recognise the song, but the rippling notes set his toes tapping and hands clapping in time. For the past three months, Shadlok had been teaching him to play the flute Jacobus Bone had left him. He had a natural ability and Shadlok was pleased with his rapid progress, but he had a long way to go before he played with such skill. *If I ever learn to play like this,* William thought, *I will die happy.*

The people in front of William moved and he caught a glimpse of the musician. William had never seen him before. The youth was maybe a year or two older than he was. His face was thin and freckled and his greenish-brown eyes were deep-set and shadowed. His hair hung over his shoulders in damp red rats' tails. He finished the tune and smiled at the applause of the people around him. A handful of coins were thrown into the woollen hat at his feet and the crowd moved away. To William's surprise the boy did not even glance at the money.

'What were you playing?' William asked, stepping forward. 'I've never heard it before.'

The boy grinned at him. 'I made it up myself. Did you like it?'

'It was very good,' William said. '*Very* good.' The exciting thought occurred to him that perhaps one day he too would be able to make up his own music.

'People always want me to play old familiar tunes, dances and carols they've grown up listening to, but I like to play a song or two of my own.' The boy began to clean the inside of his flute with a rag on the end of a stick and glanced up with a smile. 'Can you tell me the way to Yagleah? Someone mentioned that Yagleah isn't far from Weforde, and I thought I would try my luck there.'

'That way,' William said, pointing towards the West Field, just visible between the village houses. 'Follow the track through the forest and past Crowfield Abbey. It's about two hours' walk.'

It might have been his imagination, but William thought he saw an odd flicker in the boy's eyes when he mentioned the abbey.

'Do you live in Weforde?' the boy asked, putting the flute into a linen bag and pulling the drawstring tight.

William shook his head. 'I live at the abbey.'

The boy's smile widened. His face was open and friendly and William smiled back. It wasn't often he had the chance to speak to someone of his own age.

'So you will be walking home through the forest

later?' the boy asked.

'Yes, but I have a message to give to Sir Robert at the manor first.'

'Then maybe we could walk together?' the boy asked hopefully.

'All right, yes,' William said with a quick smile. He did not have to face the journey home alone. It would be very good indeed to have company on the road.

The boy nodded and seemed pleased. 'Good. It's always safer to travel in numbers, even if that number is only two. My name is Robin, by the way.'

'I'm William Paynel. Where will I meet you?'

'I will be right here,' Robin said. He tucked the flute into the leather bag by his feet and folded his arms around his thin body. 'Take your time, I will wait.'

As William sprinted across the green and along the lane towards the manor house, his spirits soared. It seemed he had made a friend today. What made it even better was that Robin was a musician, and a fine one at that. They shared a common interest, and that was a rare thing in William's life these days.

Chapter Three

The village road led up to the gates of Sir Robert's demesne farm. A ditch and thorn hedge enclosed the barns, sheds and cattle yards. A track led to a timber gatehouse set into a high stone wall. Beyond it stood the manor house.

'Hoi! You!' someone called. William looked around and saw Edmund Maudit, the bailiff of the manor, standing in the doorway of a cart shed. He was a short, thickset man whose face seemed to be set in a permanent scowl. William had seen him around the village but had never spoken to him. 'What are you doing here, boy?'

'I have a message for Sir Robert from Prior Ardo at Crowfield Abbey.'

The bailiff walked over to him. 'And what would that message be?'

'The prior wants one of Sir Robert's stonemasons

to come and look at the wall of the church. He thinks it's in danger of falling down.'

Master Maudit looked a little startled by this. He wiped his grimy hands on his tunic and rolled down his sleeves. 'Well, we'd better go and see what's to be done about that. Come with me, and remember your manners in front of Sir Robert.'

William noticed the wary looks from people working around the farm as Master Maudit passed by. It was clear that they had a healthy respect for their bailiff.

'Gate!' Master Maudit yelled as they approached the gatehouse. William heard someone scrabbling around on the other side, and the heavy timber gate swung open. A young boy ducked his head to the bailiff as he strode past, but Master Maudit took no notice of him. Sir Robert's hunting dogs barked wildly as they passed the fenced run beside their kennel, making William jump.

Weforde manor house was a two-storey stone building with a tiled roof. There was a garden beside the house, a little maze of low turf walls and wooden archways over which the rambling stems of roses had been twisted and tied. An ancient mulberry tree grew in the middle of the garden, its sprawling boughs propped up with wooden staves.

William followed the bailiff around the end of the house, past the garden and through a gateway into a cobbled yard, which was surrounded on two sides by the stables, several storerooms and a barn. The manor house and a large newly-built wing formed the remaining sides of the yard. Glancing back at him, the bailiff said, 'Wait here.'

The new building looked very different from the old part of the house. The two upper-floor windows were tall and arched, reminding William of the ones at the abbey. The walls were lighter in colour and the stones were smaller and more carefully shaped. The roof was covered in red fired-clay tiles. It looked odd and out of place against the sturdy old manor house.

There were several men in the yard. William guessed they were the stonemasons. They wore leather aprons, and the tools laid out on trestle tables in an open-fronted shed were not quite like any he had seen before. There was a pile of stone at the far end of the yard and a stack of long thin timbers nearby. The cobbles were white with stone dust and the puddles looked like spilt milk. The stonemasons took no notice of William but went about their work in silence.

A few minutes later the bailiff returned. 'Sir Robert will see you. Wipe your boots over there before you come in,' he said, pointing to a patch of grass near the gateway. William did as he was told while Master Maudit waited for him with obvious impatience. When he'd scraped off the worst of the mud, William hurried across the yard and followed the bailiff into the house.

A wooden staircase led up to a doorway that had been hacked through the thick wall of the older building. The door stood ajar. The bailiff knocked and pushed it open.

'This is the boy from the abbey, my lord,' he said. He grabbed William's sleeve and pulled him forward. A man stood by the huge fireplace, his hands clasped behind his back. He was about William's height, slight of build and probably in his late forties. He had a thin, clean-shaven face beneath closely cropped grey hair, and an unmistakable air of authority.

'Come into the light, where I can see you properly.'

William walked further into the room and stood there awkwardly. The wooden floorboards were not covered with straw or rushes, but with brilliantly coloured and patterned pieces of cloth. They didn't look as if they'd been woven or embroidered and the surface of the fabric had a glossy sheen. He wondered why anyone would put such beautiful things on the floor for people to walk on. The toes of his boots touched the edge of one and he took a hasty step backwards.

'What's your name?'

'William Paynel, my lord,' he said, ducking his head in a quick bow.

'My bailiff tells me the abbey church is about to fall down, William. Is that so?'

'I . . . I don't know for sure. There's a crack in the chancel wall and the ground on that side of the church is under water. Prior Ardo is worried that the wall might collapse. He asked if you could spare a stone-mason to come and look at it.'

Sir Robert turned to the bailiff. 'Fetch Master Guillaume.'

The bailiff nodded and left the room.

'How long have you lived at the abbey?' Sir Robert asked, after regarding William in silence for several moments.

'Since the summer before last.'

'So you met Master Bone and his manservant last winter?'

William looked at the man warily. Of all the things

25

Sir Robert could have asked him, this was unexpected. 'Yes, my lord,' he said cautiously.

'I was told that the manservant, Shadlok, stayed at the abbey after Master Bone's death. Is that so?'

'Yes.' Why was Sir Robert interested in Shadlok?

Sir Robert was quiet for some moments. 'How does he fit in there? Amongst the holy brothers?'

'Well enough, my lord,' William said. He was feeling more uncomfortable by the moment.

'I would have said he had little in common with them.' The sharp grey eyes watched him closely.

William twisted his hands together behind his back and said nothing. Did Sir Robert somehow know that Shadlok was a fay? Did he suspect that William knew it too?

Sir Robert walked over to a window and folded his arms. He looked down at the courtyard behind the house and seemed to be lost in his thoughts. His dark tunic was sombre but even William could tell that the cloth was of the finest quality. There was a heavy silver buckle on his belt and he wore a gold ring on one finger. And he was *clean*, William noticed, clean from his carefully cut fingernails to his soft calfskin boots.

William glanced surreptitiously around the room. He had never dreamt that such luxury existed. More of the vividly coloured cloths hung on the walls, showing people on horseback hunting in forest glades. There were tables and chairs, chests and two large cupboards, all richly carved and gleaming in the light from the four narrow, arched windows. A closed door in the end wall was half hidden behind the folds of a wall cloth. On either side of the window embrasures seats were piled with embroidered cushions. A richly decorated candlestick, as tall as a man and made of silver, stood beside the huge fireplace.

What would it be like to live in such a house, William wondered. To look out of the window and know that everything you saw belonged to you?

Something caught William's eye and he gasped in surprise. On a table lay Jacobus Bone's lute. Sir Robert turned at the sound. He saw what William was looking at and frowned slightly.

'You recognise it?'

'It belonged to Master Bone,' William said hesitantly. *And he left it to me when he died, but Prior Ardo gave me the flute instead,* he added silently. *It is rightfully* mine.

Sir Robert walked over to the table and picked up the lute. He held it for a moment, his fingers spread over the strings, and then he began to pick out a tune with his thumb and forefinger.

William held his breath. His heart seemed to swell inside his chest as he listened to the music. The sound was as perfect as he had known it would be.

Sir Robert finished the tune and laid the lute carefully back down on the table. 'A fine instrument,' he said softly, his fingers gently stroking the golden wood.

The hollow thump of footsteps sounded on the staircase and the bailiff came into the room, closely followed by a tall, well-built man with sun-browned skin. The mason wore a leather apron and his sleeves were rolled up, revealing muscular forearms covered with thick black hair. He pulled off his woollen hat and stood in the doorway. There was a look of distaste on Sir Robert's face as his gaze flickered down to the mason's boots, caked with mud and stone dust.

William barely listened as Sir Robert explained the situation to Master Guillaume and arranged for the mason to visit the abbey the following day. Instead, he stared at the lute and remembered the sound it had made. He was filled with a strange hunger, an urge to grab it and run. It was a sin to covet another man's possessions, but sin or no sin, it should have been *his*. He glanced up at Sir Robert with a frown. The lord of

Weforde was a wealthy man with so many fine and valuable possessions already. Why should he have the lute as well, simply because he had money to buy it?

'Tell Prior Ardo that my master mason will be there first thing in the morning,' Sir Robert said, glancing at William. He turned his attention to a sheet of parchment on the table beside him and ignored the bowed heads of William and the two men.

The bailiff nudged William in the back and pushed him towards the doorway. William hurried down the staircase behind Master Guillaume. He stepped out into the yard and glanced up with a weary sigh. It had begun to rain again.

Chapter Four

When William reached the green, Robin wasn't there. He looked around in dismay, but he couldn't see the red-haired boy anywhere. With the market over and the rain falling steadily, there were few people about. William pulled up his hood and trudged across the muddy green, past the empty pinfold, and onto the lane through the village.

The breeze was picking up. It drove the low grey clouds across the sky and set the rain hard at William's back. As he passed the houses along the lane, he could hear the sounds of busy lives going on inside: voices, laughter, shouting, dogs barking. He could smell food cooking. In one small hut, someone was singing. In the crofts behind the houses, he glimpsed chickens and pigs sheltering from the rain. Only the geese and ducks around the pond on the green seemed to like the weather. William's spirits sank lower by the minute. It seemed as if everyone was safe and warm indoors while he still had the long and lonely walk through Foxwist ahead of him.

William wasn't paying attention to where he put his feet, and stepped into a deep puddle. Cold muddy water swamped one boot. Cursing under his breath, he pulled off his boot to tip out the water. His hose was dripping. *Much more of this and I'll grow webbed feet and start to quack,* William thought, as he tried to wring out the saturated foot of his hose. He put his boot back on and set off again, trying to ignore his chilly discomfort as he squelched along.

William reached the plank bridge over the ditch between the village and the West Field. The village boys were still running about, their voices shrill and distant. He watched them with envy. It was a long time since he had felt that carefree.

He saw a figure up ahead, walking quickly towards the village from the direction of the forest, head down against the rain. Clinging to its shoulder was a white crow, dipping and swaying with each hurried step. It was Dame Alys and Fionn, William realised. The thought of meeting the wise woman on this lonely stretch of track was not a comfortable one, but she turned off onto a path skirting the West Field, heading for Weforde mill.

Dame Alys noticed William and came to a sudden halt, leaning heavily on her walking stick. She was too far away for him to see her face clearly, but he felt the sharp stab of her stare. The crow fell forward into a wide-winged swoop, landing with a bounce on the path. William's pace slowed and he watched Dame Alys warily. For the first time, he noticed that she was carrying a sack. The rough cloth and the hand gripping the neck of the sack were covered with something dark. It might have been mud, but it was hard to tell at this distance.

William jumped when someone put a hand on his arm. He turned and was surprised to see Robin. He hadn't heard the boy approach. He glanced back at Dame Alys, but the woman had turned away and was now walking quickly towards the mill, poling herself along with her stick. The sack was hidden by the folds of her cloak. Fionn flew on ahead, a glimmer of white against the grey sky.

'I'm sorry I wasn't waiting for you,' Robin said with a smile. His woollen hat was rolled up and tucked into his belt and his wet hair hung clung to his neck. He wasn't wearing a cloak and the shoulders and back of his tunic were soaked, but he didn't seem to care. 'I went to the alehouse to buy this.' He opened his battered old leather bag and took out a small loaf of maslin bread. It had been pulled apart and a thick slice of cheese stuffed inside. He tore it in half and offered a piece to William.

For a few moments, William hesitated. It was Lent and the eating of meat and anything coming from an animal, such as cheese or milk or butter, wasn't allowed other than on a Sunday, and today was only Wednesday.

'Aren't you hungry?' Robin asked.

'It's Lent,' William said reluctantly. He saw Robin's blank look and felt a flicker of surprise. 'Don't you fast for Lent?'

Robin smiled thinly and glanced at the hunk of bread. 'It seems not. Don't you want this?'

'Well, yes,' William said, 'but . . .'

'But what?'

'I shouldn't.'

Robin's eyes narrowed. 'Who would know if you ate it? I won't tell anyone.'

William was sorely tempted. Hunger gnawed with rat-sharp teeth at his stomach. Would it *really* be so bad to eat the bread and cheese? He would work extra hard in the abbey for the rest of Lent to make up for it. The prior would have his hide if he found out, but surely God wouldn't punish him too harshly?

'All right, thank you,' William said at last, grinning with delight. He took the bread and sank his teeth into it. It was still warm and the cheese had softened. There was even a smear of melting butter on the bread. Yet another sin to add to his growing list. He closed his eyes with pleasure and chewed slowly. He had never tasted anything so wonderful before. When he opened his eyes, he saw that Robin was watching him with amusement.

'Don't they feed you at the abbey?'

'If you can call it food,' William said. 'It's not like this. And there's never enough of it, especially now that Lent has begun.' He took another mouthful and, muffled, added, 'Though that's probably not a bad thing.'

He noticed that Robin didn't touch his piece of bread. Instead the boy tucked it back into his bag.

'You delivered your message safely?' Robin asked.

William nodded. 'Sir Robert is sending his master mason to the abbey in the morning.'

'And will this mason be able to stop the church from collapsing, do you think?'

William pulled a face. 'I hope so. How long will you stay in Yagleah?'

'A day, a week, who knows?' Robin looked sideways at William with the slightest of smiles. 'Perhaps I will never leave.'

William thought this was an odd thing to say. 'Where did you live before you took to the road with your flute?'

'It wouldn't mean a thing to you if I told you, but I am a *long* way from home.'

'Have you ever been to London?' William asked after a few moments. Since his brother Hugh had set out for London three years ago, he'd been curious about the city. He wanted to be able to picture in his mind where his brother was, then perhaps Hugh wouldn't feel quite so far away.

'Many times. Why do you ask?'

'My brother Hugh is there. At least, I think he is. That's where he was going when he left home.'

'It's a long journey from Iwele to London. A lot can happen along the way. For all you know he might be lying dead in a ditch somewhere,' Robin said with a shrug.

William stared at him speechlessly for several moments, shocked by the boy's callous words, but then frowned. 'How did you know we lived in Iwele?'

'You told me,' Robin said lightly.

'No, I didn't.'

'Then I must have overheard someone talking about you in the village.'

'Why would anyone in Weforde be talking about me? And most people there only know I live at the abbey, not where I came from.' William watched Robin's face closely.

'Well, somebody must have mentioned it, because I know, don't I?' Robin said reasonably, his eyes wide and innocent. Closer to, the boy's eyes seemed greener, William noticed, and not really brown at all.

William let the matter go for the moment and finished the last of his bread and cheese.

They walked up the sloping track and into the forest. The afternoon was losing light quickly. The misty gloom of the woodland made William shiver. He was very glad of Robin's company.

'We'd better hurry,' William said, squinting up at the lowering sky through the falling rain, 'if you're going to reach Yagleah before dark.'

'The darkness doesn't trouble me,' Robin said, grinning, 'nor a spit of rain.'

William knew he should warn Robin about the

dangers lurking in Foxwist but even so, he hesitated before adding, 'The forest won't be safe after dusk.'

'Forests and lonely trackways seldom are. Wherever I travel, I hear stories of wild animals, thieves and ghosts.' Robin leant a little closer to William and added, 'Not to mention tales of fay creatures ready to lead the unwary traveller astray. Do you believe in fays, William?'

William just shrugged and looked away.

'Most people don't. They are just the stuff of stories told around the fire,' Robin said. The slightest of smiles touched his thin lips. 'But I can say with all honesty that I've travelled this land from one end to the other and have never once been troubled by a fay creature.'

'Yes, well,' William muttered, feeling his cheeks redden. If Robin didn't believe in fays, there was nothing he could say to change his mind, unless he told him about Shadlok and the hob, and William had no intention of doing that.

'But if the fays *do* walk these woods,' Robin added, an odd gleam in his eyes, 'then it won't be safe whether it is night or broad daylight.'

They walked along without talking for a while. William searched for something to say to break the silence.

'What's London like?' he asked at last.

'Big,' Robin said. 'It would fill the whole of that valley behind us. Narrow streets full of houses, people jostling for space with horses and dogs, cats and rats, disease and hunger, wealth and poverty. You can watch a man being hanged on the gallows at Smithfield in the morning and see his head on a pole above the gatehouse of London Bridge that afternoon. And the noise!' Robin's face seemed to light up with a strange excitement. He turned to grin at William. 'Imagine everybody in Weforde jumping to their feet, all shouting and yelling at once. That would be just the smallest part of the noise in London. The smell of river mud is bad in winter and worse in summer. The air is thick with smoke from hundreds of fires and ovens, and ripe with the stink from cess-pits and the drains down the middle of the streets. It has a taste that stays with you long after you leave.'

William stared at him. How could Robin sound so gleeful about such horror? London sounded like something from a nightmare and not at all how he'd imagined it.

'London is a terrible and monstrous beast. It is dangerous and will devour the unwary traveller. Like your brother, perhaps,' Robin said, smiling as if he had made a joke, but it didn't reach his eyes.

William had no idea what to say. There was something about Robin that disturbed him, a streak of cruelty he did not like.

Robin stopped for a moment to take his flute from his bag. 'Nothing persuades the feet to walk a little bit faster than a lively tune.' He slung his bag over his shoulder, put the flute to his lips and began to play.

William walked along the grassy edge of the track, his footsteps keeping time with Robin's song. The music wrapped itself around him, filling him with a strange elation, and for a while he barely noticed the rain. The mud and the cold breeze were soon forgotten. He quickly picked up the tune and hummed along. Robin looked at him over the flute and nodded in approval. William grinned back. Every now and then his boots slipped on the wet grass or his cloak caught on a trailing bramble branch, snagging the wool, but he didn't slow down. He *couldn't* slow down. The notes rippling from the flute would not let him. Panic fluttered in his chest. The music was somehow pulling him along in its wake. He tried to stop but his feet no longer obeyed him; they skipped and stamped along by themselves in a dance that was getting wilder and faster by the moment. He turned to Robin in alarm but the boy was looking ahead now and his fingers flew over the holes in the flute with bewildering speed.

'Wait!' William said sharply. 'Stop!'

Robin glanced at him, eyes narrowed, but he carried on playing. His wet hair seemed a darker shade of red in the dusk and his eyes were the bright green of early summer leaves. Whatever Robin was doing, he was doing it on purpose, William realised, and he was enjoying it.

'Stop playing,' William said angrily. 'Stop *now!*'

Robin lowered the flute. His face was a mask of surprise. 'What's the matter?'

'Put the flute away.' William's hands clenched into fists. He had no idea how Robin had managed to do that to him, to make his feet move as if they were no longer his own, but he wouldn't let him do it again.

Robin's expression was unreadable. 'I just thought music would make the journey more pleasant.'

William stared back, refusing to show fear in front of the boy.

'Have it your own way,' Robin said with a shrug. He dropped his bag on the grass and squatted down beside it to pack the flute away. He took out the bread and cheese he had kept for himself and held it out to

William. 'You might as well have this. I will no doubt eat well enough in Yagleah tonight.'

William hesitated, desperate to accept the food but still wary of Robin.

'Just take it,' Robin insisted, 'by way of an apology.'

William took the bread and put it in the pocket sewn inside his cloak. 'Thank you,' he said gruffly.

Robin sighed and stood up. He hefted his bag onto his shoulder and turned to trudge away along the track. William watched him, his eyes narrowed with suspicion. The boy's thin, bedraggled figure would have wrung pity from the hardest heart, but William had the strangest feeling that there was more to Robin than met the eye. It was as if the real Robin was hiding within. It was an unsettling thought. He would be glad when they reached the abbey and parted company.

Robin walked a little way ahead of William for the rest of the journey. The silence between them was not an easy one. The rain pattered on last year's dead leaves and dripped from branches, but beyond those soft noises William noticed how quiet the woods were. There was no birdsong, he realised with surprise. The wind had dropped and Foxwist was as silent as the grave.

William glanced around with a growing sense of unease. The late afternoon shadows were creeping between the trees. He could feel a change in the air, a strange stirring that tingled through his body. The woods no longer seemed familiar. The track ahead of him *looked* the same as ever but it felt very different. He had the unsettling feeling that it no longer led to familiar places, to Crowfield and Yagleah, but to somewhere else entirely. And was it his imagination, or did Robin look different too? Taller and wider across the shoulders, perhaps, his hair longer? William fought down the fear welling up inside him. *It's just the fading light making things look strange*, he reasoned. *Not much further now and I will be safe.*

Up ahead, the rags tied to the bushes near the Hollow hung like dead hands, limp and dripping in the steady rain. Robin walked past them without as much as a glance. William hardly dared to breathe until the Hollow was safely behind him. Robin disappeared around the next bend in the track. William clambered onto the grass verge and broke into a run. Robin was waiting for him by the fork in the track leading to the abbey. He was the same skinny, lank-haired boy William had met in Weforde. Whatever William thought he had seen earlier, it must have been all in his mind, conjured out of fear and the failing daylight.

'Thank you for the food,' William said awkwardly. As strange as the boy was, he had been kind enough to share his bread and cheese with William and such rare generosity should not be ignored.

Robin's eyes gleamed. 'It's my pleasure. I hope you enjoy it.'

William opened his mouth to say he would, when he noticed a dark patch on the causeway, just a few paces away. He turned to look more closely and was disturbed to see that it was blood, mixed with small clumps of reddish fur. He crouched down beside it and picked up a tuft of fur between his thumb and forefinger. He turned it slowly and caught his breath. It was the same shade of red as the hob's fur. Fear squeezed the breath from his body and it was several moments before he realised that it was not *quite* the same, but a shade or so paler and not as coarse. It was fox fur. He glanced back down at the blood. There was a great deal of it, but strangely, there was no sign of the injured animal, and no trail of blood to show where it had gone.

William noticed something else on the blood-stained ground. Carefully he picked it up, and to his surprise saw that it was a bundle of oak twigs, tied with a length of wool. A cold chill of foreboding crept over him. He looked up at Robin and saw that the boy was staring at the abbey with a strange expression on his face.

'What do you suppose this is for?' William asked, holding up the oak twigs.

Robin glanced at them and took a step backwards. 'Who knows?' He seemed ill at ease and anxious to be on his way.

William dropped the fur and the twigs and stood up. He wiped his blood-smeared fingers on his cloak. Robin started to walk up the causeway to the track.

'I am sure the monks would give you lodgings for the night if you asked them,' William called after him. 'You could continue your journey in the morning.'

'I told you, the rain and the dark do not trouble me,' Robin said sharply. He glanced from the patch of blood to the abbey buildings and for a couple of moments his gaze lingered on the church tower. William thought he saw a flicker of fear cross the boy's face.

'I'm sure we'll meet again, William,' Robin called over his shoulder.

William grimaced and thought, *I hope not*. He

stepped over the blood stain and sprinted down the track towards the abbey gatehouse, splashing through the puddles and floodwater. He looked back when he reached the abbey gate, but Robin had disappeared into the darkening forest and the trackway was empty.

Chapter Five

William draped the wet cloak over two stools near the fire in Brother Snail's workshop to dry. The monk was washing his hands in a bowl of water after spending the afternoon weeding and digging in the herb garden. The hob stood by the open doorway to catch the last of the daylight while he scraped the mud from an iron-shod spade. An assortment of gardening tools, a hoe, a rake and a three-pronged fork, stood against the wall nearby, all cleaned and ready to be put away for the day.

Brother Snail looked at William with a frown. 'This boy Robin sounds very strange indeed. But generous, too, giving you half his bread and cheese.' If the monk had been disappointed with William for breaking his Lenten fast, he had said nothing.

William sat on the floor near the fire. He pulled off

his boots and held his feet in their soaked hose out to the warmth.

'He gave me the other half of the loaf before he went on his way,' William said. He leant over and felt for the pocket sewn inside the cloak, and pulled out the bread.

Only it wasn't bread.

William stared at the dark, seething mass in his hand in stunned silence, then with a yell, flung it away from him. He scrambled to his feet, his whole body going hot and cold in waves. He wiped his hand on the leg of his hose to try and get rid of the feel of the damp, rotting mass of . . . what was it? To his horrified gaze it looked like the remains of a small animal, long dead and crawling with maggots. A couple of them dropped from the fold of the cloak and squirmed on the floor.

Brother Snail looked up, startled. The hob threw down the spade and hurried over to see what the matter was.

'Will? What is it?' the monk asked, drying his hands on a small rag of linen. He saw the remains on the floor and caught his breath. 'Blessed God, what is *that*?'

'It's what Robin gave me . . . it's the bread,' William

47

said. *I* ate *part of that*, he thought, appalled. His stomach heaved and he ran for the door. He stumbled around the corner of the hut and hunched over, retching.

A hand grabbed William's hair, not roughly, and pulled it back from his face. Whoever it was stayed with him until every last thing in his stomach lay on the grass beneath the blackthorn tree.

'Better?' Shadlok asked, somewhere above him.

William slowly straightened up. His body trembled and tears rolled down his face. He wiped his mouth with the back of his shaking hand. 'Yes,' he said hoarsely.

Shadlok was watching him with a frown. 'The one-eyed cook's food has not improved, by the look of it.'

William shook his head. 'It wasn't Brother Martin's cooking. Maybe God was punishing me for eating cheese on a fast day.'

'Why would he do that?' Shadlok sounded mystified.

'Because it's a sin,' William said. Shadlok raised his eyebrows but said nothing.

'Are you all right, Will?' Brother Snail asked anxiously, grabbing his arm.

'Maggots are never a good thing to eat,' the hob

said, climbing up to sit on a low branch of the black-thorn and patting William on the head in sympathy.

'Maggots?' Shadlok said, sounding surprised. 'Why did you eat maggots?'

'I didn't,' William said, feeling his stomach tighten ominously. 'Well, I *did*, but I didn't mean to.'

'Would somebody care to explain what is going on?' Shadlok said evenly.

'Come with me,' Brother Snail said. 'I will show you.'

Shadlok followed the monk into the hut. William leant against the tree and breathed in deeply and slowly, trying to calm the chaos in his belly. It didn't make any sense. Robin had handed him maslin bread and cheese. It had been warm and fresh and it had tasted good. Better than good, it had been the best thing he had eaten in months. He'd seen and touched the second half of the loaf when Robin took it out of his bag. He would have wagered his soul that it had been bread, plain and simple.

So where had that rotting abomination come from? If it wasn't divine punishment on him, how had Robin managed to trick him like that?

'Maggots and black fur,' the hob said, poking the contents of William's stomach with a long stick where they lay beneath the tree. 'Not bread at all.'

William stared at the mess at his feet in revulsion. Then he began to retch again.

A short while later, William sat and shivered by the fire. Brother Snail gave him an infusion of crushed fennel seeds in warm water to soothe his stomach.

'So,' Shadlok said softly, his eyes wide and gleaming with anger, 'the king has come back. I am just surprised he has waited this long.'

Brother Snail went a shade or two paler. 'You think this boy Robin was the Dark King in disguise?'

Shadlok nodded. 'He covered his true appearance with glamour, and tricked William into seeing and tasting bread when in truth he was eating . . .'

'Don't say it, please,' William interrupted quickly, putting a hand to his mouth. He couldn't bear to think about what he'd eaten. His stomach rumbled queasily.

The hob, sitting across the hearth from William, said, 'I wonder why he didn't just kill you.'

'He made a fair attempt at it,' William muttered.

'No, he only meant to frighten you,' Shadlok said.

'Well, he succeeded.'

Shadlok gazed into the fire. The flames were reflected in the pale depths of his eyes. 'Comnath enjoys the hunt more than the kill. Like a cat with a bird, he plays with his prey and finds new and more unpleasant ways to torture it.' He looked from William to the monk and let his gaze linger on the hob for a moment. The harsh lines of his face softened slightly. 'But it is me he wants to destroy. He will hurt me in whatever way he can, and that includes coming after those close to me. None of you are safe now. You least of all,' his gaze shifted back to William, 'because you and I are bound together by his curse, and because you dug the angel from its grave and helped Bone to die. He will make you pay for that.'

William remembered the first time he had seen the king, in the Hollow last winter, with his unnaturally green eyes and dark red hair, startling against the pallor of his skin. As the boy Robin, the king had been almost unrecognisable. Almost, but not quite: the king could not fully disguise his eyes. If William had been paying closer attention, those green eyes would have given him away much sooner. *I should have trusted my instincts*, William thought in frustration. *I knew there was something not quite right about him.*

'Isn't there any way to stop him?' William asked. 'We have to fight back.'

'Oh, we will fight him, human, make no mistake

51

about that,' Shadlok said softly, 'but it will be two of us against the whole of the Unseelie Court, and I do not care for our chances.'

'Three of us,' the hob said, patting his chest.

A rare smile lit Shadlok's face. 'Your bravery does you honour.'

The hob looked delighted by the fay's praise. His face creased in a wide grin which showed two rows of sharp teeth.

'Make that four,' Brother Snail said.

William looked at him and felt a rush of affection. The monk might have the heart of a bear, but his thin body with its twisted spine and humped back was frail. He would be of no use in what was to come and they all knew it. And what chance would the hob stand against one of the Dark King's fay warriors? The truth was, William and Shadlok stood alone in this fight.

Chapter Six

William was chopping logs in the wood-shed early on Thursday morning when someone banged on the abbey gate.

'Master Guillaume to see the prior,' a voice called.

William hauled open the gate and stood aside. The mason dismounted and lifted down a large leather bag.

'We meet again, boy,' the mason said. He handed the bag to William. 'Take this, and then let your prior know I'm here.'

The bag was heavy and clanked as whatever was inside it shifted. William got a good grip on the handles and said, 'I think Prior Ardo is in the church. I'll take you to him.'

Master Guillaume tied the pony's reins to the wattle fence of the pigpen. Mary Magdalene, the abbey's elderly sow, came over to inspect the animal, grunting as she lifted her snout to sniff the pony. William leant over the fence to give her ear a quick scratch. She grunted again and settled herself in the muddy wallow by her trough. The pony found a patch of grass and began to graze.

It had stopped raining and the sky was a clear light blue. The mud in the yard was starting to dry out in the breeze. The kitchen door was propped open with a stone and William could hear Brother Martin banging around inside.

'Get out of here before I wring yer scrawny necks!' the monk yelled. 'Ye'll be in the pot feathers an' all if I catch ye in here again, ye little buggers.' There was a loud crash, a squawk, and a flurry of hens flapped out through the kitchen doorway and scattered across the yard.

William grinned at Master Guillaume's look of surprise. 'That's the cook, Brother Martin. We'll go the long way round to the church. It's best to keep out of his way when he's cooking.'

William took the stonemason through the vegetable garden to the dark arch of the passageway beside the chapter house that led to the cloister.

Brother Mark was sitting at his desk overlooking the cloister garth, his head bowed over a sheet of parchment and a goose quill pen in his hand as he copied a prayer from a Book of Hours beside him. He glanced up when William and Master Guillaume emerged from the passageway.

'Master Guillaume is here to see Prior Ardo,' William said, glancing at the mason.

'The prior is in the church,' the monk said, putting down his pen and rubbing his hands together to ease his cramped, ink-stained fingers. 'He will be glad to see you. The crack is worse this morning.'

After the bright, mild day outside, the light in the church was dim and the building was chilly. Prior Ardo, Brother Gabriel and Brother Snail were standing outside St Christopher's chapel in the north transept.

'It can't be rain damage,' Brother Gabriel was saying insistently, 'because only the saint's face has been affected.'

'I can see that for myself,' the prior said sharply, 'but what else can it be, if not damp seeping through the wall?'

'In just that one small patch?' Brother Gabriel said. His plump cheeks were pink and there was a shrill note in his voice. 'I think it might be a sign.'

The prior turned to frown down at the monk.

'A sign of what, exactly?'

'I don't know,' Brother Gabriel said, sounding flustered, 'but I don't think it's anything good.'

Brother Snail noticed William and the stonemason and touched the prior's arm.

'This is Master Guillaume,' William said, nodding to the mason.

'Perhaps we can have your opinion on the matter,' Prior Ardo said, gesturing to the chapel entrance, inviting the stonemason to come and look.

William glanced at Brother Snail and saw the worried look in his eyes. *What now?* he wondered as he peered over the stonemason's shoulder. He had never been inside the chapel before, and stared in wonder at the walls which were painted with fish beneath little blue waves, and trees and flowers on grassy riverbanks. Above the altar, there was a painting of St Christopher carrying the infant Jesus on his shoulder. The child was plump and smiling and a halo circled his head. William barely glanced at him but stared up at the saint instead. Where St Christopher's face should have been was a patch of bare stone. The plaster had fallen away from the wall in a neat circle and lay in a small heap on the altar.

'Well?' the prior asked. 'Is the wall damp?'

The mason stepped into the chapel and slowly walked around, running his hands over the walls, peering up at the ceiling and down at the floor. 'It's damp right enough. And the floor. Even so, it's strange that the plaster's come away like that, just the saint's face and nothing else. *Very* strange,' he said with a puzzled frown. He looked at the prior. 'Sir Robert told me there is a crack in the chancel wall. Can I see it?'

'This way,' the prior said, brushing past William without seeming to notice him. Brother Gabriel and the mason followed him, but Brother Snail stayed where he was, twisting sideways to look up at the damaged wall painting.

'What do the words say?' William asked, pointing to a ribbon of letters above the saint's head.

'*Cristofori faciem die quacunque tueris,*' Brother Snail read slowly, '*illa nempe die morte mala non morieris*. It means whoever looks on the face of St Christopher shall not that day die an evil death.'

'He doesn't have a face,' William said uneasily.

'No,' the monk agreed, 'he doesn't.'

Chapter Seven

William glanced around. There was an atmosphere in the gloomy little chapel that he did not like. He looked up at the painted ceiling. Two angels flew between stars and a large full moon. One was clothed in white and had sweeping feathered wings. It had clearly been painted by the same person who had decorated the walls of the chapel, but the other angel was different. It was crudely painted and looked as if it had been added by a different hand. Its robes and wings were red; it had the head of a crow and carried a sword. William found it deeply disturbing. There was something in the back of his mind, a vague feeling that he had seen something like this before, but it was gone before he could grasp it. He remembered Shadlok's reluctance to go near the church and his certainty that something evil lurked there. *Shadlok was right,* he thought. The chapel might have been a holy place until yesterday, when St Christopher watched over it, but it wasn't now. The saint was blind, and something else inhabited the chapel. They were not welcome here.

Brother Snail put a hand on William's arm. 'Come away, Will. This is not a good place, not any more.'

William nodded and followed the monk out of the chapel.

Master Guillaume stood by one of the massive stone pillars supporting the tower. He peered up as he slowly circled the pillar, and then looked down at the floor.

'This isn't good,' he said, leaning down to pick up something. William and the monks crowded round to see what he had found.

'The pier is showing signs of subsidence.' The mason held a sharp-edged piece of stone in the palm of his hand. Mortar dust and bits of stone lay scattered over the floor around his feet. Seeing four blank faces, he added, 'The ground on the north side of the church is waterlogged. Half of the building is just sitting on wet mud, more or less, which is why the wall is starting to crack. I need to take a look up in the tower.' He looked at William. 'I have two wax candles and a tinder box in my bag. Fetch them, and then you're coming up the tower with me.'

It took a minute or so to strike a spark onto the tinder and coax a flame, but at last the candles were lit. William followed the monks and the mason to a small door in a corner of the north transept. A spiral of steps curved up through the thickness of the wall. The monks stood aside and the mason nodded to William to go first. Light from his candle leapt ahead of him, chasing the shadows. The stair treads were narrow and it was difficult to get a safe foothold. William's legs burned with the effort of climbing. He could hear the mason behind him, huffing as he squeezed his stocky frame around the tightly twisting spiral.

Finally William reached a tiny landing. He pushed open the door and stepped out into the narrow triforium where a row of arched openings looked down onto the floor of the church and the wooden roof of St Christopher's chapel. A couple of startled sparrows darted out of a dark corner and sped away across the church, chirping in alarm.

The door of the ringing room was tucked in beside the column in the north-west corner of the tower. William pushed it open and stepped inside. The bell ropes hung down through holes in the ceiling and were looped back behind an iron bracket. A ladder led up to the bell chamber through a square opening in a corner of the room.

Master Guillaume walked around the room, examining the walls. From time to time he said a thoughtful 'Hmm'.

William waited by the foot of the ladder, shielding his candle flame with a cupped hand against the draughts funnelling down from the bell chamber.

'Are the walls all right?' he asked.

The mason glanced at him. 'No. The mortar is loose over there.' He nodded to the north-east pier. 'The floor boards are rotting in that corner too.'

William felt his stomach clench with fear. Noticing the look on his face, the mason grinned, showing two rows of brown teeth.

'Scared, boy?'

William stared at the mason and said nothing.

'It's a long way down,' the mason added, his eyes narrowing slyly. He jumped up and down a couple of times and the floorboards shook. William's heart missed a beat. For one awful moment, he wondered if this wasn't the mason, but the Dark King in disguise. They seemed to share the same streak of casual cruelty.

'I'm only having a bit of fun with you, boy. The floor is sound enough for now,' the mason said, holding up his candle to inspect the upper walls.

William relaxed a little.

'These walls, now, they're another matter altogether. Plaster's coming away in handfuls and the mortar is crumbling. Up the ladder with you and let's take a look at the bell chamber. Don't touch anything and stand quite still when you get up there.'

William didn't need to be told twice. He climbed the ladder and stood by the opening in the floor, almost too afraid to breathe. Master Guillaume followed a few moments later and moved cautiously around the chamber, candle held aloft.

The chamber was at the top of the tower. The huge timbers of the bell frame took up most of the space inside it. Five large bells were fixed to the cross beams. Two arched windows were set into each wall and covered with louvred shutters, to allow the sound of the bells to roll out across the countryside. Several of the shutters were broken though, and rainwater had come through the windows, soaking the frame and staining the floor. Master Guillaume frowned down at a puddle. 'Those shutters should have been mended long ago.'

William snorted. The monks had barely enough money for the most essential repairs, so a few broken shutters were not high on the list of things to be done. And quite how they were going to find the money to repair the chancel wall, and possibly the walls of the tower, was anybody's guess.

The mason turned to stare at him. 'Don't underestimate the damage rain can do, boy.' He patted a beam. 'This, for example, should be taking the weight of the bells on this side of the frame, but it's rotted away until it's barely even touching the wall any longer.'

'Could the bells fall?' William asked anxiously.

'They could, and to tell you God's honest truth, I don't know why they haven't already.'

The mason edged around and between the frame timbers, to peer into dark corners. He emerged a short while later, covered in cobwebs and bits of dried bird droppings. His face was pale and his lips clamped firmly together. He looked shaken.

'What?' William asked nervously.

'I think,' the mason said evenly, 'we should get down from here *now*. Careful on the ladder, boy, and don't hurry.'

'Why? What have you found?' William's voice was edged with fear.

'Enough to tell me this whole bloody tower could come down at any moment. And it probably will.'

Every muscle in William's body hurt as he forced himself not to clamber wildly down the ladder and make a run for the stairs.

'Slowly, slowly,' the mason said, trying to keep his voice calm.

They reached the ringing room and hurried along the triforium to the stairs. Minutes later they were in the transept, where the monks were waiting for them. The mason pinched out the candle flame between his thumb and forefinger and handed his candle to William. 'Put them back in my bag, boy.'

'Well?' the prior said. 'What did you find?'

The mason slapped the dust and cobwebs from his clothes. 'The tower is in a dangerous state. It's going to come down and there's nothing anyone can do to stop it.'

'What, *nothing*?' the prior gasped. 'Nothing at all? The whole tower?'

'Not a damn, bloody thing, begging your pardon, Prior. Though . . .' the mason hesitated and glanced upwards, 'it's not the waterlogged ground that's doing the worst of the damage.'

'Then what is it?' the prior asked in surprise.

There was an odd look on the mason's face. 'I don't rightly know,' he said slowly. 'If I were a more fanciful man, I'd say something's been scratching the mortar out from between the stones.'

A stunned silence met the mason's words. William peered uneasily upwards. He could almost hear the sound of nails on stone, scraping and scratching.

The prior was the first to speak. 'That's ridiculous!' he snapped.

The mason shrugged, but an angry flush rose to his cheeks. 'Just saying what I saw. The mortar's been gouged from between the stones in the bell chamber, and I wouldn't be surprised if it's gone in a few more places too. It won't take much to topple the tower, Prior.'

'How could such a thing happen?' Brother Gabriel asked in panic. 'Was it rats?'

The prior gave Brother Gabriel a withering look.

The mason's face was grim. 'If it was, Brother, then they were armed with chisels.'

'We must get the bells down as soon as possible,' the prior said.

The mason shook his head. 'It's too late for that. Move whatever you can carry out of the church and then keep everyone out of the building.'

'We've already taken most of the smaller statues from their niches and put them in the north alley,' the prior said. 'We'll need help to move the heavier ones.'

The stonemason shook his head. 'I wouldn't want any of my men working in this building, Prior. You might just have to leave the rest of the statues where they are and let them take their chances.'

Brother Gabriel made an odd little whimpering sound and crossed himself several times. 'We must pray for a miracle,' he said in a quavering voice, 'that God will stop our tower from collapsing.'

'Then He'd better send St Michael down with a bucket of mortar and some strong timbers,' the mason said, 'though I don't think even the archangel himself could do anything now.'

William followed the monks and the mason out of the church. The prior turned to Brother Gabriel. 'Go and tell all of the brethren to come to the chapter house immediately.'

'I'll let Sir Robert know what's happening here,' Master Guillaume said. He nodded to William. 'Make yourself useful, boy, and fetch my pony.'

William led the mason's pony to the gatehouse, where Master Guillaume was waiting for him.

'Tell the prior to send word when the tower comes

down, boy,' the mason said as he settled himself in the saddle. He settled his bag in front of him and, with a flick of the pony's reins, set off through the gateway at a smart trot. 'And remember to stay out of the church,' he called over his shoulder.

William closed the gate and pushed the bolt home. He stood with his back against the timbers, a cold dread in his stomach. It didn't seem possible that the massive stone tower could fall down, but the mason seemed quite certain that it would.

Something unholy was stirring in the abbey, William thought, something that seemed intent on destroying it. Shadlok and the hob had sensed its presence, and the forest fays were running away from it. Even the Dark King was reluctant to come anywhere near the abbey.

The image of the crow-headed angel painted on the chapel ceiling slid into William's mind and he shivered. He had the overwhelming feeling that it had been painted as a warning, but a warning against what?

Chapter Eight

Shortly before dinner William carried a pail of water to Brother Snail's workshop. The monk was busy in the vegetable garden with Peter. He gave William a wave as he walked by.

The hob was dozing by the fire and woke with a start when William opened the hut door. He yawned loudly and sat up.

'It's good to see you working so hard,' William said with a grin.

'I was helping the snail brother until the simple one turned up,' the hob said. He took something from around his neck and held it out to William. It was a white stone with a hole through it, threaded onto a length of red wool. 'This is for you. It's a holey stone and it's powerfully magic,' the hob explained. 'It lets you see through glamour. The king will not be able to disguise himself if you look at him through this.'

William set the pail on the floor and took the hob's gift. He held it up to one eye. To his astonishment, instead of the walls of the hut, he could see woodland. There was frost on the ground and the trees were bare, their branches a pattern of dark bones against the pale blue sky. William caught a fleeting glimpse of people, as pale as wisps of mist in the sunlight, walking between the trees, and he thought he heard the rhythmic thump of a drum. Startled, he dropped the stone. The hob grabbed it and held it out to him again.

William looked at the stone in the hob's leathery little paw and felt reluctant to touch it. 'I saw people,' he said uneasily, 'in a wood.'

'If you look through a holey stone, sometimes you can see the fay world beyond this one,' the hob said, 'and sometimes you see things in *this* world that have long gone.'

'Which world did I see?' William asked.

The hob thought about this for a moment. 'I don't know,' he said.

William took the stone and peered cautiously through the hole again. This time all he saw was the far wall of the hut. 'The wood's gone,' he said in surprise.

'Holey stone magic comes and goes,' the hob said. 'Keep it with you and the magic will be there when you need it.'

William pulled the woollen loop over his head and tucked the stone inside his undershirt. It was cold against his skin and he touched it tentatively. Perhaps it would be better to let the holey stone keep its secrets.

'I have to get back to the kitchen to help serve up the dinner,' William said. 'Thank you for the stone.'

The hob regarded him thoughtfully for a couple of moments. 'Don't be frightened of the magic,' he said. 'Use it wisely and it will not harm you.'

William had seen enough of magic these last few months to be cautious of it. The thought of actually using it made him feel very apprehensive.

The hob settled himself beside the fire again, curling his tail around his body and closing his eyes. 'What has the one-eyed brother man made for dinner today?' he called sleepily as William reached the door.

'A delicious thick pease pottage with bread warm from the oven and sweetmeats of honey and ground almonds to follow.'

The hob opened an eye. 'He has?'

'No,' William said, pulling a face. 'It's the last of

yesterday's vegetable pottage with a few extra leeks and a handful of barley thrown in. And no sweetmeats.'

The hob made a disgusted noise and closed his eye again. 'Then you need not bother hurrying back.'

William walked back through the vegetable garden. Brother Snail had gone back to the abbey to wash his hands before nones, the service before dinner. Peter was turning the wet, muddy earth with his spade, preparing the ground for the spring planting. He smiled at William as he passed by and gave a small wave.

William reached the garden gate and glanced up at the church tower. He put a hand to the stone around his neck and had an unsettling thought. What would he see if he looked at the church through the holey stone? Would it show him what was hiding inside? He glanced over his shoulder at Peter, but the lay brother was busy with his digging and had his back to him. William pushed open the gate and walked through the monks' graveyard, around to the north side of the church. He stared up at the cracked wall and slowly pulled the stone from beneath his shirt, then hesitated, wondering whether he really should be doing this. *If the abbey is in danger*, he told himself, *we need to know what we're up against.* He took a deep breath, closed one eye and peered through the hole.

At first all he could see was darkness, but as he watched, a light wavered into view. The abbey walls had gone. The light picked out the deeply cragged bark of an oak tree. He moved the stone to see more of the scene before him. The light was coming from a burning brand of wood, wrapped around with rags, carried by a woman with long grey hair. She was old, but her deeply lined face was fierce and her eyes wide and dark. In spite of the cold, her skinny arms were bare. Gold bracelets on her wrists gleamed in the torchlight and there was a glint of gold at her throat. Other figures, indistinct in the darkness, followed her as she walked slowly around the oak tree. Hanging from a low branch of the tree was a dark shape which glistened wetly in the flaring light. To his horror, William realised it was the remains of a deer, its throat slashed. Broken ribs bristled from a dark hole in its chest, and a bloody bowl on the ground held the animal's heart.

With a yell, William let go of the stone and stumbled backwards. He tripped on a hummock of grass and went sprawling across the waterlogged grass. Cold water soaked the back of his hose and tunic and he struggled quickly to his feet, his whole body shaking with terror. He stared around, but there was no trace of what he had just seen. He pushed the stone down the neck of his undershirt and hurried, slipping and stumbling, back around the end wall of the church.

When he reached the path through the garden he slowed his pace. Gradually his breathing steadied and he thought about what he had just witnessed. He was sure the deer had been a sacrifice, and a memory stirred at the back of his mind. The hob had once told him about a tree called the Hunter's Oak, growing in a sacred grove, where many years ago people had made offerings to some now-forgotten god. Was *that* what he had just seen, William wondered, a ghostly shadow of what had once existed where the abbey now stood? Last winter Shadlok had said Dame Alys's ancestors were the guardians of a sacred grove in Foxwist Wood. Were Dame Alys's grove and the trees around the Hunter's Oak one and the same thing?

Like the fragments of a broken pot, the pieces slowly started to fit together. Was that why Dame Alys hated the monks? William wondered. Because they had cut down the trees and built their abbey on ground that had been sacred to her ancestors?

Shadlok had seemed sure the woman had not turned her back on the old ways. What if he was right? Fear uncoiled inside William's mind: what if Dame Alys's god was the evil presence in the church?

Chapter Nine

Shortly after dawn on Friday morning, William took the handcart to the woodshed and piled it with logs to take to the kitchen and to Brother Snail's workshop. After that, the prior wanted him to help Shadlok in the new orchard. The prospect of a day spent out in the breezy March sunshine lifted his spirits and he whistled softly as he pushed the hand-cart along the path.

The hob helped William to stack the cut logs and kindling in the small woodshed beside the workshop.

'You can come with me, if you like,' William said. 'I'll be working in the new orchard with Shadlok today.'

The hob's face brightened. 'Will you bring your flute?'

'I suppose I could,' William said with a quick grin. He should be far enough from the abbey to play it without being heard.

'I will fetch it,' the hob said, his eyes alight with excitement.

William took the handcart back to the yard. The hob was waiting for him when he reached the orchard. The flute in its leather bag hung from a fence post nearby.

Shadlok had cleared the ground of scrub and weeds, and had chopped up the remains of a large old birch tree which had blown down in a winter storm. He had dug around the roots, cutting them up and unearthing them as he went. There was a huge pile of branches in the middle of the cleared patch, and a stack of logs by the sheep pasture fence. William saw the fay over by the hazel coppice, and called out to him as he climbed over the fence. 'Prior Ardo sent me to help you.'

Shadlok had taken off his tunic, rolled up the sleeves of his white linen undershirt, and tied back his hair with a strip of leather. The work was back-breaking, but in spite of that, he hadn't so much as broken a sweat. His face, with its fine mesh of scars, was as pale as ever and his shirt as fresh as if it had been newly washed and spread on the grass to dry in the sunshine.

'The monk thinks I need your help, does he?' He glanced around the bare ground of the new orchard pointedly.

The colour rose to William's cheeks. Shadlok didn't need anyone's help. 'There must be something I can do?'

Shadlok nodded towards the pile of branches. 'They have to be burned. After that you can take the cut logs to the woodshed.'

'I will fetch the tinder box from the snail brother's hut,' the hob offered.

'And some dry kindling,' William said.

The hob scurried off, leaving William to build a bonfire. Some of the wood was still green and would smoke, but the westerly breeze would carry it across the pasture and away from the abbey.

The morning passed quickly. William stacked branches and tree roots into a huge pile and pushed handfuls of kindling into gaps around the base. It took a while to coax the sparks to catch, but at last the wood crackled and spat and flames waved like yellow rags between the branches. The hob ran around in excitement, gathering up stray bits of wood and throwing them onto the fire. He capered in and out of the billowing smoke, wheezing and coughing. A piece of burning wood fell from the bonfire and caught him on his tail, singeing his fur. He hurriedly patted at the burnt patch, then ran off to find more branches.

'Brother Walter is enjoying himself.' William grinned as he watched the hob's antics.

'The creature should be tied to a fence post before he does himself some real harm,' Shadlok said, but there was the ghost of a smile on his lips.

When dinner was over and the monks were safely out of earshot in the church, William played his flute for Shadlok and the hob. He had been practising a carol that Shadlok had taught him and was feeling quite pleased with himself.

'That was an improvement,' Shadlok said, nodding. 'You no longer sound like a scalded cat.'

William glared at him. 'Thank you.'

The fay's light-blue eyes gleamed with amusement. 'Again. And this time, try and play the notes in the order I taught you.'

William lifted the flute to his lips. In spite of Shadlok's faint praise, he knew the fay was pleased with his progress. He was an able pupil and Shadlok was a good teacher.

William began again. The now familiar tune was lively and quick, the kind he remembered people dancing to on the green back home in Iwele. Step, stamp, step, stamp to the right, then one step to the left and stamp again, over and over, the dancers moving in a circle, hands linked, breathless and laughing, and trying to keep up as the tune got faster and faster.

There were no dancers today, just the sharp-eyed fay and the hob, who was sitting on an upturned pail and keeping time with the music by hitting the side of the pail with a stick. The hob's small face was creased into wide grin and his ears twitched. His tail flicked from side to side, the tuft on the end brushing across the ground.

Shadlok nodded when William reached the end of the tune. 'Better. Your timing is good and you only played two wrong notes. But that is enough for today. The monks will be finished in the church soon.'

William nodded. These smuggled minutes were all too short, but he could not risk the prior finding out what he was doing. He cleaned his flute and returned it to its leather bag.

'More music tomorrow?' the hob asked hopefully.

William smiled down at him. 'Perhaps.'

Brother Walter looked pleased. 'That's good. I will hide your flute in the snail brother's hut until then.'

After the hob had gone, William showed Shadlok the holey stone. 'The hob gave me this.'

'A seeing stone,' Shadlok said. 'Have you used it yet?'

William nodded. 'I saw something over by the church yesterday.'

He had the fay's full attention now. 'Oh?'

'I saw the body of a deer hanging from an oak tree, and an old woman with gold bracelets.'

Shadlok's face was set and tense. He said nothing, but waited for William to continue.

'I think I saw the sacred grove that grew here before the monks came,' William went on. 'I think the old woman was Dame Alys's ancestor.'

Shadlok's jaw tightened. His pale eyes were troubled. It was a while before he spoke. 'I should have guessed . . .'

'Guessed what?' William asked.

'Do you remember the bird-headed creature you saw in Dame Alys's hut last winter, and what I told you at the time?'

'You said that it was once an angel,' William said. He paused as the fay's words came back to him in full. 'You said it was evil and that the angel we found last winter had come to hunt it down.'

'I believe it is one of the Fallen, banished from the Creator's side in the dawn of the world,' the fay said softly. 'For whatever reason, it came to the forest and the people who lived here worshipped it as a god. But it did not leave this place or fade away when the monks came and cut down the trees. I believe it is still here.'

William stared at Shadlok in dawning horror. That's *what is in the church? A fallen angel?* The image of the crow-headed angel in St Christopher's chapel slid into William's mind and his heart began to beat uncomfortably fast. Had it been painted as a warning? If it had, then this wasn't the first time its presence had been felt since the abbey was built.

'Someone else knew about the angel,' William said. He told the fay about the figure painted on the chapel ceiling.

Shadlok's expression was grim as he listened.

William remembered the fox blood on the causeway, and the bundle of oak twigs, and he shivered. 'I think . . . Dame Alys might still be worshipping it.' He told Shadlok what he had found by the abbey gates, and how he had seen Dame Alys in Weforde, coming from the forest and carrying a bloodstained sack; he was certain now that the dark stains *had* been blood.

And if he'd looked inside that sack, he was sure he'd have found the body of a fox.

'She must be making blood sacrifices to help the angel become strong again,' Shadlok said.

William looked at the church, looming over the abbey and fields like a huge grey beast. 'If the angel is in the church, then why did I see it in Dame Alys's house?' he asked.

'What you saw was merely a shadow of the creature, an echo,' Shadlok said, 'not the angel itself. If she is sacrificing animals to it, then some part of it is being drawn to her.'

'But why is the angel stirring *now*?' William asked. 'What does it want?'

'That,' Shadlok said grimly, turning back to his work, 'is something I fear we will soon be finding out.'

William and Shadlok worked on until the daylight began to fade. The bell for compline had been rung long since, and the monks were in the cloister having their bedtime drinks. William carried the shovels and rake back to the tool shed, then hauled water from the well to wash his face and hands. He took his time, not wanting to run into Brother Martin in the kitchen. When at last he went indoors, the kitchen was cold and dark. A scant few embers glowed on the hearth and William knelt beside them, shivering inside his damp and muddy clothes, coaxing them back to life with a few branches from the wood basket.

A small supper had been left on the table for him. There was a piece of bread, a shrivelled apple and half a cup of small beer, not nearly enough food to fill his belly after a hard day's work in the garden, but better than nothing. He sat by the hearth to eat it. He warmed the beer with a hot poker and sipped it slowly.

Later, as he huddled on his mattress wrapped in his blanket, he tried hard not to think about the fallen angel. It was one thing talking to Shadlok about it out in the full light of day, but now, when darkness seemed to ooze from the stone walls and prowl around his bed, he felt very alone and defenceless. He pulled the blanket up to his ears and wished the hob was with him, fidgeting and snoring, a warm and solid little presence.

As he tried to settle more comfortably, he felt the holey stone dig into his chest. He took it off and hid it under his mattress. Nothing on earth would persuade him to look through the hole tonight.

Chapter Ten

Willimam woke with a start. A deep, earth-trembling rumble shook the kitchen. Pots rattled against each other, knives and ladles clattered on their hooks and the pile of fire logs collapsed and rolled across the floor. William's heart pounded as he pushed aside his blanket and clambered to his feet. His sleepy mind struggled to make sense of the terrible thunder of falling stone and timbers and the wild clang of bells. The sound shook the air and juddered through his bones.

It's the tower, he thought, flinching in terror and half expecting the kitchen to come crashing down around him. He felt his way to the door, stubbing his foot painfully against a log on the way. Outside, the grey light of dawn showed between the arches of the cloister alley. A misty drizzle was falling and there was a gritty feel to the air. A dead silence fell over the abbey, though the echo of the tower's fall still hummed in his head.

William ran across the cloister garth to the archway into the north alley. The monks were hurrying down the day stairs from their beds in the dorter, almost falling over each other in their panic. Peter stood nearby, his hair sticking up in untidy brown tufts, wringing his hands together and moaning, 'God a'mercy,' over and over again.

The south door of the church had been wrenched off its hinges and lay under a pile of rubble. Brother Mark's writing desk had fallen on its side and the broken remains of his stool stuck out from beneath a heap of stones. The statues from the church were lined up along the alley wall, a crowd of pale ghosts beneath a thick coating of stone dust.

William felt a flutter of panic in his chest. Where was the hob? Had Brother Walter been anywhere near the church when the tower had come down? Or was he hiding away, terrified but unharmed?

Prior Ardo was suddenly there, white-faced with shock, taking charge. 'Brother Gabriel, go and see if the chapter house has been damaged. Brother Stephen and Peter, see to the animals. The noise will have frightened them.'

Peter and Brother Stephen set off along the passageway beside the chapter house, but returned a few moments later.

'The passage is blocked, Prior,' Brother Stephen said. 'The roof has fallen in at the far end.'

The prior's jaw tightened. 'Go the long way round.'

Brother Stephen nodded for Peter to follow him and they set off across the cloister garth, heading for the kitchen and the door out to the yard and animal pens.

Brother Gabriel picked his way through the litter of stones to the chapter house door. He opened it and peered inside. The short passageway leading to the main chamber was cloudy with stone dust. Moving cautiously, the monk went in. He was gone for a minute or so and looked visibly shaken when he came back.

'Most of the stained glass in the window is broken, Prior,' he said, 'and there's a hole in the roof, a very *big* hole, and stones everywhere.'

William stared at the prior. A muscle twitched beside the monk's mouth as he took all this in.

'The church, Prior,' Brother Snail said anxiously. 'We have to see what damage has been done there.'

Prior Ardo nodded and when he spoke his voice

was carefully calm. 'Come with me, Brother.' He looked at the rest of the monks. 'Everybody else, wait here.'

The prior and Brother Snail covered their faces with the sleeves of their habits and stepped through the dark arch of the church doorway. Stone dust swirled out from the church on the damp air, looking like billowing smoke. The rest of the monks walked past the small crowd of statues at the far end of the north alley, away from the dust and debris, and started to pray, heads bowed and eyes closed. Brother Mark didn't go with them. He stood beside his desk, muttering, 'My books, all my pages, my work.' He turned to stare at the sacristy door, which was hanging by one hinge, then started to clamber over the rubble towards it.

The back of William's neck prickled. A sudden premonition of danger burned him like hot metal. 'Don't!' he called sharply as Brother Mark reached for the heavy ring handle. 'Don't touch the door!'

'I have to save the books,' the monk said, glancing back at William, his dust-streaked face distraught.

William darted forward, one hand reaching out to grab the monk's habit, but he wasn't quick enough. Brother Mark gripped the door handle with both hands and pulled hard. With a wrench of splitting wood, the second hinge gave way and the door fell forwards, crashing onto the rubble and trapping the monk beneath it.

William tried to haul the door aside, but it was solid oak studded with large iron nails and too heavy for him to move by himself.

'Help!' he yelled desperately. 'Quickly! Help me!'

He could see Brother Mark's right hand protruding from beneath the door. The fingers twitched and clutched at the air, and then went still. William heaved and pushed at the door. It shifted slightly, grating against the rubble on the floor beneath it.

The monks, hearing the commotion, came running to see what the matter was. Brother Gabriel rushed forward to try to help. William stumbled as Shadlok elbowed him aside. Brother Gabriel stepped hastily out of the way as the fay leant down and hooked his fingers under the door. He lifted it easily and pushed it away from Brother Mark. It slammed to the floor, sending up a choking cloud of dust.

With an anguished wail, Brother Gabriel dropped to his knees beside the fallen monk. William stared down in horror at Brother Mark's bloodied face.

Shadlok knelt down and put his fingers on the side

of the monk's neck. 'He is still alive.' He glanced up at the shocked faces above him. 'Fetch the prior,' he said, giving William a push towards the church door.

William did as he was told, stopping briefly in the doorway to look back. By now the other monks were crowding around to lift Brother Mark from the rubble.

William climbed over the fallen stones in the south aisle. He stared around in shocked disbelief at the scene of devastation in the church. A huge hole in the recently repaired nave roof let in the dusty daylight and the rain. More light came through a gaping hole in the roof of the south transept. Where the tower should have been there was just grey sky. The beautifully carved chancel screen lay smashed to rubble under a pile of stones and broken timbers. William could see one of the bells, still attached to a part of the bell frame, lying on the nave floor. The choir stalls were badly damaged and a flow of stones filled the south transept. Part of the cracked north wall of the chancel had come down too, but as far as he could see St Christopher's chapel had not been damaged.

Something white swooped through the hole in the roof and settled on a heap of rubble in front of William. It was Fionn, Dame Alys's crow. It strutted sideways along the stones and turned its head to fix William with its fierce stare. William looked around. He knew if Fionn was here, the woman wouldn't be too far away, and sure enough, he saw her standing just beyond the floodwater outside the hole in the chancel wall. Her hands were folded over the top of her walking stick and there was a look of triumph on her face.

Fionn cawed harshly and lifted into the air. He wheeled away through the church and glided in a low swoop past the old woman. She turned to follow him, giving William a smile that chilled him to the bone. On impulse, he snatched up a stone and flung it after her. Anger speared through him. How could she take pleasure from such devastation? Did she really hate the monks that much?

Two figures moved through the gloom like ghosts.

'Prior Ardo!' William called as he scrambled over the stones towards them. 'Come quickly. There's been an accident. Brother Mark is badly hurt.'

The two monks stopped and turned.

'What are you talking about, boy?' the prior said harshly. 'I saw him just minutes ago and he was perfectly well then.'

'The sacristy door fell on him.'

'Oh, dear God!' Brother Snail said softly, crossing himself with a shaking hand.

The prior clambered over the pile of rubble in the crossing, not seeming to care where he put his feet. Stones slid and rattled away, and he slipped a couple of times but didn't slow down. He didn't even glance at William as he ran for the church door, his face and habit streaked with dust. The grit-sharp air eddied around him as he passed by and caught in William's throat, making him cough.

Brother Snail followed more cautiously, edging around the rubble. William waited for him. The monk was wheezing and breathless when he reached William's side.

'How badly is he hurt, Will? Is he conscious?'

William shook his head. 'No.'

Together they left the church. Brother Mark had been taken up to the dorter and put to bed. Brother Snail scurried up the day stairs to tend to him. There was nothing William could do to help, so he went back to the kitchen. He raked out the embers and relit the fire, then went to fetch water from the well in the yard. He broke the news of Brother Mark's accident to Peter and Brother Stephen. The monk said nothing but stood tight-lipped and grey-faced, a pail of water in one hand, staring up at the ruined roofline of the abbey church. Peter started to wail in anguish. Tears slid down his face into his open mouth. He twisted his fingers together against his chest as if William's words had physically hurt him. William walked away in heavy-hearted silence.

As soon as Mass was over, Prior Ardo and Brother Gabriel set out for Weforde to speak to Sir Robert, taking Peter with them. Before he left, the prior told the rest of the monks to go about their daily work as best they could while praying for Brother Mark. Shadlok and William were given the task of clearing the fallen stones and glass from the chapter house. The monks would hold all their services and masses in there until the church could be used again.

The chapter house had been spared the terrible destruction that the church had suffered, but even so, William was shocked by the damage to the chamber. There was a hole in the roof where several massive blocks of stone had crashed through it. Bits of shattered tile stuck up from the floor like broken teeth. Several of the grave slabs of Crowfield's long-dead abbots were chipped and webbed with cracks. The stained-glass window in the east wall looked as if someone had taken a hammer to it. Many of the small panes were shattered and the lead cames that had held them together were twisted and broken. There was very little glass on the floor, so William guessed most of it was outside in the graveyard. All that was left of the Archangel Michael were his legs and part of one wing. Curiously, the dragon at his feet was mostly intact.

Shadlok rolled up his sleeves and tied back his hair. He lifted a huge ashlar block that would have taken two brawny men all their strength to shift, and set it down by the doorway, ready to take out to the yard.

'I'll fetch the handcart,' William said.

'Bring a pail too,' Shadlok said, 'to put the glass in. Some of it might be reusable.'

William nodded. He looked around to make sure they were not being overheard and added, 'Have you seen the hob today? I'm worried that he might have been in the church when the tower fell.'

Shadlok frowned. 'No. I thought he stayed in the kitchen with you at night?'

'He does sometimes, but he didn't last night. I'll go to the workshop and see if he's there before I fetch the cart.'

'Very well, but be quick.' The fay's face was set.

William knew he did not like being this close to the side chapel.

William ran all the way to the workshop. He pushed open the door and peered inside.

'Brother Walter? Are you there?'

There was no reply. William tried to ignore the fear in his stomach. What if the hob was lying beneath the rubble in the church? William ran back to the abbey to search for the hob there. He collided with Brother Stephen as he came round the corner of the south range.

'Ouf! Watch where you're going,' the monk said sharply, grabbing William's arm to steady himself. 'I thought you were supposed to be clearing the chapter house with Shadlok?'

'I am. I came to fetch the handcart,' William said.

Brother Stephen's eyes narrowed. 'Then you would be better off looking for it in the cart shed, boy, and not in the vegetable garden.'

To William's relief, Brother Martin wasn't in the kitchen. He found Brother Snail in the cloister garth, emptying out a bowl of water, red with Brother Mark's blood.

'Have you seen Brother Walter?' William asked anxiously.

'No, not since yesterday afternoon,' Brother Snail said, a frown creasing his tired face. 'Have you looked in the workshop?'

William nodded. 'He's not there.'

'I am sure he is hiding somewhere and is quite safe.' The worry in his voice belied his words. He took a bloodied rag from the bowl and wrung it out. 'Let me know if . . . when you find him.'

'I'll keep looking,' William said, trying to stay calm. 'He has to be somewhere.'

Chapter Eleven

'Well?' Shadlok folded his arms and stared at William. He had a way of looking at you sometimes, as if he could smell something unpleasant, which made William's hackles rise.

'What?' William scowled at him.

'The handcart? The one you went to fetch some time ago?'

'Oh, that,' William muttered.

'And the pail. You forgot that too.'

'Yes, all right, I'll go and fetch them now.' William turned to leave the chapter house, and then looked back at the fay. 'I can't find Brother Walter anywhere.'

Shadlok straightened up. He was quiet for a moment, and William thought he caught a brief flicker of worry in the fay's eyes. 'Perhaps he is with the pig. He often spends time with her.'

'I'll look on my way past,' William said.

'Bring the cart back with you this time,' Shadlok said.

'And the pail,' William said under his breath as he set off along the passageway.

'And the pail,' Shadlok called after him.

William grinned.

Shadlok's guess proved to be correct. The hob was in a corner of Mary Magdalene's sty. The pig was lying on her side in her mud wallow, grunting softly while the hob chittered beside her and scratched her back with a pawful of straw.

Glancing around to make sure there wasn't anybody within earshot, William leant over the fence and said, 'I've been looking everywhere for you. I was worried you might have been hurt when the tower fell.'

'I was in the snail brother's hut,' the hob said, scrambling to his feet and coming over to the fence. He climbed up to sit on the gatepost and looked pleased to see William.

'Is she all right?' William asked, nodding towards the pig.

'The noise frightened her but she is calm now. The sheep are still unsettled and the horse is nervous. She is old and the noise gave her a terrible fright. The hens have run away to hide.'

'How did they get out of the hen house?'

The hob looked guilty. 'They would have hurt themselves in their panic to escape, so I opened the door and they ran into the garden. The brother man who tends the animals has gone to look for them.'

'I suppose we should be grateful you didn't set the goats free too.'

The hob looked away. William stared at him suspiciously. 'You didn't, did you?'

The hob half shrugged and said nothing.

William stepped away from the sty and looked over at the goat pen. The gate was ajar and the pen was empty.

'It might be a good idea if you helped Brother Stephen to find them,' he said, hiding a smile.

The hob nodded and climbed down from the gatepost.

There was a loud angry yell from the direction of the vegetable garden. The hob's face split into a wide grin. 'I think the brother man has found them by himself.'

'You'd better hope Brother Stephen never catches up with *you*.'

'He can't see me!' the hob said gleefully. He scampered away, tail in the air, and disappeared around the corner of the sty.

At midday, the monks gathered in the east alley for sext, needing to keep to their daily routine in the face of the disasters that had befallen the abbey that day. They gathered at the foot of the day stairs up to the dorter, where Brother Mark lay unconscious in his bed, as if to include him in their prayers. Brother Mark's right arm and two of his fingers were broken, along with his nose and several ribs. The bones would heal, Brother Snail had assured them, but so far Brother Mark had not woken, and that was a worry.

William and Shadlok carried on with their work in the chapter house. A thought occurred to William and he asked, 'Could you use magic to heal Brother Mark? Knit his bones and wake him up?'

'I could, yes, but I am not going to.'

William frowned. 'Why not?'

Shadlok brushed stone dust from his hands and raised his eyebrows. 'What do you imagine the monks would say if Brother Mark suddenly sprang out of bed, whole and healed?'

William thought about this and said, 'Oh.'

'Oh, indeed,' Shadlok said dryly. 'If it is all the same to you, I would rather not be tied to a stake and burned by the prior for practising the infernal arts, as he would no doubt view my healing skills.'

William saw the gleam in the fay's eyes and smiled ruefully. 'I hadn't thought of it like that.'

'Brother Mark will mend in his own time,' Shadlok said, reaching down to pick up another ashlar block, 'and that is as it should be.'

By the time the prior returned to the abbey shortly before nones, the chamber was cleared of debris, though there was a large puddle on the floor and the wall paintings beneath the east window were streaked with rain. Shadlok wheeled the final cartload of stone out to the yard, leaving William to finish sweeping up the stone dust.

William leant on the broom handle and looked at the bare mortar on the floor and the damaged roof and window, and he felt sorry for the monks. The roof and floor could be patched up easily enough, but the window was probably irreplaceable. There was nobody at the abbey or in the local villages with the skill needed to put the small panes back together again, if that was even possible.

Footsteps sounded in the passageway leading to the

chapter house. William turned quickly. The prior walked through the doorway, followed by Sir Robert, Brother Gabriel and Master Guillaume the mason.

'It is very generous of you to lend us your stonemasons, Sir Robert,' the prior said. 'I am most grateful to you.'

Sir Robert waved his thanks aside. 'They will bring their tools and bedding to the abbey tomorrow and begin to clear up the mess'

The prior nodded. 'They can stay in the large barn. I will have the sacks of grain moved to the small barn, so they should have plenty of room.'

'I am sure that will be perfectly adequate,' Sir Robert said.

The look on Master Guillaume's face said that adequate was *all* it would be. The master mason paced around the room, assessing the damage with an air of detachment, while Sir Robert stood by the door, watching William intently. Indeed, he seemed far more interested in William than in the chapter house.

There was something about the lord of Weforde that made William uncomfortable. He couldn't put his finger on it, but some instinct warned him to be careful around Sir Robert.

'Where is the servant, Shadlok?' Sir Robert asked.

'In the yard, my lord,' William said, nodding his head in a quick bow.

'Tell him I wish to speak to him, in private.' Sir Robert looked at the prior. 'With your permission, Prior Ardo?'

'Of course,' the prior said stiffly. He looked surprised by Sir Robert's request, but William guessed he was not in a position to refuse. The stonemasons' labour and the building repairs would not be cheap and he would need to keep on the good side of Sir Robert if he wanted his help and money. The prior glanced at William. 'Fetch Shadlok, then go and help Brother Snail in the herb garden, boy, and don't dawdle.'

William found the fay in the open-fronted shed, unloading the stone from the cart.

'Sir Robert is here and he wants to talk to you in private,' William said, sheltering under the thatch and pushing back his hood. The drizzle had turned to rain, and a cold breeze drove it in gusts across the yard. The thought of working in the garden in this weather, on an empty belly, was dispiriting. Dinner was late, and would only be bread and cheese and the last scrapings of yesterday's pottage when it was served. If he had to wait much longer, he'd be fighting Mary Magdalene for the scraps in her swill pail.

'Then Sir Robert can come and find me.'

'I think he wants *you* to go to *him*,' William said.

Shadlok lifted another stone from the cart and said nothing.

'What does he want to talk to you about?' William asked, watching him.

Shadlok glanced over his shoulder. 'Ask him yourself and you will find out.'

William wasn't going to be put off so easily. 'It just seems odd, that's all. It can't be about Jacobus Bone, he's been dead a good three months and Sir Robert would have come to find you before now if he wanted to talk to you about *him*.'

'I have something he wants.'

'Oh? What?'

'That's none of your concern.'

Shadlok laid the last piece of carved vaulting on the ground. His dark tunic was streaked with dust and his hands were powdery white. In the cold grey light his face looked eerily pale and his eyes were an unearthly shade of blue. Strands of his white hair had come loose from the leather strip tying it back and clung to his wet cheek. William had noticed over the past months that a subtle change came over Shadlok when he was around the monks, making him look passably human, but when he was with William the mask slipped and he looked unmistakably fay, as he did now. It was unsettling to watch.

'Does he know you're a fay?' William asked after a pause.

'Yes.'

William frowned. 'Isn't that very dangerous? Can he be trusted to keep it secret?'

'Until he gets what he wants, he will do nothing to anger me.'

As far as William knew, Shadlok had no possessions other than his knife and sword. Perhaps Sir Robert wanted them. They were of fine craftsmanship and he was sure a fay weapon would be far superior to a human one. But why would Shadlok keep *that* a secret?

'Well, whatever it is, he must want it very badly,' William said, pulling up his hood.

'He does.' Shadlok's voice was soft and anger sharpened his face. 'But he is wasting his time.'

'If the prior asks, make sure you tell him I gave you the message,' William said, bracing himself to go out into the rain again. 'I don't want a flogging.'

He set off across the yard just as Brother Martin

rang a hand bell to announce that dinner was ready. William broke into a run. The herb garden could wait, his stomach couldn't.

By mid-afternoon, the rain had stopped. Patches of blue sky showed between breaks in the cloud and a mild breeze swayed through the trees. William and Peter were digging up weeds in the vegetable garden. They were both caked with mud and their clothes were wet through to the skin. William inspected his hands, running a finger over the bone-hard callouses and rough skin on his palms from the last two years of hard labour. That was how long he had been at the abbey, he realised with a touch of surprise: two whole years come the first day of May. A sudden wave of homesickness caught him off guard. He missed his family so much. Their faces were there in his mind, as clear as if he'd seen them only this morning, smiling and happy. He wished with all his heart that he could wake up to find the last two years had been just a bad dream.

'Why did God do this to us?' Peter's voice pulled him back to the present, to the chill of damp boots and muddy clothes. The lay brother's eyes were full of unhappiness. 'Why did he harm our church and hurt

Brother Mark, Will? Is he angry? Have we done something wrong?'

William patted Peter's shoulder awkwardly. 'No. The church was built on waterlogged ground, that's all. The tower fell because the ground wasn't strong enough to support it. God didn't do it, the rain did.' The lie came easily. There was no sense in frightening Peter even more. 'And poor Brother Mark was just in the wrong place at the wrong moment.'

Peter seemed to think about this as he wiped the mud from his hands with a hank of grass. 'So he's not angry about the birdman in St Christopher's chapel?'

William felt as though ants were crawling all over his body. 'The birdman?'

Peter nodded. His face was pale with fear. 'He waits in a corner of the chapel. He beckons me inside but I won't go, because I know he'll hurt me.'

Panic leapt inside William's chest. 'Don't *ever* go in there, Peter. Stay away from the chapel. Do you understand?'

Peter nodded again. 'I promise. But Will, what happens if the birdman comes *out* of the chapel?'

William drew a pail of water from the well to wash off the mud from the garden. He could see Sir Robert and Shadlok over by the gatehouse. He could not hear what they were saying but even from this distance he could see that both of them were angry. Sir Robert was talking, one hand jabbing the air as he spoke. Shadlok shook his head and this seemed to enrage Sir Robert. His hands clenched into fists and William wondered if there was going to be a fight. He wiped his wet hands on the front of his tunic and glanced around. Should he call for help before Shadlok laid out the lord of the manor on the cobbles? Before he could do anything, Sir Robert turned on his heel and strode away. Shadlok watched him go with a look on his face that was chilling to see.

Sir Robert is foolish to make an enemy of Shadlok, William thought as he walked back to the kitchen. He had no idea what Shadlok would do if he was pushed too hard, but his dealings with the Dark King had left William wary of fays and their unpredictable natures. Shadlok was not evil and he didn't have the king's streak of vicious cruelty but, if truth be told, William knew nothing of what went on inside his mind. Whatever secrets Shadlok kept, and William was sure he had a few, he kept them close. And at this moment, the biggest secret of all was what Sir Robert wanted so desperately from him.

Chapter Twelve

The stonemasons arrived at the abbey early on Sunday morning, their possessions packed onto a cart pulled by two horses. William helped them to unpack and carry bed frames, bedding and tools into the barn. As soon as they had settled into their new home, Master Guillaume and his men began the task of clearing the rubble from the church. They stopped for an hour to attend Mass in the chapter house, then trooped back to church to get on with their work.

Peter came to the kitchen to find William later that morning. William was cutting up leeks and onions. His eyes stung and tears trickled down his cheeks. He sniffed and wiped his nose on his sleeve.

'Prior Ardo wants you to go and help the stonemasons. I have to take over from you here,' Peter said, picking up a leek and holding out his hand for the knife.

Surprised and pleased by this unexpected release from the kitchen, William hurried off to the church. The nave and chancel floors were covered in a thick layer of white mud. Rain came streaming down through the gaping hole in the crossing and soaked the walls, further damaging the wall paintings. Saints and angels were slowly fading to ghostly shadows as the paint ran down the plaster in thin ribbons of colour. Many of the windows were shattered and glass lay on the floor in silvery drifts. All the able-bodied monks were piling stones onto the handcart in the nave. There was no sign of Shadlok. William assumed he had refused to work inside the church again.

Master Guillaume was talking to three of his masons. They didn't notice William at first. He stood there awkwardly, not wanting to interrupt them. One of the men was saying something in an angry undertone which William did not catch.

'There will be no more talk of ghosts, Reynaud!' Master Guillaume snapped, holding up a hand to silence the man.

'Yes, but . . .'

'Enough!'

There was an angry muttering as the stonemasons turned to go. One of them saw William and nudged

Master Guillaume. 'It's the boy.'

The master mason gave the man a warning look. 'Get on with your work. And say nothing.'

The men walked past William in silence without looking at him.

Master Guillaume looked William up and down. 'Are you frightened of hard work, boy?' The mason stood with hands on hips and a half-mocking expression on his broad, weather-beaten face.

'No,' William said.

'Good,' Master Guillaume said, 'because you will be doing plenty of it today. Follow me.'

The mason led the way across the church. William's heart sank as he saw that the mason was heading for St Christopher's chapel.

There was a basket of tools on the floor near the chapel entrance. The mason took out a hammer and chisel and handed them to William. 'You'll need these.'

Master Guillaume stared into the gloomy little chapel. He seemed reluctant to go inside. William saw the tense expression on the man's face. *He's frightened,* William thought. *He knows there's something in there. He won't go into the chapel himself but he's prepared to send me in. And I have no choice but to do as I'm told.*

'I want you to lift the floor tiles in here,' Master Guillaume said. 'We're going to use them to repair the floor in the chapter house. Just break the mortar and lever the tiles free. The mortar's damp so they should come away easily enough. Put them over there and we'll come and fetch them.' The mason pointed to the far wall of the transept, well away from the chapel. And with that, he turned and quickly walked away.

William stood at the threshold of the chapel and looked inside. The darkness and silence in the small chamber made him uneasy. Was it here that Reynaud had seen the ghost? Had William been given the job of lifting the tiles because none of the stonemasons would go near the chapel?

Taking several deep breaths, William stepped cautiously through the doorway. Apart from the bare patch where the saint's face should have been, the chapel had not been damaged at all, which struck him as odd. For several moments he stood quite still and listened. He had no clear idea what he was listening for, but the stillness wrapped itself around him like a heavy blanket, deadening the sounds outside the chapel. It was as if the church and the men working there had simply faded away. He glanced up at St Christopher and at the crow-headed angel peering down at him from the ceiling. He remembered what Peter had said, about the birdman in the corner of the chapel, and felt a tremor of fear. Steeling himself, he knelt down. The sooner he finished lifting the tiles, the sooner he could escape from here.

The first tile William tried to chisel free shattered into pieces, but the next one came away easily enough, and the one after that. As he worked, he had the unsettling feeling that there was something standing in the dark corner beside the altar, watching him. It was a struggle not to let his fear overwhelm him and send him running from the place in blind panic.

William's knees hurt from kneeling on the hard floor. He noticed an altar cloth, neatly folded on a stool against the wall. He rolled it up and knelt on it, and went back to work.

For the next hour or so, William lifted tile after tile. At last, he put down the tools and sat back on his heels to rest his aching shoulders for a minute or so. Something caught his eye. A patch of tiles near the wall was noticeably different from the rest of the floor. The tiles did not quite follow the neat lines of those around them, and there was a bird's head in the middle of each one. They were crows, he realised, and it felt as if a cold hand had closed around his heart.

Surely it wasn't by chance that these tiles were here?

William had his back to the chapel entrance, so when something passed by outside, he didn't see what it was, but a shadow crossed the wall above the altar. In the moments it took him to scramble to his feet and reach the doorway, whatever it was had disappeared. The transept was empty.

'Are you all right, boy?' Master Guillaume asked, peering at William's face.

William looked away. What could he say? *I saw a shadow on the chapel wall, but there was nothing there*? He finished stacking the tiles into small piles against the transept wall. 'Yes.'

The master mason was quiet for a few moments. William could feel the weight of his stare. 'They're coming up easily? Not broken too many, I hope?'

'One,' William said. 'The rest were easy enough to lift.'

The mason picked up a tile and turned it over to inspect it. His hands were large and his palms looked like tanned ox hide. His nails were ringed with chalky grime. 'Good workmanship, this. They'll look better in the chapter house than hidden away in that gloomy old chapel.'

'What did Reynaud see? Was it really a ghost?' The words were out before William could stop them.

The mason's face tightened and there was an angry glint in his eye. 'Reynaud is a fool,' he said at last.

'But he saw something, didn't he?' William said.

'He saw a shadow, boy, nothing more than that.'

'I saw something too . . .' William began reluctantly, but the mason didn't let him finish.

'No, you didn't,' he snapped, leaning forward. His breath smelled of rotting teeth and the sour tang of small beer. 'Understand? If my men get it into their heads that this church is haunted, then they won't stay and we won't get paid. A word of this to anyone and I'll tell your prior I caught you stealing. You'll be out on your ear without a rag to call your own.'

William's cheeks flamed with fury. 'I've never stolen anything in my whole life!'

'Then keep your mouth shut and you'll keep your good name. But cross me on this, boy, and you'll regret it.'

William watched the mason walk away, a sick feeling in the pit of his stomach. Master Guillaume meant what he said. The sooner he was finished with the tiles and away from the side chapel, the better.

*

By the time the hand bell for sext rang out, William had lifted all the crow tiles. He had broken up the thick layer of mortar with the hammer and scraped the bits aside. He looked around the chapel and saw that he still had just under half the floor to go. He would need to hurry if he wanted to finish by dusk. He picked up the chisel and shuffled across the floor to start on the next row of tiles. Light from the doorway behind him showed a patch of loose earth where the crow tiles had been. He prodded it with the chisel and to his surprise, he realised that a hole had been dug into the hard-packed earth. It was roughly square and each side was a little over three hand-spans in length. It was too small to be a grave. His curiosity roused, William scraped and hacked at the earth with the chisel, scooping it out of the pit and piling it up on the floor beside him. As he dug down, a feeling of misgiving stole over him. *I shouldn't be doing this*, he thought, but something made him carry on.

A harsh voice behind him made him jump.

'*What* in the name of God are you doing?'

Turning quickly, William saw Prior Ardo and Brother Snail standing in the chapel doorway, staring down at him in astonishment.

'Well?' demanded the prior, nodding at the hole by

William's knees.

William looked up at the two monks in dismay. 'Taking up the tiles, as Master Guillaume told me to.'

'Did he tell you to dig holes too?' the prior said angrily, stepping over the threshold.

William got to his feet. The prior noticed the now-grubby altar cloth and with tightly pursed lips, picked it up, refolded it and put it on a corner of the altar. William flushed guiltily. Brother Snail, his small hunched body moving stiffly, leant down and picked up one of the crow tiles. He examined it for a few moments, and then turned his head sideways to look at William.

'Why did you dig the hole, Will?' There was a worried look in the monk's eyes.

With a wary glance at the prior, William said, 'I noticed some loose earth and wondered what was buried there.'

Prior Ardo crouched down and inspected the hole. He picked up some of the earth and ran it through his fingers. His thin face was tight with suspicion. 'What did you find?'

'Nothing. It's empty.'

'You got right to the bottom?' The prior managed to make it sound like an accusation.

'I don't think so,' William said uncertainly.

'Then dig deeper.'

William's stomach sank in dismay. He felt a curious reluctance to go near the hole again.

The prior gave him a warning look. 'Now.'

William glanced at Brother Snail. The monk must have realised from his expression that something was wrong.

'Perhaps William should get on with taking up the tiles for now,' Brother Snail said quickly. 'Master Guillaume seemed most anxious to see them all so he could decide how best to lay them in the chapter house, and I fear we are delaying him. William can dig out the hole later.'

William smiled briefly at Brother Snail, grateful for his quick thinking, but his relief was short-lived.

'Master Guillaume can wait,' the prior said dismissively. He stared at William coldly. 'Do as I told you.'

William slowly continued to scrape up handfuls of earth.

'Hurry, boy,' the prior snapped.

The two monks stood by silently to watch William as he worked. He had to lean into the hole to reach the bottom, and was wondering how much deeper it would go when the chisel blade scraped against something flat and hard. He felt it with his fingertips. As far as he could tell, it was made of wood, with strips of metal running across it. Small rounded objects, about the size of a fingernail, were set into the metal here and there. Nail heads, perhaps? He was not sure; they felt more like stones than metal.

William sat back on his heels and brushed the earth from his hands. He was filled with deep foreboding. The atmosphere in the chapel had changed subtly. The air felt heavy and his skin prickled unpleasantly, as if a storm was coming. 'There's something down there. A wooden box, I think,' he said hesitantly.

'Bring it up.' There was quiver of excitement in the prior's voice.

William glanced up at Brother Snail. The monk's face was grave.

'Perhaps we should leave it where it is,' Brother Snail said quietly.

William saw the prior's look of surprise. 'The box might hold the bones of a saint for all we know. Maybe God in His infinite wisdom has seen fit to reveal it to us in our time of need.'

This box has nothing to do with God, William thought with fearful certainty. *It should be left alone and the hole filled in.*

'The bones of a saint will bring pilgrims and their money to our abbey,' the prior said, his eyes gleaming. 'Our church is in a sorry state and what money we have for repairs will not go far. Perhaps God has taken mercy on us and has sent us our salvation.'

Brother Snail's glance flickered over the pit in the floor, but he said nothing. He clearly did not share the prior's optimism.

Prior Ardo's sallow cheeks were flushed with anticipation. 'Lift the box.'

It took several minutes of struggling to work the box up and out of the pit. It wasn't particularly big but it was heavy, and there were no handles to grab hold of. William huffed and grunted with the effort, scraping his knuckles painfully against the stones sticking out of the sides of the pit. The prior helped him to drag it onto the floor and into the light near the doorway. He knelt down beside William and brushed the scatter of earth and stones from the top of the box. He looked around for something to clean it with.

'Pass me that,' he said, waving a finger impatiently towards the altar cloth. Brother Snail handed it to the prior, who set about rubbing the mud from the box, all regard for the embroidered linen forgotten in his excitement.

The box was made from oak. The wood was dark and as hard as iron in spite of having been buried deep in the earth. The corners were protected with gold mounts. Thin bands of gold, set with small polished stones, criss-crossed the lid and side panels. The stones glowed softly in a rich rainbow of colours and the gold bands were exquisitely carved with tiny, strange-looking animals and birds, leaves and curving branches. The box was beautiful and clearly very valuable.

William glanced up at Brother Snail and met his worried gaze for a moment. He could guess what was going through the monk's mind: why would anyone bury such a treasure as this? Why hide it at the bottom of a muddy hole in a little-used side chapel?

The prior lifted the lid. Inside, the box was tightly packed with layers of straw and raw wool. The prior's hands were shaking as he carefully pulled it all out, releasing a musty smell into the chilly air. William peered over the prior's shoulder to see what lay beneath the packing.

The prior straightened up slowly and stared down into the box. The hoped-for saint's bones were not there. In their place was a small wooden bowl, old and plain, like countless others that could be found on any table in any house in England. The prior's disappointment was almost palpable.

'What's that?' Brother Snail asked, reaching down into the box.

He took out a tightly coiled strip of lead. Carefully he unrolled the soft metal. William could see letters carved into it.

'What does it say?' William asked.

The monk stared at the lead strip for a few moments in silence. His cheeks were the colour of ashes.

'It says,' he began with obvious reluctance, *'Cave: ira dei. Domine miserere nobis.'*

William heard the prior draw a sharp breath and panic fluttered in his stomach. 'What does that mean?'

'It means,' Brother Snail said softly, *'Beware: wrath of God. Lord have mercy upon us.'*

For a few moments, nobody spoke or moved. William stared at the bowl in its nest of wool. The words on the lead strip were a warning, but against what? Was the bowl cursed? And even if it was, what harm could a small wooden bowl possibly cause?

'We should bury it again,' Brother Snail said, his voice trembling slightly.

The prior picked up the bowl and turned it over to examine it. 'There are words here,' he said, peering at the underside. He handed it to Brother Snail. 'Your eyes are sharper than mine. Can you make out what they say?'

With obvious reluctance, Brother Snail carried the bowl over to the doorway, where the light was a little better.

'It says, *Velieris cecidum* . . . I'm not sure what the next word is.' He angled the bowl to catch the light. '*U . . . n . . .* I think it says *unum . . . in eterno . . .* the last word is *obscuro. Velieris cecidum unum in eterno obscuro.*'

'*Hide the fallen one in eternal darkness*,' the prior said softly, a puzzled look in his eyes.

William drew a sharp breath. *The fallen one.* Shadlok had said the god that was worshipped in the sacred grove, right here where the abbey now stood, was a fallen angel. Were the words on the bowl and the lead strip a warning of some kind? But what possible connection could there be between a wooden bowl and a fallen angel?

'There is more,' Brother Snail said. 'Patterns of some kind. Symbols or ciphers, perhaps. I don't recognise them. And more words, difficult to read.' He peered at them for several moments. '*Deus indulgeo nos*. God forgive us.' With one shaking hand, he quickly crossed himself. 'We must rebury it, and we must do it *now*.'

'No,' the prior said firmly. 'We will keep it in the sacristy for the time being. The box is worth a small fortune. We can sell it, and decide what to do with the bowl later.'

Brother Snail shook his head. 'I think you are making a mistake.'

'A few idle words, probably written in mischief, and we imagine the worst,' the prior said dismissively, but there was a look of uncertainty in his eyes. 'Neither of you will mention the lead strip to anyone, or the words on the bowl, do you understand?'

Brother Snail's mouth drew into a hard line and he said nothing. The prior looked at William, and William nodded.

'Prior?'

They all turned quickly. Master Guillaume stood outside the chapel. His gaze flickered from the box to the hole in the floor, then up to the prior's face.

'Found that in there, did you?'

The prior seemed lost for words. William could see he was angry that the mason had seen the box, but it was too late to try to hide it now.

Master Guillaume nodded towards the bowl in Brother Snail's hands. 'Was that inside the box?'

'Yes,' the prior said stiffly.

'Well now, that's a curious thing, isn't it?' Master Guillaume said. 'A plain little thing like that inside a box fit to grace the treasury of the king himself.'

Brother Snail leant down and put the bowl back into the box, closing the lid. 'These things are none of your concern. They're abbey property and we are merely removing them to a place of safety while the work continues.'

'Oh, is that so?' Master Guillaume said, raising his eyebrows. 'You left it until *now* to take them to a safe place?'

It was obvious that the master mason did not believe him. Master Guillaume was nobody's fool. He knew perfectly well they had only just discovered the box.

'What are you doing here anyway?' the prior snapped, clearly annoyed by the man's insolence.

'I came to see where the boy had got to with the tiles,' Master Guillaume said.

'Very well.' The prior gave William a warning glance. 'Get on with your work, boy.'

Without another word, the prior picked up the box and left the chapel, sweeping past the mason. Brother Snail followed, but he paused in the doorway. 'Fill in the hole, William.' He gave William a meaningful look and set off after the prior.

Master Guillaume waited until the monks had gone before turning to William.

'A strange thing to bury under the floor of a side chapel, wouldn't you say, boy? A valuable box like that?'

William was scraping the earth back into the pit. He said nothing.

'And all it held was that bowl? Nothing else at all?'

'No,' William said. 'Nothing.'

'No clue as to what was so special about the bowl? Because it must be very special indeed to be placed in such a box, don't you think?'

William didn't answer. The master mason squatted down across the pit from him, his hands linked between his knees.

'Keeping silent when I ask you a question is as good as lying,' he said pleasantly.

William glanced up at the mason. 'I don't know who buried the bowl or why. Maybe it's a relic.' He didn't know what made him say that but he regretted it as soon as he saw the look on the mason's face.

'A relic! Of course, and an important one at that,' Master Guillaume said, a thoughtful look in his eyes. 'It would explain why such an ordinary little bowl would merit a box adorned with gold and precious stones. But why then hide it away beneath the floor of such a small and insignificant abbey?'

William straightened up and shrugged. He looked around for the chisel and hammer, to get on with lifting the tiles.

'Unless, of course, the relic is something very precious indeed,' Master Guillaume went on. 'And what better place to keep something safely hidden than *here*, where nobody would ever think of looking? Where better to hide, say,' the mason paused for a moment, a strange light in his eyes, 'the bowl Jesus himself used at the Last Supper?'

The words hung in the cold air of the chapel and echoed inside William's shocked mind. Was Master Guillaume suggesting the bowl was the Holy Grail?

It couldn't be, surely? William thought. Whoever had carved the warning onto the lead strip had called it the Wrath of God. The bowl was cursed, not blessed.

'It isn't the Grail,' William said, staring up at the mason.

But Master Guillaume was not listening. The tiles were forgotten as he hurried from the chapel, excitement shining in his face.

William scraped the last of the earth and broken bits of mortar into the pit and sat back on his heels. He stared down at the scatter of crow-headed tiles in dismay and thought: *What have I done?*

Chapter Thirteen

At dusk, Brother Gabriel rang the hand bell to call the monks to the chapter house for vespers. William heard it clanging far off in the cloister and suddenly felt very alone. He was uneasily aware of the huge empty church around him. The masons had finished work for the day but he still had half a row of tiles to lift before he could leave the chapel.

Hours spent kneeling on the rough mortar floor had taken their toll and he stood up for a few minutes to ease his aching legs. The afternoon light had faded and it was almost too dark to see what he was doing, but if he didn't lift all the tiles today, he would have to come back tomorrow, and that didn't bear thinking about. For the last hour or so he had caught fleeting glimpses of shadows flitting across the walls and heard soft rustling noises. An image of flexing wings had formed in his mind and it had taken every last bit of courage he could muster to stop himself from making a run for the safety of the cloister.

As he stood there, a soft sigh breathed out close to his ear. William stared around the dark little chapel, eyes wide with terror, but there was nothing to see. His heart hammered in his chest as he forced himself to kneel down again and reach for the chisel. Fear made him clumsy and he broke the next two tiles. Fighting back his panic, he wiped the sweating palms of his hands on his tunic. His gaze was drawn to the dark corner beside the altar and his breath caught in his throat, threatening to choke him. There was something there, a patch of darkness just a little denser than the shadows around it. He was sure that it hadn't been there a few moments ago.

Slowly, William put the hammer and chisel on the floor and crawled cautiously away from the altar. He felt behind him for the door jamb and pulled himself to his feet. His breath was coming in short ragged gasps and he forced himself not to turn and run in wild terror through the church. The shadow moved again. William's foot touched the threshold and, moving as stealthily as he could, he stepped over it and out of the chapel, then he turned and fled across the transept, glass and broken stone grating under his feet.

William reached the nave and skidded to a halt. It was too dark to pick his way through the rubble towards the cloister door with any measure of safety. Instead, he ran the length of the church to the west door. Moments later, he was in the yard and running across the wet cobbles towards the abbey kitchen.

Peter was warming the monks' evening drink of small beer in a cauldron over the fire. His face brightened when he saw William.

'Brother Martin said you were working in the church today, Will. I was worried about you.'

William forced a smile as he pulled up a stool to the hearth and warmed his shaking hands. 'I've been lifting tiles in St Christopher's chapel.'

'You mustn't go in there,' Peter said anxiously. 'You mustn't go near the birdman.' He wrapped a rag around the handle of the cauldron and lifted it from the hook. He set it on the table and started to ladle the warmed beer into waiting cups.

'I didn't have any choice,' William muttered as he pulled off his boots and held his hosed feet out to the fire. The wool steamed gently in the heat. Painfully itchy chilblains on his toes ached as the warmth slowly returned, and he rubbed them for a few moments.

'Did you see anything?' Peter asked. 'Was the bird-man there?'

William shook his head. Peter didn't need to know what he'd seen and heard in the chapel.

'That's good, Will,' Peter said earnestly. For a while, he concentrated on ladling the beer without spilling it. When he had finished, he stood the cauldron on a hearthstone. He glanced at William. 'The stonemasons from Weforde said a bowl was found in the church today. They said it was the Holy Grail and that the prior brought it out of its hiding place to bring pilgrims to the abbey.'

William frowned at him. '*I* found the bowl, and it isn't the Grail.'

'It isn't? How do you know?'

William thought of the words on the bowl and the warning scratched onto the lead strip, and remembered the prior's order not to tell anyone about them. 'It just isn't.'

'But the masons say it is,' Peter said, sounding confused.

William said nothing. He could not stop Master Guillaume from claiming the bowl was the Grail, if that was what he wanted to do, but he wouldn't add to the lie.

*

At dawn on Monday morning William woke from a restless sleep and strange, confused dreams about his family, but the dreams dissolved like smoke in the wind before he could grasp them. He lay huddled on his mattress until the cold draught under the yard door forced him to sit up, dragging his blanket around his shoulders. He put a foot on the floor and gasped in surprise as the damp wool of his hose touched cold stone. Where were his boots? He had been wearing them when he'd gone to sleep last night, as he did every night, but they weren't there now.

William stared at his feet in bewilderment. Who would have taken his boots? And *how*? Both of the doors into the kitchen were firmly bolted. He searched the room but the boots were nowhere to be found.

What do I do now? he wondered, running his hands through his hair. Boots or no boots, he would certainly be punished if the fire wasn't blazing beneath a cauldron of water when Brother Martin arrived in the kitchen. William fetched a pail and unbolted the door. A thin mist drifted across the yard in the grey dawn light, but at least it wasn't raining. He picked his way slowly and awkwardly over the cobbles, trying to avoid the worst of the puddles. *This is ridiculous,* William thought in exasperation. Of all the strange things that had happened at the abbey lately, the disappearance of his boots felt like the most baffling.

He hauled up a bucket of water and filled his pail, then began the ankle-jarring walk back to the kitchen, the sodden and muddy wool of his hose chafing uncomfortably against his skin. He set the pail down by the door and went to fetch wood for the fire. When he returned to the kitchen, he saw a pair of boots standing by the hearth. For several moments, he stared at them in astonishment. He picked them up and turned them over to examine them. They couldn't be *his* boots, surely? The holes in the soles and the toes were covered by neatly stitched patches and he could smell the tallow that had been rubbed hard into the leather to keep the rainwater out. He gazed at them in amazement and realised they *were* his boots. Someone had mended them while he'd been sleeping.

'They will keep your feet dry now,' someone said behind him.

William grinned as he turned and looked down at the hob, sitting on the mattress, wrapped in William's blanket. 'Thank you! Where did you get the leather for the patches? And how did you mend them so quickly?'

The hob grinned back and looked very pleased with himself. 'The snail brother gave me an old boot that had lost its fellow and I cut the patches from that. Hob fingers work quickly.'

'Well, these look almost as good as new,' William said. 'Hob fingers are clever too.'

The hob looked at the puddle forming around William's feet. 'The snail brother gave me some tallow. Perhaps you should rub it onto your feet to keep them dry as well.'

'That's a very good idea, but people don't put tallow on their feet.'

'Why not?'

William shrugged. 'I don't know. They just don't.'

The hob pulled a face to show what he thought of this bit of folly.

William made up the fire and filled the cauldron with water.

'You'll have to move from there,' he said to the hob. 'Brother Martin will be here at any moment and he won't be pleased to see my bedding all over the floor.'

The hob bundled up the blanket and pushed it under the small table in the corner of the kitchen, then he walked to the yard door and reached up to lift the latch.

'How did you get into the kitchen last night to take off my boots?' William called after him. 'The doors were still bolted when I woke up his morning.'

The hob pointed to the rafters.

'Through the roof?'

'There are holes up there, if you know where to look.'

'And you do, I suppose?'

The hob nodded. 'I follow the rats and the spiders. They know all the hidden ways in this place.'

The sound of footsteps in the cloister outside the kitchen warned them that Brother Martin was approaching. In a heartbeat, the hob had gone and the yard door creaked slowly closed.

William was scrubbing the greasy pottage cauldron with water and ashes when Brother Snail came to find him later that morning.

'These are for you, Will.' The monk held out what looked like a bundle of rags. 'I found them in a chest in a storeroom. They're old and are more patches than clothing, but at least they're wearable.'

Smiling broadly, William wiped his hands on the front of his tunic and took the clothes. He was going up in the world, it seemed. As well as nearly-new boots, he now owned a second tunic, undershirt and two pairs of hose. 'Thank you,' he said with genuine delight. He plucked at the front of his damp tunic. 'I might get a chance to dry these things out at last.'

The monk nodded and smiled. He glanced at William's feet. 'The hob has mended your boots, I see.'

'He's made a good job of it, too.'

'He has nimble fingers. If it was not for the fact it would be too hard to explain away, I'd ask him to mend all the monks' boots.'

William put his new clothes under the table with his bedding. He was already looking forward to the wonderful moment he would be fully clean and dry again. He could barely remember how that felt.

Brother Snail stood by the fire and stared down into the embers. He was quiet for several moments and seemed preoccupied. 'It has been a strange morning,' he said at last. 'A disturbing one in many ways. Some of the brethren have seen or heard things which have troubled them.'

'Oh? What kind of things?'

'Several people have seen shadows and heard whispering or rustling noises in odd corners of the abbey. Brother Gabriel swore he saw the shadow of a huge crow in the church, spreading its wings. It was gone in a moment and he didn't stop to search for it, he just took to his heels and ran, and wasn't ashamed to admit it.' The monk held thin hands out to the fire. 'But that's not the worst of it. Brother Stephen found a dead lamb in the graveyard. Its throat had been cut, and it wasn't the work of an animal.'

'No, and I think I know who did it,' William said.

Brother Snail's eyes widened in surprise. 'You do?'

William nodded. 'I think it was Dame Alys.'

Brother Snail stared at him in thoughtful silence for several moments. He pulled up a stool and sat down. 'I see. Perhaps you would like to tell me why you believe she would do such a thing.'

William squatted by the fire and told Brother Snail about the sacrificed fox and the bloodied sack he'd seen Dame Alys carrying.

'But how can you be sure the two things were connected, Will? You didn't actually *see* the woman kill the fox, did you?'

'No,' William agreed, 'but I saw other things.' He took the holey stone from around his neck and held it up. It twirled slowly on the woollen cord. 'The hob gave me this. It's a holey stone. Shadlok calls it a seeing stone.'

Brother Snail listened in silence as William told him what he'd seen through the stone, about the Hunter's Oak and the sacred grove. The monk's face paled when William told him about the crow-headed god and how Dame Alys's family had been the guardians of its grove for longer than anyone could remember.

'Shadlok believes it is a fallen angel,' William finished, 'and that it's still there, in the chapel, keeping close to its holy place.'

'One of the Fallen?' the monk breathed, horrified. 'Oh, dear God, no! That is what the words on the bowl must have meant! *Hide the fallen one in eternal darkness.*' They stared at each other in silence. Brother Snail crossed himself slowly. His thin fingers fumbled beneath his cowl for the cross he wore around his neck, and he held it tightly. 'The bowl and the fallen angel must be bound together in some way, Will.'

'When I saw the sacrificed deer, I saw a bowl, too. It was being used to hold the deer's heart.'

Brother Snail looked appalled. 'Was it the bowl we found?'

'I didn't see it clearly, but I wouldn't be surprised if it was,' William said. 'Where is the bowl now?'

'Prior Ardo is keeping it under lock and key in

Abbot Simon's old chamber until the sacristy door is repaired.' The monk held out his arm for William to help him to his feet. 'There has been something . . . unclean in the side chapel for the last few months, Will, but I never imagined it could be something so terrible. But *somebody* knew about the angel, *someone* carved the words of warning on the bowl and buried it beneath the chapel. I will search through the abbey's books to see if I can find out who it was and what they knew. There might be something written about it somewhere.' Brother Snail closed his eyes. 'And in the meantime, we must pray that we can find the way to banish this angel . . . this *demon* back to hell where it belongs.'

Chapter Fourteen

Tuesday dawned bright and windy. Doors and window shutters rattled and draughts whistled through gaps. William crawled out of bed, tired after another bad night's sleep. Fleeting images of beating wings had chased through his dreams, and the dark outline of a monstrous bird, perched on the broken rafters of the church, its harsh cries filling the air. Several times he had woken suddenly and had lain there listening, heart pounding in cold terror, with no idea what it was that had woken him. He went about his work in heavy-eyed silence. Lack of sleep made him clumsy and he quickly fell foul of the equally tired cook when he dropped a water jug and it smashed into pieces on the kitchen floor.

'Clear that up,' Brother Martin growled, landing a stinging blow across the back of William's head.

'Give me a chance, then,' William snapped.

The monk's bloodshot eye widened and his lips curled in the snarl of a mad dog. His big hand bunched into a fist and he drew back his arm. William ducked just in time but the monk's hand kept going until it hit the wall and he let out a yell of rage and pain.

William was out of the door and halfway across the yard before the monk knew he'd gone. He wasn't looking where he was going and ran full tilt into Prior Ardo, sending the monk flying. Brother Gabriel was behind the prior and broke his fall, but there was nobody to stop Brother Gabriel from landing heavily on the cobbles. He lay there, winded and dazed.

Brother Martin, in hot pursuit of his kitchen boy, tripped over Brother Gabriel and grabbed the prior to stop himself from falling, only to bring the prior crashing to the ground with him. William stared in horror at the three monks floundering in a heap at his feet.

The commotion in the yard brought people running to see what had happened. Reynaud the stonemason and Brother Stephen helped the monks to their feet. William looked from the furious prior to the even angrier cook and felt an overwhelming urge to turn and run. Before he could do so, Brother Snail was there. The small monk stood between William and the others and tried to calm everyone down.

'The boy meant no mischief, Prior, I saw what happened and it was a simple accident.'

'Get out of my way,' Brother Martin snarled. He made a grab for William, but Brother Snail stood his ground.

Shadlok, who had been working with the stone-masons, walked over to stand beside William. He said nothing, but simply folded his arms and stared at Brother Martin, his gaze chillier than the brisk March wind whipping across the yard. The cellarer took a step backwards. An angry flush of colour mottled his face and he watched Shadlok warily.

'Enough,' the prior said loudly. He seemed to struggle with the impulse to take William by the scruff of the neck and shake him until his teeth rattled. Instead, with a visible effort, he said, 'Brother Snail is right. It was an accident. The boy does not deserve to be beaten for that.'

Brother Martin scowled at the prior's mild words but held his tongue.

William was as surprised as Brother Martin by the prior's leniency. Normally Prior Ardo was all in favour of the redeeming qualities of a sound beating, and he had *never* taken William's side against one of his monks before.

The prior glanced around. 'Well? Haven't any of you got anything better to do than idle here in the yard?'

There were a few raised eyebrows as people went back to their work. With a last glare at William, the cellarer stumped back to the kitchen and slammed the door behind him.

'You are no longer needed in the kitchen,' the prior said, staring coldly at William. 'From now on you will work with the stonemasons, or with Brother Snail or Brother Stephen.' As if he felt the point needed to be emphasised he added, 'Stay away from Brother Martin.'

William nodded and tried to hide his delight.

Prior Ardo turned to Brother Snail. 'It might be as well if the boy slept in your workshop for now.'

William opened his mouth to protest. He *couldn't* sleep in the hut, away from the safety of the abbey walls . . . but then he thought, *it isn't any safer* inside *the walls.*

'Yes, of course, Prior,' said Brother Snail.

The prior turned back to William. 'Find Master Guillaume and ask him what you can do to help.'

William watched the prior walk away with Brother Gabriel limping along beside him.

Brother Snail gave William a reassuring smile, but it didn't quite reach his eyes. William knew the monk was worried by the thought of him being alone in the hut at night. 'It really is for the best if you stay away from Brother Martin for now, Will.'

Something in the monk's voice hinted that there was something else behind William's banishment from the kitchen. 'This is about more than just a broken pot, isn't it?' William asked with a frown.

Brother Snail hesitated, then sighed and said, 'Brother Martin has been having nightmares these last few nights. About you.'

'Me?' William stared at him in astonishment.

'The prior knows about the bad dreams and he most probably feels things will settle down if you are away from the kitchen for a while. Brother Martin is tired and his temper is short, so it's probably for the best.' Brother Snail patted his arm. 'You will be far more comfortable sleeping in my workshop, I am sure.' The monk turned to go but looked back at him with a gleam in his eye. 'But don't break too many of *my* jugs or bowls, will you?'

William grinned. 'I can't make any promises.'

*

William waited until Brother Martin left the kitchen for vespers before fetching his mattress and blankets and his spare clothes. He felt as if a weight had been lifted from his shoulders. He didn't realise until that moment just how much he had come to loathe working alongside Brother Martin. He hefted his bundled belongings more securely in his arms and, without a backward glance, set off for Brother Snail's workshop. In an odd kind of way, it felt almost as if he were going home.

Shadlok and the hob were sitting by the fire when William reached the hut. The hob had taken William's flute from its hiding place and was trying to play a tune. Shadlok was watching him with a gleam of amusement in his eyes. William carried his bedding over to a corner of the room and dumped it on the floor.

'You are sleeping here now?' Shadlok asked.

William nodded. 'Brother Martin doesn't want me in the kitchen any more.'

'You can share the floor by the fire with me,' the hob said, looking very pleased with this turn of events. He laid the flute across his knees and grinned up at William.

'Thank you,' William smiled back.

'What did you do to anger Brother Martin this morning?' Shadlok asked.

'I dropped a jug.'

Shadlok looked surprised. 'He tried to kill you just for that?'

'He'll use any excuse to beat me,' William said tightly. He was quickly coming to hate Brother Martin.

'I could put a curse on him,' Shadlok said. There was a gleam in his eye, and William wasn't sure if he was being serious.

'What kind of curse?'

'Whatever you want,' he said, shrugging. 'I could turn him into a fish or make his hands shrivel to stumps. I could make him fall asleep and not wake again.'

William smiled uncertainly. 'You could really turn him into a fish?'

Shadlok nodded. 'Just say the word and it will be done.'

'Or a frog,' the hob suggested hopefully. 'Or a worm.'

For a moment, William was sorely tempted to accept the fay's offer. He could imagine Brother

Martin as an ugly old carp, mouth opening to bite on a sharp hook . . .

It was a struggle but reluctantly he shook his head. 'No, it wouldn't be right.'

'It is your choice,' Shadlok said with the hint of a smile. 'Just tell me if you change your mind.'

Oh, don't tempt me, William thought with feeling.

The hob stared up at William. 'The one-eyed brother man is full of anger, like a boil waiting to burst. One day he will go *sploff*.' He clapped his paws together with a sharp slap.

'Well, I really hope I'm not there when he does,' William said, shuddering.

The hob picked up the flute again. His fingers were too small to cover the holes properly, so the tune he played consisted of just a couple of notes, but he played them with his usual enthusiasm. William sat down across the fire from Shadlok.

'Brother Martin has been having nightmares about me. The prior thinks it'll be better if I keep out of the kitchen for now.'

'The prior is right.'

'Do you dream?' William asked curiously. 'Do you even *sleep*?'

Shadlok shook his head. 'Not in the way humans

do. When I sleep, it is more a stilling of the mind.'

'What about you?' William reached out a foot and nudged the hob.

'I dream about the forest,' the hob said, lowering the flute. There was a look of sadness in his eyes as he stared into the fire, and a faraway look on his face.

'You miss it, don't you?' William said gently.

The hob looked up at him. 'Sometimes I do. But I would miss you and the snail brother and Shadlok just as much if I were back in the forest.' He held the flute out to William. 'I would like you to play now.'

For a while, William played and peace settled around the hearth. At last, Shadlok stirred himself and said, 'It is time you learnt a more challenging tune.'

He took the flute and began to play a tune William had never heard before. His long fingers moved gracefully over the holes in the instrument, and the song lilted and spun and glowed through the firelit room.

William listened, rapt. He had never heard such heart-meltingly beautiful music before. Not even Robin's playing had been *this* good. The hob sat perfectly still for once, a look of awe on his face.

When the last few notes died away, William shook his head. 'I will *never* be able to play like that.'

The fay handed the flute to William. 'That does not mean you cannot try.'

And try William did. With Shadlok's patient instruction, he caught a shadow of the song. Frustration welled up inside him as he strove to get closer to the beauty of Shadlok's playing, but his fingers felt clumsy compared to the fay's and at last he lowered the flute and frowned at Shadlok.

'It's just too hard.'

Shadlok sat forward and threw a stray branch into the fire. 'Few things worth having are easily won. You must practise until playing comes as naturally as breathing.'

William snorted. 'That's easy for you to say.'

The fay raised an eyebrow and a smile lifted the corner of his mouth. 'I had to learn once, just as you are now.'

William looked at him curiously. 'Who taught you?'

Shadlok looked away and the light left his face. It was if a shutter had closed between them. He stared into the fire in silence for a while, then he got to his feet and walked over to the door. 'Be sure to bolt this behind me,' he said without looking back at William and the hob, and he was gone.

William stared at the closed door thoughtfully. He

had touched a nerve, it seemed. 'He doesn't like talking about the past, does he?'

The hob leant over and poked a finger into William's chest. 'It hurts him, in here.'

'I wonder if he'll ever trust us enough to tell us what happened to him, why he was exiled from his own world,' William said, 'and why he and the Dark King are such enemies.'

The hob yawned sleepily. 'One day, he will.'

William fetched his bedding and unrolled his mattress. He bolted the hut door, then pulled off his boots and settled himself for sleep. With a contented sigh, the hob lay down beside him and within minutes, they were both sound asleep.

Chapter Fifteen

L ife at the abbey settled into a sort of routine over the next few days. Peter was sent to Yagleah with a message from Prior Ardo to Edgar the carpenter, asking him to come and start boarding up the church and chapter-house windows. He arrived with his son, Hal, and a cartload of timbers on Wednesday morning and set to work.

William divided his time between helping Brother Stephen with the animals, Brother Snail in the garden, and working in the church with the stonemasons. On Saturday morning, a week after the collapse of the tower, William was wheeling another cartload of stone from the church to the stonemasons' shed when he saw a group of people emerge from the passageway beneath the gatehouse. There were four men, a woman and two young children. They were dressed in ordinary working clothes and carried

151

baskets and a couple of sacks. Brother Stephen herded them across the yard. He saw William and waved him over.

'Fetch Prior Ardo,' Brother Stephen said. There was a bemused look on his face. 'Tell him we have . . . pilgrims, here to see the holy relic.'

William frowned. They'd come to see the bowl? Closer to, he recognised two of the men. They were from Yagleah, and he often saw them at Weforde market.

'Hurry, boy!' the monk said, flapping a hand at William. He seemed at a loss to know what to do with the pilgrims and the gifts they'd brought. William glimpsed a couple of chickens squashed into a wicker basket, and a honeycomb in an earthenware pot. The villagers had washed their faces and hands and cleaned the worst of the grime off their clothes. They stood close together and stared around at the abbey buildings, openly curious.

Prior Ardo was in the cloister, sitting on the stone bench by the chapter-house doorway, eyes closed and hands clasped. It was almost time for nones and Brother Gabriel stood nearby, bell in hand, ready to call the monks to prayer.

'Pilgrims,' William said, running up to the prior,

'out in the yard.'

'What?' The prior's eyes snapped open. He stared at William as if he had taken leave of his senses.

'Pilgrims from Yagleah, to see the bowl. Brother Stephen sent me to fetch you.'

The prior looked startled, but then his face lit up with excitement and he turned to Brother Gabriel. 'God has answered my prayers! The first pilgrims to our abbey, Brother. The first of many, God willing.'

The prior and Brother Gabriel went to greet the villagers and accept their offerings. William stared after them in dismay. It no longer mattered that the bowl was not the Grail. Word of the abbey's holy treasure had spread quickly through the surrounding villages and excitement was growing. He could shout the truth from the rooftops but nobody would listen. The people in the yard had come to see the Grail and that was just what the prior intended to give them.

A makeshift shrine was set up at the western end of the north aisle. William was sent to fetch a small table from a storeroom and the bowl, in its jewelled oak box, was placed on it. Brother Gabriel set wax candles in silver holders on either side of the bowl.

'Do you want me to light them?' Brother Gabriel asked.

The prior shook his head. 'No, there's no need for that.'

The prior was not going to waste the abbey's precious wax candles on villagers from Yagleah, William thought wryly, even if they *were* pilgrims.

Brother Gabriel nodded in agreement. He looked at William. 'Go about your work, boy. You're not needed here now.'

William walked away across the nave. On impulse, he hid behind one of the huge pillars, to watch as Brother Stephen led the pilgrims into the church. The villagers stared around in shock at the ruined building as Brother Stephen herded them towards the shrine. They crowded around to peer into the box, their faces shining with awe, then knelt in front of the table and bowed their heads as the prior began to pray.

The cold air stirred as something drifted past William, an unseen presence that made the hair on the back of his neck stand up. A foul odour wafted along behind it and he caught his breath in disgust. It smelled like rotten cabbage and meat that had gone bad, with more than a hint of a ripe cess-pit thrown in for good measure. *Oh, that is* disgusting, William thought, putting his hands over his nose. It was so bad it made his eyes water. He breathed through his mouth and watched as, one by one, the pilgrims and the monks looked around uneasily and sniffed the air. Cloaks were pulled more tightly around shivering bodies, and noses were held as the stink reached them. One of the children started to cry.

Prior Ardo, his face strained and his nose wrinkled with distaste, crossed himself hurriedly and urged the villagers to their feet. Brother Stephen led them out of the church. The prior closed the box and handed it to Brother Gabriel. William darted back behind the pillar and hid as the monk scurried across the nave towards the cloister door. William risked a glance around the edge of the pillar and saw the prior standing near the west door, his head to one side, listening to something. He crossed himself again, then turned and quickly left the church.

William edged away from the pillar. Brother Gabriel had left the door to the cloister ajar and a thin shaft of grey light cut through the gloom in the south aisle. A small dark shape crossed it and William's heart almost leapt out of his chest in fright. Something touched his leg and he jumped.

'Has it gone?'

To his relief, William saw that it was the hob. 'I

don't know,' he said softly, 'but I don't think we should wait around to find out.'

The hob ran ahead of him and reached the cloister door first. Thankfully, there was nobody about.

'Ugh, I can *still* smell it,' William said in revulsion. True, the foul odour wasn't quite so bad here in the cloister and had more of a fishy tang now, but it still turned his stomach. The hob climbed onto a stone bench nearby and sat hunched up and shivering in the chilly breeze that chased its tail through the arches of the cloister alley.

'I was looking for you,' the hob said, wrinkling his nose against the lingering smell. 'The snail brother sent me to tell you that he found some writing hidden in there.' He pointed to the sacristy door. Edgar the carpenter had rehung it that morning and someone had scrubbed Brother Mark's blood from the timbers. 'He wants us to go to his hut this afternoon and he said Shadlok must come too.'

Whatever it was, it must be important for Brother Snail to call William and the fay away from their work.

'Shadlok is helping the carpenters. I'll find him and give him the message. Tell Brother Snail we'll be there as soon as dinner is finished.'

The hob nodded, jumped down from the bench and, with a flick of his tail, he was gone.

Out in the yard, the bell rang out calling the monks to the frater for dinner. William suddenly realised that the smell in the cloister had nothing to do with the fetid stench of the demon in the church. It was Brother Martin's fish stew, and the reek of it seeped through the abbey like marsh mist. Quite what the cook had done to the stew to make it smell so bad, William couldn't imagine, but one thing was for sure: he didn't think he would *ever* be hungry enough to want to sit down and actually eat it.

After dinner, William went to find Shadlok. 'Brother Snail's found out something about the bowl in the sacristy. He wants us to meet him in his workshop this afternoon,' he said.

'Very well,' Shadlok nodded. 'The carpenters will be returning to Yagleah soon to fetch another load of timber. I will go to the monk's hut then. You will need to make some excuse to get away from the stonemasons.'

William had already planned his escape. He would plead a belly gripe and say he needed to ask Brother Snail for something to soothe it. It wasn't so far from the truth either, he thought queasily, remembering the bowl of stew and the glassy-eyed fish head that had stared back at him from the thin grey stock in his bowl.

Shadlok lifted a plank onto his shoulder and carried it up the steps to the church door. He paused and seemed to take a deep breath before stepping over the threshold. William followed a few moments later, one hand clutching his belly and his face pulled into a suitably pained expression.

Luck was on his side; Master Guillaume had smelled Brother Martin's fish stew and readily believed that William was an innocent victim of the cook's food.

'But don't make a habit of this, boy,' the mason warned. 'Gripes or no gripes, there's more than enough work to do here.'

William grinned to himself as he left the church and set off for Brother Snail's workshop.

'Come in, come in, Will,' Brother Snail said, ushering him into the hut and closing the door behind him. 'I was beginning to worry that you wouldn't be able to get away from Master Guillaume. What excuse did you give?'

William grinned. 'Belly gripes.'

Brother Snail smiled, but there was a look of sadness in his eyes. 'So many lies.'

'Well, I couldn't tell him the truth.'

'No, of course not, that wasn't what I meant. But small lies have a habit of growing into bigger lies and tripping you up.'

The hob was sitting on a hearthstone. Shadlok, arms folded, stood by the fire. William glanced at him in surprise, wondering how he'd managed to get here so quickly. Brother Snail took William's arm and led him over to the table, where a small leather-bound book lay beside a lantern. The stub of tallow inside was lit and the smoky flame flickered and guttered. The book's shadow flapped like a little black wing on the table beside it.

'I found this in a cupboard in the sacristy. It is a history of the abbey, written more than a hundred years ago.' Brother Snail opened the book and slowly turned the exquisitely decorated vellum sheets.

The hob climbed onto the table and squatted between William and the monk. William had to peer over his head to see the book.

Brother Snail seemed to be searching for a particular page. He found it and smoothed it flat with his fingertips. There were lines of writing and a small painted picture of the abbey. The workmanship was impressive, but the look of the page was spoilt by the untidy scrawl of words in black ink at the foot of the page and the small drawing beside it. It showed a bowl above what looked like a stick with a bundle of feathers tied to the top.

'This was added after the book was finished,' Brother Snail said. 'I think this drawing is meant to be the bowl we found in the side chapel. The words at the bottom of the page say *Verum est ad sanctum pedem*. That means, *The truth is at the saint's foot*. I think whoever buried the bowl may have written a full account of why he did so before hiding it somewhere here in the abbey, at the feet of a saint.'

'Yes, but which saint?' Shadlok said with a trace of impatience. 'There are a great many to choose from.'

'I don't know,' the monk admitted.

William pointed to the drawing of the feathered stick. 'What's that supposed to be?'

The hob traced the drawing with a fingertip, his curved claw scratching the vellum. 'It is a tree.'

Three pair of eyes turned to stare at the hob in surprise.

'It looks nothing like a tree,' William said.

'The painted man in the church is carrying a tree with feather leaves at the top, just like this one,' the hob said with a shrug.

Brother Snail frowned thoughtfully for some moments and then said slowly, 'I believe you're right.' He turned to William and Shadlok in sudden excitement. 'It's a palm tree. It's one of St Christopher's sacred symbols. They don't grow in England, but in the Holy Lands far to the east they are as common as weeds. So I have heard, anyway.'

'Why did he go around carrying a tree?' William asked, baffled.

'He was a giant of a man and he used the tree for a staff,' the monk explained. 'But the point is that it was drawn as a clue. The truth is at *St Christopher's* feet.'

'It is likely that whoever drew this wrote down in secret what he could not say in this book,' Shadlok said. 'If we're looking for a sheet of parchment, it could be hidden in the smallest of spaces, though there is a fair chance it will not have survived the damp rising through the walls or the destruction of the tower.'

'Even so, we have to try to find it,' Brother Snail insisted. 'And the side chapel is the only place in the abbey linked to St Christopher.'

'There was nothing else buried in the chapel,' William said. 'I took up all but the last few tiles and there were no more holes dug into the floor.'

'Then we must have missed something,' Brother Snail said, with a helpless little shrug.

'Maybe it's under the feet of the *other* holy man with a feather tree,' the hob suggested innocently. He jumped with fright when William leant down and grabbed him by the arms.

'*What* other holy man?' William demanded. 'Where?'

'There is another St Christopher in the abbey?' Brother Snail asked, his cheeks pink with excitement.

The hob nodded. 'He has no head and the small man on his shoulder has mostly broken away, but he still has his tree.'

'Where did you see him?' William asked.

'In the square place where the brother men sit sometimes,' the hob said, 'with the garden in the middle.'

'The cloister?' Brother Snail sounded surprised, but then his eyes widened and he turned to William. 'Of course! There must have been a St Christopher among the small statues on the chancel screen. It must have been taken from the church and put in the north alley with the other statues.' He turned to the hob with a wide smile. 'Your sharp eyes might well have solved this riddle, Brother Walter.'

The hob looked delighted. His ears twitched and he smiled back at the monk.

William grinned and poked the hob in the ribs. 'Even so, you might have told us about the statue before now.'

'No matter,' Brother Snail said, still smiling. 'At least we know now. Will, can I ask you to find the statue and bring it back here? The brethren will be in the chapter house, and the stonemasons will have finished for the day. You won't be disturbed. Brother Walter will show you where to look.'

The hob nodded but he looked worried. 'We won't have to stay there long, will we?'

'Only as long as it takes us to find the saint,' William assured him. The statues from the chancel screen were small, barely the length of his arm. St Christopher would be light enough to carry back to the workshop.

A problem suddenly presented itself to William. 'But what if the writer hid whatever it was in the chancel screen itself? The screen is just a pile of rubble now.'

'One thing at a time, Will,' Brother Snail said briskly. 'Let's just find the statue and take it from there.'

William peered around the corner of the passageway. The east alley was deserted. He could hear the murmur of voices coming from the chapter house. The daylight was fading and shadows were creeping through the cloister. He looked down at the hob. 'Show me where you saw the statue.'

Glancing around fearfully, the hob crept out of the passage and along the alley. William followed close behind him. They turned the corner into the north alley.

The statues were eerily lifelike in the half-light, their painted eyes watchful. Some of them were as small as the hob; others were the size of a fully grown man. Many of them were chipped and cracked, or missing hands or noses. Their colourfully painted robes and faces gave a rainbow glow to the gloom of the cloister walk.

Countless stone eyes seemed to follow William as he picked his way carefully between the throng of saints and angels. The hob disappeared for several moments, but then he reappeared, dust and cobwebs on his fur and a look of panic on his face.

'The holy man has gone!'

'Are you sure?' William asked. 'Perhaps someone's moved him?'

The hob shook his head. 'Other stone people have gone too. Look.' He pointed to a patch of empty floor between an angel playing a recorder and a small statue of St Catherine carrying a wooden cartwheel. Bits of broken stone and dust marked the gaps where other statues had been.

'The stonemasons must have taken the most badly damaged statues out to the rubble heap in the yard,' William said. 'We'll have to search there.'

The hob looked dubious. 'There is a *lot* of stone in the yard and the holy man is very small. It might take a long time to find him, and it's getting dark.'

'Then we'll have to do it tomorrow,' William said. 'We *have* to find whatever was hidden at his feet.'

The hob pulled a face. 'Then it's just a great pity his holy feet aren't a good deal larger.'

William managed to find a few minutes to speak to Brother Snail as he brought the monks their warmed bedtime beer that evening.

'The statue's disappeared,' William said, keeping

his voice down. 'I think the stonemasons have taken it out to the yard to break up for rubble.'

The monk gave an exasperated sigh. 'We were so close,' he murmured. 'Is there a chance they haven't smashed it yet, do you think, Will?'

William shrugged. 'I don't know, but I'll go and search for it tomorrow, when I get a chance. There are usually a couple of men working in that part of the yard and they won't want me climbing all over the rubble heap, so it might take a while.'

Brother Snail nodded. 'Well, just do your best.'

William nodded. 'I'll try.'

But later, as he carried the tray of empty cups back to the kitchen, William admitted to himself that finding one small and possibly broken statue amongst the vast pile of stones would be difficult, if not downright impossible. There was a more than fair chance that whatever secrets St Christopher had guarded, they were lost for good.

Chapter Sixteen

William slept well that night. He was woken shortly after dawn by the hob patting his cheek with a leathery paw. The fire was already crackling cheerfully under a cauldron of water. William rubbed his eyes and peered blearily up into the hob's face.

'You were sleeping snorily,' the hob said. 'I did not want to wake you until I had to.'

William sat up and stretched. The hut was warmer than the kitchen had ever been. It felt right somehow, sleeping inside timber walls again, on a wooden floor.

The hob bustled about, adding wood to the fire and putting a piece of bread on a hearthstone to warm. William wondered where he'd got it from, then decided it didn't matter. It smelled appetising and he was hungry enough to eat a sheep.

The hob turned the bread on the hearthstone so

that it didn't burn. 'I heard shouting coming from the brother men's sleeping room in the night. More bad dreams, I think. The snail brother makes sleeping potions but they do little to stop the nightmares.'

The hob wouldn't let him out of the workshop until he'd had some bread and a mouthful of hard cheese. There were even a few hazelnuts roasted in the embers, and a couple of small apples which still held the lingering sweetness of late summer.

The hob scolded him for eating his food too quickly, making William grin. It was almost like being at home in Iwele, being told by his mother to at least *try* to chew his food before swallowing it.

I'm going to enjoy living here, William thought as he finished the last of the nuts. He pulled on his boots and stood outside the hut for a minute or two. The breeze still had a cold edge to it, but the sky was blue and shards of sunlight glittered on the fishpond. New green growth speared through the dense mats of last year's dead reeds around the water's edge. The trees in the forest across the river were flushed with a faint haze of spring green. Crows wheeled across the sky, little black rags tossed on the wind above Two Penny Copse. William felt his spirits lift. On a day such as this it was easy to pretend that all was well with the world, that there were no fallen angels or fay kings with evil in their hearts and death in their eyes. Today there was just the feel of sunlight on his face and the smell of wet earth and wood smoke on the breeze. And if his body ached tonight, it would be from a day of honest work and not from another of the cellarer's hard-fisted beatings.

Later that morning William went to fetch a pail of water for Brother Snail. Peter was already at the well, tipping water from the bucket into the pail by his feet.

'Are you helping Brother Martin in the kitchen now?' William asked.

Peter nodded. He tried to pull his hood forward to hide the blackened swelling around his eye, but he couldn't hide the cut to his lip. William grabbed the lay brother's hood and pushed it back. Peter flinched but stood there, mute with misery.

'What happened to your face?' William asked sharply, though he already knew the answer. 'Did Brother Martin hit you?'

Peter turned to leave but William caught hold of his arm. 'Did he?'

'I have to go,' Peter mumbled, trying to push him away. He glanced nervously over his shoulder at the kitchen door, which stood ajar. William could hear the cellarer moving about inside and the low rumble of his muttered, angry curses. 'I have to get back to work.'

William's mouth tightened angrily. It was one thing for the monk to hit *him*, but quite another if he was using his fists and venting his anger on Peter. He could imagine only too easily how angry Brother Martin would be with Peter's clumsiness. William's earlier elation at being away from the kitchen disappeared like water on a hot stone. How could he enjoy his freedom when Peter was paying the price for it?

Perhaps I should ask Prior Ardo to be allowed back to work in the kitchen, he thought, a sick feeling in the pit of his stomach. But he knew he would be wasting his time. Brother Martin didn't want him there.

Peter pulled up his hood, covering his wind-reddened ears. His face was pinched with anxiety, his eyes frightened. 'I have to go *now*, Will.'

William nodded and watched the lay brother shamble away across the yard, water slopping from the pail and soaking his boots. He would beg Brother Snail to help Peter, but that was all he could do, and he feared it was not going to be enough to save the lay brother from the cellarer's vicious temper.

William dropped the bucket into the well, then

hauled it up, heavy with water, and rested it on the wall. He glanced over towards the rubble heap on the far side of the yard. Two of the stonemasons were busy sorting the usable stone from rubble. He had no hope of searching for the statue while they were there.

Brother Stephen walked past him carrying an axe. 'When you've finished, boy, fetch the wood cart and meet me by the gateway. A tree's come down across the trackway and we're going to cut it up for firewood.'

William carried the pail of water to the workshop and ran back to the yard to get the cart. Brother Stephen was already walking along the causeway, the hem of his habit lifted clear of the floodwater, when William caught up with him. William wheeled the cart up the slope to the trackway, grinning to himself when he realised that his newly mended boots hadn't let in any water and his feet were dry.

A dead ash tree had split its trunk and the crown had come crashing down across the track, shattering the brittle branches and scattering wood everywhere. Brother Stephen set to work with the axe while William stacked the cut wood on the cart. At last the monk stopped to wipe the sweat from his face. He handed the axe to William.

'I'll take this lot back to the abbey. You cut up some of the smaller branches while I'm gone. And be careful with the axe, boy. The prior won't thank me if you end up chopping off your foot.'

Brother Stephen lifted the handles of the cart and wheeled it away. William hefted the axe and swung it into a branch. Chips of wood shot off in all directions and he quickly ducked out of the way.

'The monk is right, you need to have a care,' someone said behind him.

William glanced around, and to his dismay he saw Robin standing a few paces away, watching him with a smile that sent a shiver down his spine.

'What are you doing here?' William gripped the handle of the axe tightly and held it across his body.

'That is not a very friendly way to greet an old friend,' Robin said. He was the same thin boy with stringy red hair whom William had met in Weforde, but his green eyes were icy with malice. 'Especially after I shared my food with you the last time we met.'

Anger surged through William at the memory and he felt his cheeks redden. 'We're not friends, and it *wasn't* food.'

Robin grinned. 'Yet you took it readily enough.'

William felt the weight of the axe in his hands and

knew he would use it against the Dark King if he had to. 'You tricked me, but I know now who you really are.'

Robin regarded him coldly. 'So?'

'So why are you still pretending to be human?' William asked, sounding a good deal braver than he felt. 'And why are you here?' This wasn't just a chance meeting, he was sure.

'I want you to give Sceath-hlakk a message from me: tell him I will not forgive him for releasing Bone from my curse. I am leaving the forest, but our paths will cross again, and I will show him then what I do to those who defy me.'

William remembered how ill at ease the king had seemed when they had reached the abbey gatehouse the other day. It dawned on him that the Dark King was as frightened of the fallen angel as the rest of them.

'You're running away,' William said scornfully. 'You're scared of what's in the abbey.'

A look of murderous anger twisted the king's face. For a few heart-stopping moments William thought he'd gone too far.

'How dare you!' the king spat. '*No* living creature questions my courage!'

William realised that he had touched a nerve and recklessly took advantage of it. 'All the forest fays have been leaving Foxwist these last few weeks, and now you're running away too.' *Stop it!* a voice inside William's head said in alarm, *stop baiting him, or this won't end well.*

The king's eyes narrowed and his lips curled in a sneer. 'And why shouldn't I leave? I know what is stirring in the abbey. To stay in the forest is to risk something far worse than death.'

What could possibly be worse than death? William wondered uneasily.

A shiver of light crossed the king's body and the red-haired boy vanished. Comnath, king of the Unseelie Court, stood in his place. He looked just as he had when William had first seen him, last winter in the Whistling Hollow. There was a fleeting resemblance to the boy Robin in the sharp-boned face and unnaturally green eyes, but this creature could never have been mistaken for a mortal man. His dark red hair was swept back from his face and it hung straight and sleek over the shoulders of his green tunic. Lean of build and disturbingly beautiful, he had the look of a dangerous wild animal. The king walked forward slowly and came to stand in front of William. Close to, he seemed to radiate a painfully icy chill. William shivered and took a step backwards. His hands were damp with sweat and shaking as he held the axe to his body.

'The question I must ask myself is this,' the king continued, his voice soft and oozing malevolence, 'do I kill you now and be done with it, or do I wait? But you *will* die, of course, sooner or later, and it will be by my hand.' The green eyes narrowed as he gave this some thought.

William stared back at him, refusing to lower his eyes. It was a struggle, but he had no intention of giving the king the satisfaction of seeing just how frightened he was.

'But not today, I think,' the king said contemptuously. With that, he turned towards the forest. In the blink of an eye he had gone and William was alone on the trackway.

Chapter Seventeen

That night William dreamed he was back home in Iwele. It was a bright May morning, full of warm breezes and hedges foaming with blossom. He was standing in the vegetable garden beside the mill house listening to the sound of voices and laughter coming from inside the building. His mother and his sister, Cecily, stood in the doorway, beckoning to him. Behind them, he could see his father and his younger brother Matthew, smiling and happy. Joy flooded his body in a hot rush; they weren't dead! He tried to run to them, but found that no matter how hard he tried, he couldn't move.

Someone called his name and with a huge effort, he managed to turn his head. On the far side of the mill-race stood his older brother Hugh, waving to him. He tried to shout back but no sound came. The laughter in the mill house turned to screams. Dragging his gaze away from Hugh, William stared at his home in horror. Smoke billowed from the roof and flames roared high into the sky. The doorway was the mouth of a furnace and against the red-hot glow he could see the black shapes of his family.

No! Not again! Don't let them die again, please!

The timbers of the old mill burned fiercely and in a matter of minutes the building had collapsed in a pile of charred wood and ash. There was no sign of his family. Hugh, still on the far bank of the millrace, pointed to William and screamed in a voice scorching with hatred, 'Why didn't you save them? Why did *you* survive, but not them?'

William woke with a start. His body was damp with sweat even though the workshop was bitterly cold. With a shaking hand he pushed back his blankets and rolled off the mattress to kneel on the floor by the hearth. He lifted the *couvre-feu* aside and the glow from the embers cast a little light. Enough light to see the dark outline of someone standing by the hut door.

William froze with terror. The figure was so tall it touched the rafters. There was a soft rustle and a dark red gleam as the firelight shone on glossy feathers.

And then, in the space of a heartbeat, the creature was gone.

How long he crouched there, trembling and terrified, William didn't know. When at last he forced himself to stand up, his body was stiff with cold. There was a scraping noise in a corner of the hut. William spun around in fright. The hob, his eyes huge with fear, crawled out from behind the wood basket.

'I did not think it would *ever* leave,' the hob said shakily. 'It stood by your mattress and watched you while you slept.'

William poured himself a cup of water and knelt by the hearth to drink it. The hob crept over to sit beside him. He leant against William and shuddered from time to time.

Had the demon somehow put the nightmare in his mind, William wondered? The worst thing about it was how clear the faces of his family had been. It was as if they had really been there with him. Seeing them again had been almost too painful to bear and his sense of loss was a knife in his heart. Watching them die in the fire was a torture he had been spared two years ago; seeing it now was agony.

William wiped away the tears that blurred his eyes. If the demon had been responsible for the nightmare, then it had looked inside his mind and knew what memories to use to hurt him. And if it could do that, what else could it do?

William was in a quiet mood as he went to fetch the wood cart from the shed early on Monday morning. The nightmare had left a heaviness of spirit that he couldn't shake off, and his thoughts were of his brother Hugh. He was filled with a painfully strong need to see him again. *Where are you, Hugh? Please come home. Please come and find me.*

Peter emerged from the kitchen carrying the wood basket and walked towards the shed. William waited for him, but the lay brother didn't reply to his friendly greeting and wouldn't look at him.

'Peter? What's wrong?' William asked, catching hold of Peter's sleeve.

'I have to fetch the firewood for the kitchen,' Peter mumbled, pulling away from him. He looked terrified. William was disturbed to realise that the lay brother was frightened of *him*.

'Peter, what is it?'

'Brother Martin told me not to speak to you,' Peter blurted out, twisting his hands together anxiously around the handle of the basket.

'Why not?' William asked in surprise. He saw the confusion in the lay brother's eyes as he struggled to decide whether or not to answer him.

'You don't have to be scared of me,' William said gently. 'We're friends, aren't we?'

Peter nodded reluctantly.

'Did Brother Martin tell you . . . something bad about me?'

After a moment's hesitation, Peter nodded again.

'What did he say?'

William didn't think the lay brother was going to reply but at last, in a voice small and hoarse with fear, Peter spoke. 'He says . . . you are in league with the devil.'

'He said *what*?'

'He says that you get into his dreams to torment him, and that the devil is there with you.'

'I get into his dreams? Are you sure that's what he said?'

Peter nodded. 'You did last night.'

William stared at the lay brother, appalled. It felt as if there were a lump of ice lodged in his chest. The creature was turning the cook against him through his dreams. How could he possibly defend himself against that?

'Listen to me,' he said, reaching out to touch Peter's arm again. The lay brother flinched as if he had raised a hand to hit him. 'Listen, Peter, I'm not in league with the devil, I promise you.'

'But I've seen you too, Will, in *my* dreams,' Peter whispered, 'with the devil standing behind you. It looks like a crow but its wings are red and it is so *tall* . . . it looks like the birdman in the chapel.' Panic flashed in his eyes and he took a couple of stumbling steps backwards. 'Brother Martin says you will hurt us all, like you hurt Brother Mark.'

William was speechless. He merely stared at Peter, his body cold with shock. Peter seized his chance. The firewood forgotten, he turned and ran across the yard as if the whole of hell was at his heels.

William sat on the chopping block by the shed door, his head in his hands as he tried to make sense of what Peter had told him. What if Brother Martin managed to persuade the rest of the monks that William was evil? He had appeared to Brother Martin in his nightmares, and everyone at Crowfield knew how terrible *they* had been lately. And Peter claimed to have seen him with the demon in his dreams too. But the very worst of all was the suggestion that he had somehow harmed Brother Mark.

A shadow fell across William's face and he glanced up. Brother Snail stood by the door.

'Will!' the monk said in surprise. 'What are you doing hiding away in here?'

'Have you heard what Peter and Brother Martin are saying about me now?'

Brother Snail didn't need to ask what William meant. He sighed and lowered himself onto a stump of wood. He gazed at William with a look of compassion. 'Yes, I have.'

'It's not true,' William said defensively. 'It's the demon. It's getting into people's dreams and it's making them think that I'm there too.'

'I know.' Brother Snail reached out to put a hand on William's arm. 'I've been telling them so but they are too frightened to listen.'

'Did you tell them the demon is a fallen angel?'

The monk shook his head. 'No, and until we find something to prove what we suspect, I can say nothing.'

William leant back against a stack of cut logs and stared bleakly out at the yard. 'Why is the demon doing this? Why has it picked on me?'

'Perhaps the demon knows you had a hand in releasing the angel from its grave last winter,' Brother Snail said, 'and if the angel had come here to hunt it down, it won't thank you for that.'

William frowned at the monk. 'Then why hasn't it turned on Shadlok? It was his idea to dig up the angel, not mine.'

Brother Snail was quiet for a while. There was a troubled look in his eyes.

'There's something you're not telling me, isn't there?' William said suspiciously.

'I just wondered . . .' the monk began. He cleared his throat and started again. 'I just wondered if the demon wants . . . more from you.'

'More? What do you mean?'

'Do you remember what Abbot Simon said on his deathbed, Will? About you?' the monk asked. 'He said that the light shines brightly in you, and that it marks you out from those around you. What if the demon is drawn to you precisely because of that? What if it is trying to take that light for itself?'

'How can it possibly do that?' William asked, and then he suddenly realised what Brother Snail was saying. 'You think it means to kill me?'

The monk's face crumpled with unhappiness. 'I pray I'm wrong, but I believe . . . the demon wants your soul, Will. By isolating you from the people around you, it leaves you vulnerable. It will try to make sure there will be nobody to help you when the time comes.'

William stared at the monk in shock. It all sounded too horribly plausible. 'Shadlok won't turn his back on me,' he said, but there was a worm of doubt in his mind. Was he so sure of that? What if Shadlok had had enough of life at the abbey and saw this as a way of ridding himself of a tiresome burden? He could easily find someone else to be bound to by the Dark King's curse.

'You will never be alone, I promise,' Brother Snail said. 'I will be there, and the hob too, and unless I have gravely misjudged him, I truly believe Shadlok will stand by you. But be on your guard constantly, Will.'

William stood up. He gazed down at the monk, touched by his loyalty, but really, what could Brother Snail do against a fallen angel?

'I'd better go. Brother Stephen will be wondering where I've got to with the wood cart.'

Brother Snail nodded and got to his feet. William grabbed the cart handles and started to wheel it out of the shed. 'I haven't had a chance to search through the rubble heap yet. The stonemasons are always around. But I'll keep trying. The sooner we find whatever was hidden at St Christopher's feet the better.'

'Good lad. We'll fight this demon, Will, never you fear,' Brother Snail said, forcing a smile, but William wasn't fooled. What possible chance did any of them stand against a creature who had defied God Himself?

Chapter Eighteen

Brother Stephen had cut up several of the larger branches and the trackway was littered with logs. He stopped to lean on the axe handle when William arrived with the wood cart.

'Finally decided to turn up, have you?' he said sharply. 'Well, now that you're here, you can start loading the logs onto the cart.'

With that, Brother Stephen got back to work and didn't speak to William again for the rest of the morning. The silence between them was not a comfortable one, and William wondered if Brother Stephen believed what Brother Martin had been saying about him. It seemed likely that he did. When the bell for sext clanged out, faint and distant, the monk leant the axe against the tree stump and set off back to the abbey without a word, wheeling the laden cart ahead of him.

William got on with cutting up the last few branches. With luck, he would finish them before dinnertime and wouldn't have to spend an afternoon of awkward silence working alongside Brother Stephen.

The pile of logs grew and William stopped for a few minutes to rest. He laid down the axe and stretched his arms above his head, easing out his stiff shoulder muscles.

There was a rustling behind him and he turned to see a figure emerge from a holly thicket. It was Dame Alys. She pulled her cloak free from the spiky leaves and clambered down the grass bank onto the track, steadying herself with her walking stick. Fionn swooped down from the branches of an oak tree and landed beside his mistress. He flapped his wings and cawed loudly. William eyed the bird with dislike.

'I saw you here yesterday with the fay,' Dame Alys said. She shook her head slowly. 'I don't know what you've done to make an enemy of that one, but I would not care to be in your shoes. Fays are tricksy at the best of times, but *him*, he's the worst of them all.'

'You don't need to tell me that,' William said gruffly.

Dame Alys walked over to stand in front of him,

almost close enough to touch. And certainly close enough to smell. She reeked of death and blood. He wrinkled his nose and turned away.

'I hear the monks have found the Holy Grail in their church,' the woman said. She stepped sideways, forcing him to look at her. 'But that's a lie. The bowl belongs to *me* and I want it back.' She peered into his face and her eyes narrowed in suspicion. 'But I think you knew that already, didn't you?'

William didn't reply. He watched her warily and tried not to breathe in her gamey odour too deeply.

'A clever boy like you can surely find a way to return the bowl to its rightful owner, can't you?' she said with a sly smile that deepened the web of wrinkles around her mouth.

'You want me to steal it?' William asked.

The woman jabbed a finger towards the abbey. '*They* are the thieves, not me!'

'Then you go and take it, if it's yours,' William said. He wanted nothing to do with any of this.

The woman's oddly-coloured eyes narrowed dangerously. 'You don't want to get on the wrong side of me, boy.'

William was about to say he had to get back to work when she suddenly reached out and raked a fingernail across his cheek.

There was a sting of pain and William yelped. He clapped a hand to his face and jumped back. 'What was that for?' he demanded angrily.

The woman ignored him. She fumbled in the pocket sewn inside her cloak and pulled out an oak twig. With great care she wiped the blood from beneath her nail onto the twig, then returned it to her pocket.

William remembered the bundle of oak twigs and the fox's blood he'd found on the causeway and he recoiled. What did she want with his blood? He made a grab for her cloak, but she brought her stick down hard on his arm and he stumbled backwards. In the same moment Fionn rose into the air with a clap of wings, his claws reaching towards William's face. William dropped into a crouch. Fionn's claws skimmed his head, raking his scalp painfully. The bird swooped upwards to land on a branch.

'Bring me the bowl, boy,' Dame Alys said, 'or I swear, Fionn will feed on your eyes one of these days.'

William grabbed a branch and stood up. He swung the branch from side to side. If the crow came near him again, he wouldn't think twice before bringing it down. 'I know what the bowl is, and I know what your ancestors used it for,' he said, glancing at the woman, but keeping a careful eye on the crow.

Dame Alys looked surprised. 'Too clever by half, you are,' she said, baring brown teeth at him. 'Too clever for your own good.'

'And I know about the demon,' William added recklessly.

Her face quivered with rage and she spat at his feet. 'Belinus is not a demon! You have had your chance to help me, boy. I won't ask again.'

In a whirl of fury, she turned and stamped away. She pushed aside the holly branches with her stick and forced her way back into the forest. Fionn flew after her.

For a long time after she had gone, William stood on the track, waves of sick dread churning through his belly. *She has my blood*, he thought. It was only a smear, but perhaps that was all she needed for an offering to the demon. The question was: what would the demon do with it?

When the bell rang for dinner, William returned to the abbey. He passed Brother Stephen and Brother Gabriel in the yard. They watched him walk by in silence, their eyes hostile. He heard them whispering behind his back and glanced over his shoulder. He saw Brother Gabriel cross himself.

The hob was in his usual perch in the blackthorn. He saw the cut on William's cheek and his face puckered with concern.

'You're hurt,' he said, reaching down to prod William's cheek gently.

'I met Dame Alys in the forest,' William said. 'She scratched me.'

'Why?' The hob sounded surprised. 'Did you do something to make her angry?'

'No. She wanted some of my blood as an offering to the demon,' William said, his stomach tightening at the memory, 'and she also asked me to steal the bowl for her.'

The hob clambered quickly down the tree, as surefooted as a cat. His eyes were wide with alarm. 'Nonono! You must not give her the bowl, and you must keep your blood to yourself.'

'Well, I didn't run up and offer it to her,' William said. 'As for the bowl, I've no intention of giving it to her.'

William followed the hob into the hut. He sat on a stool while the hob fetched a bowl of water.

'Bad, bad woman,' the hob muttered as he dipped a rag into the water and climbed onto the table to dab at William's cheek. The wet cloth was soothingly cold against the burn of the cut. William smiled at him.

'That's much better, thank you.'

The hob patted the cut dry, then dried his paws with a linen rag. 'The scratch is not deep. It will heal quickly. But she is still a bad woman for doing this to you.'

'She won't get close enough to me to do it ever again,' William said, a little of his anger returning.

'Good,' the hob said. He pointed to the basket of food that had been left on the table. 'The one with the simple wits brought that for you.'

William took a covered earthenware pot from the basket and sniffed the contents cautiously.

'What's in it?' the hob asked, leaning down to take a look inside the pot.

'I don't think I want to know.' William sniffed again and wrinkled his nose. He was sure that even Mary Magdalene would turn her snout up at today's dinner. In truth, it smelled like something the old pig had been rolling in.

The hob was deeply unimpressed by the cold and watery vegetable pottage and burnt bread. William prodded a lump of what might have been turnip and felt his spirits sink. The pottage would barely take the edge off his hunger and he still had an afternoon of hard work ahead of him. He was sure Brother Martin had deliberately held back the bigger pieces of vegetables and chosen the smallest, most charred hunk of bread out of spite.

'This is very bad,' the hob said, shaking his head and scattering breadcrumbs over the table. He brushed them away with the tuft on the end of his tail and then scowled down at the blackened crust in his paw. He tapped it with a fingernail. It was as hard as stone and sounded hollow. 'This does not taste good at all.' He pointed to William's mouth. 'And it has made your teeth black.'

'And yours, too,' William said. The hob curled back his lips to reveal black teeth and gums. The hob's tongue was black as well.

'It still tastes better than *this*,' William said, prodding a thick cabbage stalk. It was solid and woody and floated like a drowned slug beneath the surface of the pottage.

The hob dropped the bread back into the basket and wiped the soot off his paws. 'Nasty.'

William grimaced. Nasty indeed. Brother Martin could not have made his dislike for William any plainer.

He was scraping the last spoonful from the bottom of his bowl when Brother Snail came to find him. The monk's expression was grim.

'Prior Ardo wants to see you, Will, in the chapter house, right away.' He paused for a moment and peered more closely at William. 'What happened to your face?'

William told him briefly. The monk looked horrified.

'We are going to tell Prior Ardo the truth, now, before this gets completely out of hand, and before that woman does you some serious harm. I will also tell him that Shadlok is a fay, and before you say anything, Will, I have Shadlok's permission to do so. Indeed, he will meet us at the chapter house in a few minutes' time. We need to get the prior on our side if we are to have a hope of dealing with this terrible mess.'

'Are you sure this is the best way?' William asked doubtfully.

'It is the *only* thing we can do,' Brother Snail said. 'Several of the brethren have asked the prior to turn you away from the abbey and unless we give the prior a reason not to, I fear he will do so.'

Chapter Nineteen

Shadlok was waiting when William and Brother Snail reached the chapter house.

'We are to go straight in,' the monk said. He looked up at Shadlok. 'Are you sure about this?'

Shadlok's gaze flickered to William briefly. 'I am sure.'

Brother Snail nodded. 'Very well. Follow me.'

They walked along the short passageway to the inner door of the chapter house. Brother Snail knocked and pushed it open. Prior Ardo was sitting on the stone seat beneath St Michael's stained-glass feet, the only part of the window not boarded up. He was alone. There was a lantern hanging by the door and a second lantern on the stone seat beside him. In the soft half-light, the prior's face looked haggard and old. He beckoned them forward and stared at William for some moments.

'Do you know what is being said about you?' the prior said, his voice hard, his eyes cold. 'That you torment Brother Martin in his sleep? That you are in league with the devil?'

William's mouth was dry. He licked his lips and nodded.

'What do you have to say about these accusations?'

'Prior,' Brother Snail began, but Prior Ardo held up a hand to silence him. His eyes never left William's face.

'I want to hear what the boy has to say.'

William cleared his throat. 'It's not true, any of it. At least . . . Brother Martin may have dreamed about me, but that wasn't any of my doing.'

'Nevertheless, something unholy is here among us and both Peter and Brother Martin believe it has something to do with you.'

William glanced at Brother Snail. He had no idea where to begin or how much to say. His desperation must have shown in his face because the monk stepped forward and said in a tone that brooked no argument, 'I will tell you what we should have told you long before now, Prior, and I speak for us all. Will unwittingly released something the day he found the bowl in the side chapel. We believe that it is a fallen angel.'

The prior looked startled but let the monk continue

without interruption.

'This creature was worshipped as a god before Christianity came to this land, in a grove which once stood on the site of our church. Only now, with the floods and the collapse of the tower, the fallen one is beginning to stir again. William is entirely innocent in all this. He is no more in league with this demon than you or I.'

A muscle twitched beside the prior's mouth and beads of sweat prickled on his upper lip. He wiped them away with a trembling finger. There was a tremor in his voice when he spoke. 'And how do you know this?'

The monk hesitated. 'Some of it comes from the wise woman with the white crow, Dame Alys. Some of it was told to Shadlok by local people.'

Anger shook through the prior's body. 'You have spoken with that . . . *woman?*'

Brother Snail shook his head quickly. 'No, Prior. The woman approached Will in the forest this morning.' He took William by the arm and pulled him into the circle of lantern light. 'She cut his face. She wanted his blood to offer to the demon.'

A look of revulsion crossed the prior's face as he stared at William. 'This will not be tolerated,' he said hoarsely. 'The woman is a heretic. She should be tied to a stake and burned to ashes.'

'To kill a weed, you must kill the root. The demon is the root and we have to find a way to be rid of it,' Brother Snail said. 'Then we can decide what to do about Dame Alys.'

Prior Ardo sat in stony-faced silence for a while, then flicked a finger towards William. 'Why is the demon so interested in *him?*'

'I believe the fallen angel is drawn to the boy because his soul is pure,' Brother Snail said, 'not because he is evil or damned. Do you remember what Abbot Simon said on his deathbed last winter, when Will helped to carry him down to the church?'

The prior's face was haggard in the lantern light. 'He said the light shines brightly in the boy.' The prior had been paying attention that day, William realised in surprise.

Brother Snail put a hand on William's arm. 'I believe the fallen angel wants William's soul. It is trying to turn us against him, but we must not be tricked into believing he is evil.'

The prior stared at William for a long time in silence. At last he nodded. 'I believe you are speaking the truth.'

Brother Snail looked relieved.

'But do not call this . . . creature an *angel*,' the prior said, anger snapping in his eyes. 'It is a *demon*.'

Brother Snail nodded. 'As you wish, Prior.'

The prior turned to look at Shadlok, a look of dislike souring his expression. There was deep suspicion in his eyes.

'You are not human.' It wasn't a question. 'I have always known you were . . . different. You are a fay?'

Shadlok inclined his head slightly.

The prior's sharp gaze flicked back to Brother Snail. 'You have known his true identity all along?'

'Yes.'

'But you didn't think to tell me?'

The monk said nothing, and that gave the prior his answer. None of them had trusted him enough to tell him the truth, and they had only done so now because they had no other choice.

'Why did you stay at the abbey after Master Bone died?' the prior asked. 'Why didn't you return to your own . . . kind?'

Shadlok nodded towards William. 'I stay here because of him. I was bound to Jacobus Bone by an ancient curse. The same curse now binds me to the boy.'

'I see,' the prior said on a soft breath. 'So that was what Abbot Simon meant, that boy wouldn't walk his path in life alone. It seems that, somehow, the abbot knew about *you*. Who placed this curse on you?'

'I was cursed by Comnath, the Dark King of the Unseelie Court. I am exiled from my own world and my fate is bound to that of a human until I die. For now, it is this boy.'

The prior stared at him in silence while he took this in. 'Why did the king punish you this way?'

Shadlok's expression hardened. 'He had his reasons.'

The prior's eyes narrowed but he didn't pursue the matter. He turned to Brother Snail and asked in a hard voice, 'Is there anything else you haven't told me?'

Brother Snail took the leather-bound history of Crowfield Abbey from the pocket inside his cloak and handed it to the prior. 'There is hope we can find out more about the fallen . . . demon, and hopefully discover a way to protect ourselves from it.'

The prior opened the book and leafed through the pages. He read the hastily written words at the foot of the final page and glanced up at Brother Snail. 'What does this mean, the truth is at the saint's foot? Which saint?'

'St Christopher, Prior. The palm tree is his symbol. Whatever was hidden is not in the chapel, though. We've searched it thoroughly. But there was a statue of St Christopher on the chancel screen,' Brother Snail explained, 'and we're trying to find it.'

'I see,' the prior said, gazing down at the book with a thoughtful frown.

'In the meanwhile, the bowl should be locked away,' Brother Snail said, but the prior didn't let him continue.

'No! Absolutely not.'

'But Prior, the bowl is at the heart of what is happening here. There were warnings carved into it.'

'About the *demon*, Brother, but that doesn't mean there's anything wrong with the bowl itself, does it?' the prior said sharply.

'It's a thing of evil,' Brother Snail said, an angry flush colouring his pale cheeks. 'It was used to hold the blood of creatures slaughtered as offerings to the demon.'

'How can you *possibly* know that?' the prior demanded.

Brother Snail started to say something and then stopped. He glanced at William and gave the smallest shake of his head. William guessed the monk didn't want any mention of the holey stone. The prior had accepted William's innocence in all this, but if he found out that William was using fay magic to look into the past, that could soon change. If he discovered that William had the Sight, he would be in deep trouble. So Brother Snail said nothing.

The prior stood up. 'The bowl is the only thing of any value that this abbey has left. It will bring pilgrims to our gates. Their money and gifts will help to rebuild our church. I will not hide it away on a superstitious whim. Do you understand? And as for this,' he handed the book back to Brother Snail, 'we have more important things to do with our time than go search-ing for something that has, in all probability, long since disappeared. We know what is haunting the church. All we need to do is have faith in God, and pray for salvation.'

'The bowl is cursed, Prior!' Brother Snail protested.

Prior Ardo held up a hand. 'That's enough! I will decide what is best in this matter, Brother. Just be grateful that I believe what you've told me about the boy's innocence and that I am allowing the fay crea-ture to live within these walls with impunity. Do *not* push me any further!'

The prior turned to William. 'I accept that none of

our misfortunes are of your making, but others may not believe it so readily.' He glanced at Brother Snail. 'I will tell the brethren the bones of what we have talked about today, but no word of any of this must leave the abbey, or reach the ears of the stonemasons and carpenters. Is that understood?'

'As you wish,' Brother Snail said stiffly.

The prior looked at Shadlok. He seemed very wary of him. 'You must find a way to break the curse binding you to the boy and leave the abbey. A house of God is no place for your kind.'

Shadlok's eyes narrowed and he leant towards the prior. 'If I knew the way to break it, I would have done so a long time ago,' he said softly.

The prior flinched and gazed at Shadlok as if he was a feral creature from the forest which might attack at any moment.

Which, William thought, wasn't so far from the truth.

The prior hurried from the room, closing the door behind him with a bang that echoed around the walls.

Brother Snail's face was white with anger. 'I hope for his sake that the prior is not making the worst mistake of his life.'

Chapter Twenty

William peered around the corner of the barn. The yard was deserted. It was late afternoon and the monks were in either the vegetable garden or the cloister. The stonemasons were working in the church.

'There's nobody about,' William said. 'Run!'

The hob scampered across the yard ahead of William, heading for the rubble heap. William pushed aside any lingering feelings of guilt and ran after him. Prior Ardo hadn't actually *forbidden* them to search for the statue, so if he and the hob just *happened* to be near the rubble heap, and just *happened* to see the statue . . .

The mound of broken stones rose like a small white hill in the far corner of the yard. William stared at it and his spirits sank. He didn't even know what the statue had looked like, so how was he going to find bits of it amongst all this?

A patch of ground beside an elder tree was covered with stone chippings and dust. Beside it was a pile of stones and damaged statues waiting to be smashed into smaller pieces, with one of the heavy hammers propped up against the tree. William started to search through the stones and found fragments of several statues: a face with smooth cheeks and wide, blue-painted eyes whose nose had sheared away; two stone hands pressed together in prayer; part of a foot . . .

'Do you recognise any of these?' he asked, holding them up for the hob to see.

'They are too big,' the hob said. 'The holy man was smaller than me.'

For a while, they searched in silence. William was beginning to think they were wasting their time when suddenly the hob saw something.

'There! Look!' the hob said, waving a paw at a stone by William's foot. It was St Christopher's neck and chest, with the remains of the holy child on one shoulder and part of the tree staff at his side.

'The rest of him has to be here somewhere,' William said, hauling the larger pieces of stone aside. The hob watched in a fever of excitement, jigging up and down and chittering. Every now and then, he darted between William's legs to grab some bit of stone.

'Will you stop getting under my feet!' William said in exasperation after he nearly tripped over the hob for the third time. 'Just stand over there, out of the way.'

The hob did as he was told with obvious reluctance, but it wasn't long before he was pointing to stones and telling William where to look next.

William leant down to lift a large piece of broken tracery from the chancel screen.

'There! *There!*' the hob gibbered, almost bursting with impatience as he pointed to something William had just uncovered.

William worked the stone free and held it up. It was a statue base with two legs, the hem of a robe and the lower part of a tree staff. Crudely carved waves curled beneath the saint's bare feet. William turned the statue over to examine it. If he hadn't been looking so closely, he could easily have missed the carefully applied patch of plaster in the middle of the stone base. He tapped it with a fingernail. It sounded hollow.

'We've found it! This is it!' William said, jubilantly.

One of the stonemasons emerged from the church, wheeling a laden handcart. William quickly pushed the statue base down the front of his tunic. 'Find

Shadlok and tell him to meet us at Brother Snail's workshop as soon as he can.'

The hob nodded and disappeared around the corner of the shed. It wasn't likely that the stonemason would be able to see him, but it wasn't a chance worth taking.

William glanced over his shoulder as he walked quickly away across the yard, but the stonemason was unloading the cart and taking no notice of him.

Brother Snail was washing his hands in a pail by the hut door after an afternoon spent working in the vegetable garden.

'We found the statue!' William said, hauling it from inside his tunic and lifting it in the air.

The monk's eyes lit up with excitement. 'You clever boy, Will! Quickly, bring it into the workshop.'

'The hob's gone to find Shadlok; they'll be here in a minute.'

Brother Snail nodded. 'Good. Build up the fire and light the lanterns, Will, and let's see what secrets St Christopher has been guarding so carefully.'

He took the statue base from William and, using the blade of his small herb knife, he began to chip away at the plaster. With growing excitement, William watched as it cracked and a large chunk fell to the floor. He caught a glimpse of a tightly folded square of parchment wedged into the hollow in the base. Brother Snail pulled it free and stood the base on the table. He carefully unfolded the parchment then nodded slowly. 'Good, it's still readable.' He looked up at William. 'As soon as the others arrive, we will see what it says.'

Brother Snail settled himself on a stool by the fire. He angled the fragile parchment sheet to catch the light and began to read.

'*Written on the twentieth day of January in the Year of Our Lord 1236, at the Abbey of St Michael the Archangel at Crowfield in the Forest. This is the last testament of Abbot Bartolomeo de Albasiis. May God have mercy on my soul, which I believe to be damned for all eternity by the actions I have been forced to take to protect all who live in this place.*' The monk paused and cleared his throat. He glanced around at the faces of his three listeners. 'The abbot writes in Latin. I will have to translate the words as I go, so please be patient.'

William nodded. The hob said nothing, but sat close to the hearth and listened intently. Shadlok stood silently just beyond the circle of firelight, arms folded.

Brother Snail turned back to the parchment. '*I came*

to Crowfield Abbey on All Souls' Day in the Year of Our Lord 1235. The sweating sickness had taken the lives of the previous abbot and prior of this house, and many of its brethren. Grave misfortune had befallen the abbey for almost two years and the surviving brethren believed it to be cursed.'

William felt the hairs on the nape of his neck rise. He saw the Brother Snail's fingers tremble slightly. The parchment wavered for a moment, but the monk seemed to gather himself and his voice was steady when he continued.

'Cattle sickened and died, the wheat and barley crops failed and ewes miscarried their lambs. The brethren were sorely troubled by evil dreams and waking visions of a crow-headed demon with wings of the deepest crimson. This abomination, I most truly believe, is one of the fallen angels, cast from God's presence for rebelling against Him during the War in Heaven. It is the demon Raum, who takes on the form of a crow. I have seen this creature for myself.'

Brother Snail looked up. His eyes were wide with shock. 'So, the creature has a name,' he whispered. 'Raum. I admit I have never heard of it.'

'How did the abbot find out who it was?' William asked softly.

Brother Snail quickly scanned the parchment. 'It seems Abbot Bartolomeo was sent here by the abbot of Crowfield's mother house in France. He was chosen to fight the Great Evil at Crowfield because he had experience in exorcising demons. He had in his possession a grimoire, a book of magic, called *Ars Goetia*, which lists many demons. Presumably he learnt about Raum from this book. *Before disaster fell upon this abbey, a new tiled pavement was laid in the church and a chapel dedicated to St Christopher was built in the north transept. It was during the building of this chapel that a bowl was discovered beneath the floor of the transept. It was curiously marked with magical symbols, and Abbot Henry ordered it to be destroyed. By some dark art, the bowl remained unharmed, and thereafter a Great Evil came to the abbey.*'

'Does it say how they tried to destroy it?' William asked.

'No,' Brother Snail said. 'Nor does it tell us who buried the bowl originally, or *why* they did so.' He smoothed a fold in the parchment and continued to read.

'*On St Martin's Day in 1235, Thomas Bolewyn, a freeman from Weforde, was caught trying to steal the bowl from the sacristy of the abbey. He was brought before Sir*

Guilbert de Tovei at the manor court in Weforde, where he claimed that the bowl belonged to his family. Under duress, he admitted that his ancestors were the guardians of a sacred grove which had been cut down and burned when the first abbey was built at Crowfield. Thomas admitted, after further persuasion, that the bowl was used to hold the blood of those sacrificed to his heathen god. The man was then taken out and hanged and his body was buried in a pit of quicklime.'

'Why did they do that?' William asked.

Frowning at the parchment Brother Snail said, 'It seems Sir Guilbert and Abbot Bartolomeo were frightened men. They wanted to destroy everything to do with the demon and the cursed bowl, including Master Bolewyn.'

'Except they did not succeed,' Shadlok said, stepping forward into the light. 'The bowl could not be destroyed, and Dame Alys is most likely the descendant of Thomas Bolewyn, so his bloodline survives too.'

'So it would seem.' Brother Snail sat quietly for a few moments, one hand holding the cross around his neck. At last he lifted the parchment and continued to read. 'Abbot Bartolomeo goes on to say that after Thomas was hanged, the demon attacked the abbey and the surrounding villages with renewed vigour. *The brethren of this abbey prayed day and night in the church for God to come to our aid, then in the December of that year a fever caused many of them to sicken and take to their beds and I prayed in the church alone. I begged and pleaded and bargained with God, until at last, on Christmas Eve, He answered my prayers. He sent an angel of vengeance to Crowfield but it was struck down in the forest by some unseen and unknown enemy, and that which I hardly dare put into words came to pass: the angel died. Two of my most trusted brethren struggled from their sickbeds and between us we carried the angel to a place in the forest shunned by the people who live hereabouts, and we buried it. It is our burden to keep this most terrible of secrets. I fear God has turned his face from us.'*

There was a stunned silence in the hut. William stared at Brother Snail. 'So that *is* why the angel was in the forest a hundred years ago,' he whispered. 'It was here to hunt down the demon. It came in answer to Abbot Bartolomeo's prayers.'

'And it might have succeeded if Comnath hadn't shot it with an arrow,' Shadlok said.

'At least we now know what happened that terrible night,' the monk said softly. 'William, kindly pour me a cup of water.'

William took a cup from a shelf and dipped it into

the pail of water near the door. He handed it to the monk. Brother Snail nodded his thanks and sipped it. Abbot Bartolomeo's story had visibly upset him. It was a minute or two before he was ready to continue. '*On the feast of St Stephen in 1236, I walked through the snow to Weforde and spoke with Sir Guilbert. He was rumoured to be an alchemist and indeed this proved to be true. I gave him a book of magic I had in my possession, Ars Goetia, and bade him keep it, and in return he agreed to bind the demon to the bowl, as I believe it to have been bound once before. I assisted him in his dark magic and for that I have forfeited my eternal soul. The demon was imprisoned in the cursed bowl and both were buried beneath the floor of St Christopher's chapel. The place is marked by tiles carefully chosen to give a warning of what lies below. I crave God's mercy and pray that never again will the demon be free. If that hope proves to be a false one, and the demon is released, then at least you who are reading this testament will know the name of your enemy and the means by which we overcame him once before. May God have mercy on your souls.*' Brother Snail tapped the foot of the parchment with a fingertip. 'Someone has added a line at the end of the page. It simply says that Abbot Bartolomeo died at the abbey on Easter Sunday, 1237.'

Nobody spoke for a long time. The hob put a paw on Brother Snail's humped shoulder and patted it in silent sympathy.

'I wonder what happened to the abbot's book of magic?' William asked at last. Without it, there was no hope of binding the demon again.

'It is still in the manor house at Weforde, along with several other books of magic,' Shadlok said. 'I saw it when Bone and I stayed there last winter. Sir Robert is an alchemist, like his ancestor before him.'

William heard Brother Snail gasp in surprise. 'What's an alchemist?' he asked.

'A conjurer, a magician,' Brother Snail said, his voice sharp with disapproval. He looked up at Shadlok. 'Are you sure about this?'

The fay nodded. He squatted down by the hearth. The firelight was reflected in his eyes and threw shadows across the sharp planes of his face. His long silver-white hair hung down over his shoulders and gleamed like moonlight in the gloom of the hut. 'He takes great care to hide it. His books are kept in a locked room in his house and only he has a key.'

The monk frowned. 'But he let you go in there?'

Shadlok nodded again. 'Once. He thought I might be . . . of use to him in his work.'

214

'His work? And what would that be, exactly?' Brother Snail asked softly. There was a look of distaste on his face which surprised William. He had never known the monk to judge someone harshly for their beliefs before.

Shadlok gazed at the monk as if trying to decide whether or not to answer the question. 'He is searching for the al'iksir of life.'

William was thoroughly baffled now. 'The what?'

Before Shadlok could explain, Brother Snail cut in angrily. 'What use did he think you could be to him in such a quest?'

'Fay folk live longer than humans. He thought I might know the secret of immortality.'

'I see. And do you?' There was a dangerous glint in the monk's eyes.

'No,' Shadlok said evenly, 'I am mortal, as you are. And it is for the Creator alone to decide the lifespan of all living things. It is not within my power to bestow that gift on another creature.'

'The Dark King made Jacobus Bone immortal,' Brother Snail said, 'so it is clearly a secret known to *some* of your kind.'

'But not to me.' Shadlok's gaze was steady and unblinking, as if challenging the monk to argue with him. William interrupted before Brother Snail had a chance to reply.

'What is the al'iksir of life? And why is so terrible that Sir Robert is an alchemist?'

'Alchemists practise dark magic of the worst kind,' Brother Snail said. 'They conjure demons to do their bidding and they seek to change the nature of matter, whether it is changing lead into gold, or a human life into an eternal one. The al'iksir of life is believed to bestow immortality on the one who discovers it, but that is for God alone to do, not man.' He fixed Shadlok with a hard stare. 'And not fays. Alchemy is against nature, and against God.'

Shadlok stared down into the fire. His face was set and his mouth drawn into a thin line. He picked up a stick and prodded the logs, sending up a shower of sparks. Flames danced over the shimmering wood as the fire murmured and crackled.

'If Sirobbit is an alchemist and can conjure demons,' the hob said, 'then perhaps he can make them go away too, like the other man did.'

'Only if he has the skill and the knowledge to use what is written in the *Ars Goetia*,' Shadlok said.

Brother Snail did not look at all happy about this. He shook his head slowly. 'We should not use this kind of magic. It is utterly wrong.'

'Magic is simply a tool,' Shadlok said with a lift of one shoulder, 'it is neither wrong nor right.'

Angry patches of colour rose to the monk's cheeks. 'We are meddling with a *demon*!'

'I would say the demon is meddling with *us*,' Shadlok said sharply, 'and the only weapon we *can* use against it is magic.'

'Shadlok is right,' William said. He nodded towards the parchment. 'You read what happened back then. The monks had no choice but to use magic to fight the demon. If Sir Robert can help us, then I think we should let him.' He thought of the oak twig smeared with his blood and he shivered. The sooner they found a way to get rid of the demon, the better. And preferably before Dame Alys used him as a sacrifice.

'Abbot Bartolomeo believed himself to be eternally damned for using spells to bind the demon, Will,' Brother Snail said. 'We will very likely be damned too.'

'No,' Shadlok said, 'the abbot thought he was damned only after he found the angel's body in the snow. He probably thought its death was a judgement upon him for failing to rid the abbey of the demon.

He never knew what really happened in the forest that night.'

'He didn't know about the Dark King,' William said.

'Exactly,' Shadlok said. 'The abbot used magic to defeat Raum, but his intentions were pure. The Creator, I am certain, would never have turned away from him for that. The pity is that he went to his grave believing that he was damned.'

Brother Snail closed his eyes and bowed his head. 'Of course, you're right. God would not turn His face from Abbot Bartolomeo for fighting this terrible evil in the only way he could. If we must use magic to defeat Raum, then so be it. God will understand and forgive us for it too, I am sure.'

Shadlok's eyes narrowed. 'I never doubted it.'

'I'm sorry, I did not mean to insult you,' the monk said, looking up at the fay, his face flushed.

It was hard to tell if Shadlok had taken offence at the monk's words. 'Magic is a part of fay nature. It is how the Creator made us. I have never felt I needed to ask forgiveness for that.'

There was a tense silence in the hut. It was only broken when the hob asked anxiously, 'What if Sirrobit won't help us?'

'Why would he refuse?' William asked.

'Perhaps he doesn't want people to find out he can do magic,' the hob replied.

'Brother Walter is right,' the monk said, his gaze softening as he looked at the hob. 'We can't force Sir Robert to show us his books or to help us.'

William remembered the argument between Shadlok and Sir Robert in the yard the other day.

'You have something that he wants,' William said, turning to Shadlok. 'Perhaps you can give it to him in exchange for his help?' He saw the flash of anger in the fay's eyes and knew he had said the wrong thing.

'Oh?' Brother Snail said, looking up at the fay hopefully. 'What is it?'

'Something I have no intention of giving him.'

'But . . .' William began.

The fay turned on him furiously. 'I said no!'

Brother Snail struggled to his feet. 'Don't talk to the boy like that! His suggestion was well meant.'

'Do *not* interfere in things that do not concern you,' Shadlok said, glaring at William and ignoring the monk.

'It does concern me,' William said, staring back at Shadlok. 'It's not *you* who's in danger of being sacrificed.'

Anger burned brightly in the fay's eyes. 'You do not know what you are asking of me, or the trouble it will bring if I give in,' Shadlok said.

'No,' William agreed, 'but I know the trouble we're facing if Sir Robert refuses.'

Brother Snail shuffled forward to stand between them. 'Hopefully Sir Robert will agree to help us without expecting anything in return.' He folded the parchment and tucked it into the pocket inside his cloak. He looked weary and the burden of what lay ahead seemed to weigh heavily on his shoulders. 'I will go and speak to Prior Ardo now and tell him what we've discovered. Let us hope that he is willing to listen.'

Chapter Twenty-One

William was unrolling his mattress after vespers, ready to settle down for the night, when Brother Snail came to see him. The monk's breath rasped in his throat as he lowered himself onto a stool to rest for a few moments.

'The prior has refused to ask Sir Robert for help,' Brother Snail wheezed. 'He wants nothing to do with alchemy or magic of any kind. I suspect he would have nothing more to do with Sir Robert either, if he didn't need his help rebuilding the church.'

William stared at him in dismay. 'Did you tell him there's no other way to defeat the demon?'

'Of course I did, Will, but the prior was adamant. He believes that what we must do is pray for the angel to come again and help us. We begin this evening after compline. The brethren will keep vigil in the church, just as Abbot Bartolomeo and his monks did.'

'That's *all* he's going to do?' William asked in disbelief.

'It worked once before,' the monk reminded him gently. 'The angel came to Crowfield when Abbot Bartolomeo prayed for help.'

'And look what happened *that* time,' William muttered. 'I wouldn't be in a hurry to come back here if I was him.'

The monk said nothing. His eyes were clouded with unhappiness and William felt sorry for him. He sometimes forgot that this was Brother Snail's home, and that the monks were his family. Watching what was happening to them must have been hard for him.

'The demon isn't just going to sit around and do nothing while you keep your vigil,' William said. 'It'll try to stop you.'

The monk's jaw tightened. 'We'll just have to take that chance.'

'All you're going to do is make it angry,' William persisted, '*really* angry.'

'I know, but the prior has made up his mind,' Brother Snail said softly, his expression bleak. He got to his feet and stood for a moment, one hand on the table for support. 'I have to go. It is almost time for compline.'

'Are you going to be praying in the church all night?' William asked, looking at the monk's frail body and listening to him struggle for breath.

Brother Snail nodded. 'We all are.'

'Is that a good idea?' William asked after a brief hesitation. 'I mean . . .'

The monk seemed to understand his concern and smiled. 'A little discomfort is a small price to pay for divine help, Will. I will be all right.'

William wasn't convinced by this. He didn't like the thought of Brother Snail spending a night kneeling on the floor of the bitterly cold church, under the malevolent gaze of the demon. It was madness. It would do more harm than good to the monk's already fragile health. William knew he would be wasting his breath, though. Brother Snail would do what the prior asked of him with quiet dignity and he would neither ask for, nor expect, special treatment.

'Is there anything I can do to help? William asked.

'Stay away from the abbey tonight, and keep Brother Walter close by you.'

William watched the monk walk to the door, a small figure in a habit that seemed to have grown too big for him these last few weeks. He felt a surge of anger at Prior Ardo's stubbornness. What if the only thing the monks succeeded in doing tonight was goading the demon into a rage?

And even if by some miracle their prayers were answered and the angel came back to Crowfield, what if it failed to defeat the demon?

With the fire built up to a crackling blaze, the hut was warm and comfortable. The hob sat by the hearth, roasting some small wizened apples on a stick.

'Will you play your flute?' the hob asked hopefully.

William started to say no, that he wasn't in the mood, but then decided it was a good way to take his mind off what was happening in the church. He fetched the flute from its hiding place and pulled a stool over to the fireside.

The hob grinned in delight. 'Play the summer song, and I will sing the words.'

William smiled. He knew which one the hob meant. It was the first tune Shadlok had taught him and it was the hob's favourite.

'*Summer is a-coming in,*' the hob sang as William played. '*Loudly sing cuckoo!*'

William tried not to laugh as the hob added several

more cuckoos, though they weren't in the song. It was the bit the hob liked the best.

'Cuc-KOO! Cuckoo, cuckoocuckoocuckooo-ooo.'

'That's not how it goes,' William said, lowering the flute for a moment and grinning.

'*Groweth seed and bloweth mead, and spring the wood anew*,' the hob trilled, and with a triumphant look on his face, he took a deep breath and finished, '*sing CUCKOO!*'

William resisted the hob's pleas to continue playing. He cleaned the flute and put it back in its bag. It seemed all wrong to be making music when the monks were risking their lives in the church. The hob was disappointed, but he seemed to pick up on William's sombre mood and sat quietly by the fire to turn the apples on their sticks.

William felt oddly restless. He stood up and paced around the hut. Outside, an owl hooted, its call quivering on the damp night air. In the distance, a fox screamed, an unearthly sound that made him shiver.

William lay down on his mattress and stared up at the thatch between the rafters. In his mind he could imagine the monks kneeling in the chancel of the church, huddled inside their habits against the damp and draughts. He could almost smell the incense and hear the murmur of prayers rising on the candle-hazed air, and see the dark shape of the demon high up on the church roof, wrapped in its crimson wings, watching and waiting. He pushed aside his blanket and sat up, too unsettled to lie still.

'Will the good nangel come back?' the hob asked, pulling a hot apple from the fire and holding it out to William.

William frowned. 'I don't know.' The apple burnt his fingers and he rolled it from hand to hand to try to cool it. The heat didn't seem to bother the hob, though. William watched him take another apple from the stick and bite into the peel with his sharp teeth, holding it cupped in his paws. 'The prior seems to think it will.'

For a while, they ate in silence. William almost jumped out of his skin when the latch rattled suddenly.

'Open the door!'

Recognising Shadlok's voice, William scrambled to his feet and hurried over to draw back the bolt.

Shadlok pushed past him, fury in every line of his body. 'Did you know what the monks intended to do?' he demanded, his eyes burning like blue flames.

'Brother Snail told me this evening.'

'And you did not think to tell *me*?'

'I didn't know where to find you,' William said.

'Then the monk should have told me.'

'Why?'

'Because I would have tried to stop them. It is too late now, the fools are already in the church and the demon is there with them. They have no idea what they have done. This will not end well.'

William felt as if he had been doused in cold water. He heard the hob whimper quietly behind him. 'Can't you go and warn them?'

'I would be dead before I crossed the threshold.'

'What will the demon do to them?' William asked unsteadily.

Shadlok didn't answer. His silence said more than any words.

William started towards the door. 'Then I'll go. I'll *make* the prior listen to me.'

Shadlok grabbed his arm as he passed by.

'There is nothing you can do to help them now.'

William tried to pull his arm free but the fay's grip was too tight. He turned on Shadlok angrily. 'I can't just stay here and do nothing!'

Shadlok started to say something but his words were lost when a gust of wind suddenly slammed into the hut, shaking bits of thatch and dust from the roof and flinging open the door, which crashed back against the hut wall. The fire guttered and the lantern went out. William gasped in shock and Shadlok let go of his arm. The wind howled through the hut, raging like a wild boar, sweeping jars and bowls from the shelves. William crouched down, his arms shielding his head, as things flew through the air, sharp-edged and deadly. Hot embers from the fire pit were scattered across the floor. Something hit him painfully hard on the arm. A moment later, a stool caught him on the back, sending him sprawling. Bits of broken pottery cut into his hands and face. Panic-ridden, he rolled into a tight crouch and lay there, battered and bleeding, as the world was torn apart around him.

A hand grabbed the scruff of his tunic and he felt himself being hauled to his feet. He was dragged across the hut and out into the raging dusk. Rain lashed his face and stung his eyes. The wind howled and broken branches slashed through the air. William stumbled away from the hut and fell to his knees in the wet earth of one of the herb beds. Moments later, the hob was there, wrapping his thin arms tightly around William's neck and clinging to him for dear life.

William looked back at the hut just in time to see

the thatch lift from the rafters and scatter into the wind. He hugged the hob to his chest and crouched forward as a rafter wrenched free and cartwheeled across the garden, missing them by a whisker.

'Run!' Shadlok shouted, grabbing William's arm. 'Follow me!'

William ran after the fay, skidding in the mud and slipping on the wet grass. The hob hung on grimly, his head knocking painfully against William's jaw as he was bounced around.

It wasn't until he saw the dark arch of the passage beside the chapter house up ahead that William realised they had run towards the abbey.

Shadlok bundled him into the shelter of the passageway. William's ears rang as the noise of the storm was dampened by the thick stone walls.

'Go to the warming room, you should be safe there,' the fay said. 'I will try to get the monks out of the church.'

William ran along the passage behind Shadlok and took a deep breath before following him out into the east alley. The wind hit him like a hammer blow, almost knocking him off his feet. Keeping close to the wall, William fought his way to the door of the warming room and scrabbled for the heavy latch. He managed to lift it and threw himself headlong into the small chamber.

For a long time, he stood with his back to the door, his breath ragged and harsh in his throat, and hugged the hob tightly. He was trembling from head to foot. The hob lowered himself to the ground unsteadily. William felt for the lantern and tinderbox on a shelf by the door and lit the tallow candle with shaking fingers. He lit a second lantern hanging from a bracket near the fireplace. Light wavered over the walls and flickered across the vaulted ceiling, and shadows turned the empty fireplace to a dark cave. When the shock and fear had finally cleared a little, William realised Shadlok had chosen their refuge well. The walls of the warming room were solid and thick, and there were no windows. William had no doubt that the storm had been raised by the demon. It still howled outside the door, but it couldn't reach them in here.

'Are we safe?' the hob asked in a whisper, looking up at William with frightened eyes.

'I think so,' William said. 'For now, at least.'

The hob glanced at the door. 'What about the brother men? And Sceath-hlakk?'

'I don't know,' William said. Should he have gone

with Shadlok? It did not seem right, somehow, hiding in the warming room when the monks and the fay were in the church, at the mercy of the demon.

'There must be *something* I can do to help them,' William said.

'No, no, no,' whimpered the hob. 'Don't go out there!'

William opened the door cautiously and looked out. The wind had dropped and the rain had eased. An unnatural silence hung over the cloister, as if the evening was holding its breath. William glanced back at the hob. 'I have to find Brother Snail.' Perhaps the hob heard the desperation in William's voice because he didn't argue. 'I'll be back as soon as I can. Stay here. Don't be tempted to follow me, no matter what.'

William closed the door behind him and stood for a moment, peering down the empty alley. He could just make out the south door of the church, a patch of darkness against the stone walls. It was closed and there was no sign of Shadlok.

William gathered together the few shreds of courage he could muster and walked towards the church. He breathed in deeply, trying to steady the wild thump of his heart, then reached for the handle and slowly pulled open the door.

Chapter Twenty-Two

The church was lost in darkness. Rainwater dripped into puddles in the nave. The sound echoed eerily around the building. Somewhere close by, a stone crashed onto the floor, making William almost jump out of his skin. He froze in terror as a violent gust of wind blew open the great west door. The icy wind rushed up the nave and there was a thunderous sound of falling planks, clattering and thudding onto the floor at the east end of the church. The terrified screams of the monks sent the blood pounding through William's body. Someone collided with him, almost knocking him over. He heard the desperate scrabble of feet on rubble as more of the monks ran past him, heading for the south door. He was shoved roughly aside and stumbled against a pillar. He decided it was safer to stay there until the escaping monks were out of the way.

The wind whipped between the pillars and slammed the south door shut with a crash that seemed to make the whole building shudder. William crouched by the pillar, half expecting the aisle roof to come down on his head. There were shrieks of terror as the monks tried to open the door, but they were driven back by the savage wind. Someone stumbled against William.

'Who's that?' a frightened voice called.

'It's me, William.'

'Open the door, boy, quickly!' It was Brother Gabriel. He pushed William into the aisle. 'Go on, hurry!'

William elbowed his way through the knot of monks by the door and felt for the latch. With a howl, the wind caught him and sent him sprawling. He landed heavily and hit his head on the floor. Tiny points of light sparked behind his eyes. A wave of dizziness left him feeling sick, but he forced himself to crawl back to the door. He had no idea what had happened to the monks, but the doorway was clear. Slowly, he got to his knees and reached for the latch. Desperately, his fingers slipping on the bitterly cold iron, he tried to lift it. The wind threw itself at him like a frenzied dog and William fell sideways. He tried again, reaching up for the latch, and again the wind tossed him aside.

William slumped on the floor, his back against the wall. *The demon isn't going to let us go,* he thought in despair. Forcing himself to move, William crawled towards the door once more, keeping as close to the wall as he could. He had to keep trying. He reached the door and slowly slid his fingers up the wood, edging his way towards the latch. An ear-splitting crash reverberated around the church. William flinched and closed his eyes. It was a couple of moments before he realised the sound had come from the chancel. Someone started to scream in pain, then more stone thundered down and the screaming stopped. Heart pounding, William seized his chance and made a desperate grab for the latch. He pushed it up and rolled aside as the heavy door swung open.

'Quickly!' he shouted. 'Get out of the church!'

There was a scurry of movement as the monks closest to the doorway made a run for the cloister alley. William scrambled after them. 'Into the warming room!' he shouted above the angry howl of the wind. 'It's the safest place!'

Like a flock of terrified sheep, the monks jostled and pushed their way into the small chamber. William followed, with Shadlok close behind him. The fay closed and barred the door. In the lantern light, William could see that Shadlok's face was bruised and bloodied from a cut above one eye, and there was blood in his hair. William looked at the monks. Not one of them had escaped unscathed. Their habits were soaked through, torn and streaked with mortar dust. Their faces and hands were battered and bleeding. Brother Mark's broken arm and ribs were giving him a lot of pain, to judge by the agonised look on his face. Peter huddled silently into a corner of the room, eyes wide with shock. Blood dripped from his nose and mouth and he wiped at it with shaking fingers. William felt a cold twist of fear in his chest as he realised that Brother Snail was not there. There were others missing too.

'Brother Snail is still in the church,' he said, turning to Shadlok, 'so are Brother Odo and the prior.'

'There is nothing we can do for them now,' the fay said bleakly. He wrapped his arms around his body and stared blindly into the shadows.

Brother Gabriel started to pray. One by one, the rest of the monks picked up the Latin words. Even Brother Martin mumbled along, though he managed to make the holy words sound like curses. None of them could see the hob, sitting near the door, a miserable bundle of ruffled fur. William sat down beside him, his back against the wall, and the hob shuffled across to lean against him. William felt the small body shiver. Keeping a wary eye on the monks, he put his arm around the hob to try and warm him, but the others were too lost in their misery to notice.

Was Brother Snail still alive? William felt sick with fear for the monk, but Shadlok was right: there was nothing anybody could do to help Brother Snail, or the prior and Brother Odo. He closed his eyes, leant his head against the wall and tried not to think about what might be happening to them.

Shadlok remained on his feet, his back to the door. Glancing up at him, William saw the tense set of the fay's face and the distant look in his eyes. Wherever Shadlok's thoughts were, they weren't in the warming room.

Gradually the exhausted monks fell asleep, propped against the wall or curled up on the floor in front of the fireplace.

William slept fitfully. When he woke at dawn, the monks and Peter were still asleep but Shadlok and the hob had gone. William left the warming room and closed the door quietly behind him. He stood in the alley and looked around.

The wind had blown itself out during the night and the misty grey morning was still and silent. The cloister garth was littered with broken branches and last autumn's dead leaves, scoured out from hidden corners. Several branches had snapped off the old walnut tree. Rainwater flooded the herb beds, turning them into small ponds. It would take a full day's work to clear it all up.

William saw that the south door of the church was ajar. He walked slowly towards it and peered cautiously around the edge. It seemed peaceful enough inside the building. He could hear voices somewhere over towards the chancel. He jumped when a figure loomed out of the gloom. To his delight he saw that it was Brother Snail, bruised and cut, but still alive.

'You're safe!' William grabbed the monk in a tight hug.

The monk patted William's back. 'It's good to see you too, Will, but perhaps you could let me go now?'

William blushed and released the monk. 'I'm sorry, it's just . . .'

Brother Snail put a hand on his arm and nodded. 'I know.'

'Most of the monks are in the warming room. None of them are badly injured,' William said.

'I am relieved to hear it,' the monk said quietly. 'Brother Odo was not so fortunate.'

'Is he badly hurt?'

'He's dead. Part of the chancel wall collapsed on him.'

William felt a stab of pity for the old monk. What a terrible way to die. 'What about Prior Ardo?'

'His arm is broken and hē has some deep cuts, but he will live.' Brother Snail sat on the stone bench in the cloister alley, exhausted and drained. 'Forgive me, Will, I need to rest for a moment.'

William looked down at the monk. His pitifully small body was hunched forward and his thin hands rested in his lap. There was a large bruise on the side of his face and cuts on his tonsured head. He needed more than a few moments' rest, William thought anxiously.

'I'll fetch you some warmed beer,' William said, but Brother Snail shook his head.

'Time enough for that later, Will. Your help is needed in the church. I will go to the warming room. There'll be cuts to clean and salve.' He raised his arm. 'Help me up, please.'

William steadied the monk as he rose slowly to his feet. 'Someone else can see to them, you should go and lie down.'

Brother Snail smiled briefly. 'I will rest later. Hurry along now. The prior has need of you. Oh, and I sent the hob back to the workshop. He told me what happened there last night and he is going to see what can be salvaged.'

With deep misgivings, William stood aside and watched Brother Snail shuffle away. The monk struggled to put one foot in front of another. The night in the church had cost him dearly but at least he had survived, and for that William was deeply grateful.

William was horrified by the state of the church. All the recent hard work by the stonemasons and carpenters had been undone in a frenzy of destruction. Boarded-up windows were once more open to the raw morning light. Rubble and timbers littered the floor of the nave and chancel. Puddles reflected the sky like the shattered pieces of a vast mirror. William looked up at the paintings on the walls and his heart seemed to miss a beat. The faces of the saints and angels had gone, leaving patches of bare stone above rain-streaked but otherwise untouched bodies. It looked as if they had been gouged from the plaster with something sharp. He shivered and looked away, sickened by the lingering feeling of hatred that poisoned the air in the ruined church.

Another stretch of the chancel wall had come down and William could see Shadlok and Prior Ardo pulling stones from a large heap of rubble. The prior moved awkwardly, his broken arm held tightly to his chest. His face twisted with pain as he slowly reached for a stone. He crouched there for a moment, eyes closed and breathing through his open mouth, before throwing the stone aside.

'Over here, boy, we need your help,' he called when he noticed William. His voice sounded tired and small.

William stared at the rubble. Somewhere under the stones lay Brother Odo. He pushed aside all thought of what they were going to find and set to work.

Nobody said a word when at last a foot in a scuffed old boot was uncovered. As William quickly pulled smaller pieces of rubble aside, he felt a stir of cold air against his face. Just for a moment, he thought he heard the rustle of wings. A small red feather floated down to settle for a moment on the rubble by William's feet, several shades darker than the monk's blood staining the stones around it. A draught lifted the feather and sent it tumbling away. William glanced up at the gaping hole in the roof. The demon was up there and it wanted him to know that it was watching.

Chapter Twenty-Three

Brother Odo was carried to the guest quarters and laid out on a trestle table, where Brother Snail washed the body and prepared it for burial.

William built up the fire in the kitchen and warmed small beer in a cauldron. He poured the beer into a jug and Peter carried the jug and a tray of cups to the warming room for the monks. William took two cups of beer to the guest quarters. The prior was standing beside Brother Snail, praying over Brother Odo. His broken arm was held in a sling made from a torn linen strip. The smell of blood and death made William's stomach churn. He breathed through his mouth to try and block it out, but the smell had a taste, thick and cloying. He stood uncertainly in the doorway until the prior beckoned him forward.

The monk accepted the cup with a nod and sat on

a stool nearby to sip the warming drink. Brother Snail wiped his bloodied hands on a wet rag and took the other cup from William. His face was grey with exhaustion and there was a smear of blood on his cheek.

'This is very welcome,' he said with feeling.

William glanced down at Brother Odo's body, then quickly looked away. What was left of the monk barely looked as if it had once been a man. Brother Snail took his arm and drew him away from the table. 'You should leave now, Will. Ask Brother Stephen if he has any work for you. I am sure he'll be glad of your help.'

As William turned to go, there was a loud rap on the door.

'Come in,' the prior called wearily.

The door opened and Master Guillaume stepped into the room. He saw the body on the table and froze, a look of horror on his face. He crossed himself quickly.

'Yes? Did you want something?' the prior asked sharply.

Master Guillaume dragged his gaze away from Brother Odo and stared blankly at the prior. 'What? Oh. I . . .' He cleared his throat and squared his shoulders. 'I've come to tell you that I'll be taking my men back to Weforde as soon as we get our belongings packed away and onto the cart. We won't be coming back. Not after last night.'

The prior stared at the master mason in silence for several moments. There was a look of resignation on his dirt-streaked face. 'Very well.'

The mason looked ill at ease. 'I don't know what's haunting this abbey, Prior, but it's too dangerous to stay here a day longer. We're leaving before ...' Master Guillaume's gaze slid back to the bloody mess on the table, '... before it's too late. You might want to think about getting your monks away, too.'

'Thank you, but I will decide what is best for the people in my care,' the prior said stiffly.

'Please yourself,' the mason muttered. With that, he left the room, and the door closed quietly behind him.

'I think it is fair to say your prayers for help did not work.' Shadlok folded his arms and stared at Prior Ardo. The monk sat on a stool by the newly laid fire in the warming room, cradling his broken arm. Abbot Bartolomeo's sheet of parchment lay in his lap. He'd read it in bitter silence. He looked up at the fay and scowled. 'So it would seem,' he said stiffly.

'It is time to ask Sir Robert for help,' Shadlok said.

William saw the look of revulsion on the prior's face. Even now, with his church all but reduced to rubble and the abbey facing ruin, the prior was still reluctant to use magic to fight the demon.

'I will not do that,' the prior said. 'I don't know why God didn't answer our prayers, but it's not for me to question the Almighty's decisions and I will *not* go against Him by asking an alchemist for help.'

'Then you will stand by and watch as the abbey is destroyed around you and your monks die one by one, because that is what will surely happen.' There was an edge to the fay's voice. The cuts and bruises William had noticed earlier on Shadlok's skin had already faded. He stood there, clean and unmarked, in stark contrast to the filthy, bloodstained monk. 'Abbot Bartolomeo knew he had no choice but to use magic against the demon. Do you claim to be wiser than him?' Shadlok didn't try to hide the biting contempt in his voice.

Spots of angry colour rose to the prior's cheeks. 'I claim nothing! And the abbot only lowered himself to using magic after he found the angel lying dead in the forest.' He paused and stared at Shadlok with something close to hatred. He snatched up the parchment and shook it at the fay. 'He never knew who fired the arrow and that added a terrible burden to his anguish. He never found out that it was brought down by an arrow shot by one of *your* kind! But God answered his prayers, and I believe He will answer ours.'

'Then he had better do it while there is something left to save.'

'Prior,' Brother Snail began. The prior shot him a warning glance. The monk seemed to brace himself as he continued. 'Perhaps God means for us to help ourselves. Perhaps there will be no angel to rescue us this time. We are defenceless as we stand now, so we should at least find out if Sir Robert can do the binding spell.'

'I said no!' The prior got to his feet. The parchment slipped to the floor. 'We will burn the bowl. We should have done so long before now. I will fetch it.' He turned to William. 'You, boy, build up the fire.'

'No, Prior, you can't do this!' Brother Snail said in alarm. 'Abbot Bartolomeo wrote that his attempt to destroy the bowl failed. We have already angered the demon enough. Who knows what it will do if we provoke it any further?'

'The bowl and the demon are bound together,' the prior said furiously. 'Destroy one and you will destroy the other. We will try again, and this time we *will* succeed.'

'He's gone mad,' William said, after the prior swept from the room.

Brother Snail shook his head. 'He is simply trying to fight something he does not understand.'

'The man is a fool,' Shadlok snapped.

'Build up the fire, Will,' Brother Snail said. 'Let the prior try to destroy the bowl. Maybe after that he will allow us to speak to Sir Robert.'

It was with deep misgivings that William did as he was told.

The prior returned a few minutes later. He bolted the warming-room door and stood by the fireplace, the bowl in his hand. He leant forward, flinching away from the heat of the flames, and dropped it into the heart of the fire.

'More wood, boy,' he called sharply. 'Quickly!'

William grabbed a couple of logs from the basket and threw them onto the blaze. The wood cracked and spat and sparks scattered across the floor. The prior took a branch from the pile of kindling beside the wood basket and prodded the logs, sending a huge rush of sparks and flames up the chimney. He threw the branch into the fire and stepped back.

For a while, the only sounds in the room were the roar of the fire and the hissing and spitting of the logs as they shimmered in the fierce heat. William's damp clothes began to steam gently and he felt the sweat trickle between his shoulder blades. Brother Snail lowered himself onto a stool and sat there, a hunched bundle of dark robes, his eyes closed and his lips moving in silent prayer. Shadlok stood by the door, his face set, his body tense. The prior stared down into the fire with wide, unblinking eyes, as if willing the inferno to consume every last bit of the accursed bowl.

Perhaps Abbot Bartolomeo was wrong about the bowl, William thought as he felt the searing heat on his face. Surely nothing could survive this blaze?

The minutes passed until at last the fire began to burn down. The logs turned to ashy grey ghosts, fragile and spent on the hearth. Prior Ardo leant forward to peer into the embers.

'I can't see the bowl,' he said after several moments.

William took a stick from the wood basket and poked through the ashes. The stick touched something hard. With a terrible sense of helplessness, William scraped through the embers. The bowl lay on its side, the wood not even scorched. William picked it up on the end of the stick and it dangled there, covered in ash but whole and unharmed. He set it down on the hearth.

'We have no choice but to speak to Sir Robert now,' Brother Snail said softly.

The prior said nothing. He crossed himself slowly and turned away from the fireplace. 'Very well,' he said at last. It sounded as if the words were being dragged from him. 'I will gather the brethren together for Mass. Afterwards we will decide how best to approach Sir Robert with our request.'

With that, he left the room. There was a look of defeat on his sallow face that William had never seen there before. Brother Snail stood up and shuffled over to pick up the bowl. For a long time, he held it in his cupped hands. 'Such a small thing,' he murmured, 'and so full of evil.'

He placed the bowl on the stool and followed the prior to the chapter house.

William and Shadlok left the warming room and stood for a while in the cloister alley, breathing in the cold, fresh air. The early-morning sky above the garth was cloudless and blue. Sunlight polished the puddles in the herb beds to sheets of silver. Raindrops beaded the branches of the walnut tree and sparkled like tiny stars. Spring was just a breath away and William felt a brief lift of his spirits.

'We should go and see if there is anything left to salvage in the workshop,' Shadlok said at last.

William nodded. He was bone weary and his body ached from the night spent on the cold floor of the warming room, but he needed to keep busy. Maybe that way he could block out the images and sounds that crowded into his mind, if only for a while. But he didn't think he would ever forget the noise and the blood and the fear of the last few hours, not if he lived to be an old man. And *that* was looking less likely by the day.

Chapter Twenty-Four

All that was left of Brother Snail's workshop were four walls which had shifted sideways to lean against the blackthorn tree. Shadlok used broken roof timbers to shore them up, trying to stop them from collapsing altogether. The hob carried out the few pots of salves and bundles of dried herbs that had survived and lined them up on the grass nearby.

'Your flute is broken,' the hob said unhappily, handing William the leather bag. 'The music has gone. No more dancing and singing.'

William opened the bag and tipped the shattered bits of flute onto the grass. It was beyond repair and he felt a pain beneath his ribs at its loss, but it wasn't just the beautiful old flute he'd lost, it was the hope of a different future. He looked at the wreckage strewn across the garden and felt a surge of despair. Almost nothing had survived the storm. As he looked there was a loud creak and a sharp crack of splitting wood. William turned just in time to see the walls of the hut fold in on themselves and collapse in a heap. A cloud of dust rose from the broken daub, and bits of wattle poked up like thin fingers from the wreckage.

The hob grabbed William's leg and whispered, 'Oops!'

William stared at the remains of the hut in dismay. For the second time in two years, he had lost his home.

Shadlok stood with his hands on his hips and glared at the fallen walls, his frustration plain on his face. He leant down and picked up a piece of the flute. He turned it over in his hands. 'I made this for Bone a long time ago.' A brief look of sadness crossed his face. Without looking at William, he said, 'I will make you a new one. It will not be as fine as this one was, but it will suffice.'

For the first time that day, William smiled. 'You will?' In the midst of all the terrible things that were happening at the abbey, the fay's kind gesture shone the more brightly. William tucked the leather bag into his belt. 'I'll keep this, then.'

'I still have hopes of turning you into a good

musician one day,' Shadlok said, throwing the broken flute onto a pile of wattle and timbers. 'And when that day comes, we will leave this place.'

'It can't come soon enough for me,' William said grimly. There was a small cough somewhere by his knees. Looking down, he saw the offended expression on the hob's face.

'You can come with us,' he said, squatting down beside him.

'Will there be a forest where we are going?' the hob asked, his green-gold eyes apprehensive.

William remembered what Robin had told him about London and his heart sank. How could he take the hob there? How could he take him anywhere where there would be more people than trees? The hob was a woodland fay. He wouldn't be happy in the noise and bustle of a town, nor would he be safe. William glanced helplessly up at Shadlok. The fay seemed to understand what was going through his mind because he turned to the hob and said in a surprisingly gentle voice, 'We have time enough before we need to think about leaving.'

The hob nodded and looked relieved. 'I would like to see the world, but I don't think I would like to live where there are no trees to talk to.'

William got to his feet. He was filled with a great sadness at the realisation that one day he would have to say goodbye to the hob.

But not yet, he told himself fiercely. Not for a long time yet.

Brother Snail came to find William, Shadlok and the hob after the chapter meeting finally finished.

'Prior Ardo is taking everyone to Bethlehem,' the monk said. 'They will be safer there for the time being. Brother Stephen and Peter will come back to tend to the livestock and chickens every day, but other than that, the abbey will be abandoned.'

Bethlehem was the larger of the abbey's two granges; it was over near Yagleah, and home to John Holcot the freeman and his family. William could just imagine the look on John's face when the monks turned up at his door and told him they had come to stay.

'So the demon has won,' William said bleakly.

'For now, perhaps,' Brother Snail said. The bruises on the monk's face were an ugly mottled blue in the morning light, and there were dark shadows beneath his eyes. 'There is still hope, Will. The prior has finally given me permission to go and talk to Sir Robert, to see if there is anything he can do to help us. You and Shadlok are to come with me and we are to leave immediately.'

'What about me?' the hob asked anxiously.

'You're coming with us,' William said.

Shadlok went on ahead with the hob, leaving William and the monk to follow along more slowly. Brother Snail leant heavily on a stick and moved stiffly; it seemed his joints and twisted back were hurting him. When William and the monk reached the yard, Shadlok was waiting for them by the stables. Matilda stood patiently beside him, saddled and bridled. There was no sign of the hob but William knew he would not be far from Shadlok's side and would be hidden with fay glamour. William noticed the sword and knife hanging from the fay's belt. Shadlok was taking no chances on their journey to Weforde.

Edgar the carpenter had arrived for work as usual that morning, unaware of what had happened during the night. His load of timber had been stacked against the kitchen wall and the monks were now lifting sacks of grain and baskets of vegetables onto the back of his cart. Brother Matthew hurried over to William and pushed a bundle of blankets into his arms. 'Here, boy, put these on the cart.' The monk sprinted back inside the abbey to fetch another load.

Edgar helped William to pile the blankets on top of a stack of mattresses. 'Much more an' ol' Scrat here'll wind hisself tryin' to pull this lot to Beth'lem,' Edgar said, watching Brother Stephen staggering across the yard with a stack of cooking pots and bowls, all crammed into a large iron cauldron and black with soot from the kitchen fire. 'Always s'posing Scrat can shift it at all.'

William glanced at the sturdy brown horse standing patiently between the cart shafts. The animal rolled a baleful, white-rimmed eye in William's direction and blew loudly through flared nostrils.

Seeing William's wary look, Edgar grinned. 'Yer wise to keep away from ol' Scrat, lad. Nastier beast ye won't find if ye look 'til Christmas Day.'

As if to back up the carpenter's words, the horse bared his teeth at William.

Edgar gazed at the animal affectionately. 'But he's a good worker, and I can't ask for better'n that.'

William helped Brother Stephen to wedge the cauldron between a large chest containing the abbey's few pieces of silver and a basket full of the abbey's books.

'Ye forgot summat,' Edgar said, eyeing the monk sourly.

Brother Stephen wiped the soot from his hands onto the front of his habit and glanced at the carpenter. 'Have I? What?'

'The font. It's 'bout the only thing you *ent* piled onto the cart.'

The monk coloured and looked awkward.

'Mebbe we should make two journeys,' Edgar suggested, but Brother Stephen glanced fearfully at the abbey buildings and shook his head.

'The prior wants to take whatever we can carry in one journey.'

''Cept it ent *you* carrying it, it's me poor ol' horse,' Edgar muttered as he watched the monk hurry back to the kitchen. He turned to William. 'The holy brothers are tight-lipped 'bout what's happened here but I ent blind, lad. The stonemasons have packed up and gone, now this lot are leavin' and takin' everything that ent nailed down and it don't look like they're coming back in a hurry.' He eyed William narrowly. 'I know there's summat wrong in the church, 'cause I seen things in there these last few days that ent *Christian*.'

'Oh?' William said cautiously, remembering the

prior's order not to talk about the demon to anyone outside the abbey.

The carpenter put his face close to William's and whispered, 'I think, whatever it is, it's guardin' the holy relic. It's got wings like a gret big crow and a beak that could pin a man to a barn door, and *that* ent summat you see every day.'

'No, it isn't,' William muttered.

'We're ready to leave, Will,' Brother Snail called. He was over by the stables with Shadlok and Matilda.

'Eh well, you're better off away from here, lad,' Edgar said. 'The abbey's got a mite too many secrets for my likin'.'

William remembered that it was the carpenter's ancestor who had found the angel dying in the snow and had run to the abbey for help. Edgar knew Crowfield's secrets better than almost anyone.

Brother Matthew staggered towards the cart, carrying more mattresses. With a heavy sigh, Edgar turned to help him and William sprinted away.

Chapter Twenty-Five

Illiam crossed the yard to the gatehouse where Brother Snail was sitting uncomfortably in Matilda's saddle. 'This is really not necessary,' the monk was protesting mildly. 'I *can* walk.'

'You will slow us down,' Shadlok said brusquely, as he guided Brother Snail's foot into a stirrup.

A leather bag hung from the pommel of the saddle. A feeling of evil seeped into the air around it and William guessed that it held the bowl. He saw Matilda shiver when it touched her shoulder. One gentle brown eye rolled in panic.

'I'll carry the bag,' William said. It was an effort to force the words out. 'It's scaring Matilda.'

Brother Snail untied the bag and held it out to him. 'It might be for the best.'

William took it and caught his breath. It felt as if

he had plunged his arm into a pail of freezing water. He pulled his sleeve down to cover his fingers and gripped the neck of the bag tightly.

Shadlok took Matilda's bridle and led her towards the gate. William hauled it open and stood aside to let them pass. The horse shied away from the bag and Shadlok had to hold tightly to stop her from bolting. Brother Snail clung to the pommel as the horse's hooves slipped and skidded on the wet bridge timbers. For one terrible moment, William thought she was going to fall into the river, taking the monk with her. Shadlok moved quickly. He hauled her to a standstill, talking softly to her in his own tongue and running a hand gently down her nose. The wild look gradually left her eyes and her ears pricked forwards as she listened to his voice. Shadlok guided her onto the causeway and up to the track. William kept his distance as he followed them into the forest, not wanting to scare the horse again.

When they reached the oak tree at the fork of the track, Shadlok made the hob visible again. He lifted him up to sit behind Brother Snail and the hob settled himself comfortably on Matilda's broad back. He grinned over his shoulder at William, clearly very pleased with this unexpected bit of comfort.

The day warmed as the sun rose in the sky, but it was going to take more than one spring day to dry out the muddy track. William trudged along, keeping to the grass along the edges whenever he could. Up ahead, he saw Matilda struggle through the mud, her large hooves sinking deep into the oozing ruts. A short distance beyond the rag-hung bushes near the Whistling Hollow, Shadlok turned the horse's head and led her into the undergrowth. Brother Snail and the hob ducked low to avoid a tangle of elder branches. William followed them into the woodland and to his surprise saw that Shadlok had found a dry path leading away between the trees. It narrowed to the width of a fox in places and disappeared completely into the undergrowth in others, but Shadlok's pace never faltered and they always picked it up again.

The lightest of breezes swayed through the branches high overhead, and sunlight dappled the forest floor with light and shadows. New green growth unfurled beneath the trees, and here and there blackthorns were covered in clouds of white blossom. The woods were full of the sound of birdsong, and somewhere close by a woodpecker hammered. William breathed in the damp scent of old leaf mould and warm bark and felt a stir of anticipation. Spring was creeping through the forest and summer would be close behind. If it wasn't for the chill from the bag numbing his arm, William would have enjoyed the walk. He hummed to himself to keep his spirits up, and wondered how long it would take Shadlok to make his new flute. In an effort to keep his mind from dwelling on everything that had happened, he went through all the tunes he had learnt, the fingers of his free hand moving to form the notes on an imaginary flute.

They reached a clearing and Shadlok pulled Matilda to a halt. He helped Brother Snail down from the saddle.

'When nature calls . . .' The monk smiled sheepishly at William. He hurried over to the ivy-smothered hulk of a dead tree, and disappeared behind it. William hung the bag on a branch and stood in a patch of sunlight, rubbing his hands together to try and get the feeling back into his fingers.

Shadlok stood in front of Matilda, stroking her head. She closed her eyes and rested her nose against his shoulder contentedly. The hob shuffled forward onto the saddle and began to plait Matilda's mane.

'Why hasn't the demon come after the bowl?'

William asked. The further they travelled from Crowfield, the more he wondered why the demon had made no move to follow them.

'What makes you think that it has not?'

William glanced around uneasily. '*Is* it following us?'

Shadlok's long fingers continued to stroke the horse's face, but his expression was grim. 'It has been keeping pace with us since we left the abbey.'

The hob turned in the saddle to look around the clearing with frightened eyes. William felt as if he had been doused with cold water. 'Why hasn't it attacked us?'

'I do not know,' Shadlok said softly. 'It must know where we are taking the bowl and what we intend to do, but for some reason it is not trying to stop us.' He stared at William for a few moments. 'And that worries me.'

Brother Snail hurried over to them. 'There is something in the trees over there,' he said, keeping his voice down and pointing towards a stand of birches on the edge of the clearing.

'It's the demon,' William said softly. He peered between the trees but couldn't see anything.

'God help us,' the monk whispered, crossing himself quickly.

William fetched the bag and waited while Shadlok helped Brother Snail back up into the saddle. They set off again, picking up the path on the far side of the clearing and moving as fast as they could through the undergrowth.

'Are we going the right way?' William called. It seemed to him they were travelling east, but he was sure Weforde lay more to the south.

'This path should cross the Old Way a short distance from here. We will turn south then,' Shadlok said over his shoulder.

William glanced around as he pushed his way through dense thickets of blackthorn and hazel. Thin branches whipped back at him and tangled in his hair. He stumbled over tree roots and for a couple of heart-stopping minutes he lost sight of the others when the path wove its way through a grove of oaks. He felt a sudden snatch of panic when he caught a glimpse of something red off to his left. He was certain it was the demon. It was moving silently through the under-growth, shadowing him. Terror burned through him like wildfire. He tried to run, but the harder he tried, the more entangled in branches he became. Fighting down his terror, he pulled himself free from the sharp spines of a blackthorn and pushed his way through a hazel thicket. He glimpsed Matilda's rump and tail up ahead and called out, 'Wait!'

Three surprised faces turned to look back at him.

William caught up with the others and stopped for a moment to catch his breath. He pointed into the undergrowth behind him. 'The demon . . . I saw it.'

'You *must* keep up with us,' Shadlok said. 'The Old Way is not far now. The going will be easier when we reach it and it should afford us some protection. Stay close.'

They walked along in silence until at last they came to a wide, shallow ditch. Shadlok pulled Matilda to a halt. He seemed to be listening for something, but other than the call of a blackbird, the forest around them was silent.

Careful to keep his distance from the horse, William stood by the ditch and looked around. There were fewer trees here and the undergrowth was sparse. A wide strip of flat and treeless ground stretched away on either side of him, running from north to south. He could see a second ditch on the far side of it.

'This is the Old Way?' he asked. 'Where does it lead to?'

'Nowhere in this world,' Shadlok said, 'not any longer.'

'Is it a fay path?' William had heard of such places, where you trespassed at your peril, but he had never come across one before.

'It is now, though it was made by humans hundreds of years ago.' Shadlok's head jerked around and he held up a hand in warning. William followed the direction of the fay's stare and saw a wisp of mist coiling out of the woodland on the far side of the Old Way. It gathered itself into a more solid shape that looked troublingly human.

'Stay silent, all of you,' Shadlok said softly. 'Do not move.'

William didn't need to be told twice. He watched the misty figure drift towards them, until it drew level with Shadlok. By now, William could see that it was a woman, but it bore only a fleeting resemblance to a human woman. William stared in revulsion at the gaunt face with its gaping mouth and cloudy white eyes. She wore a loose robe of fragile and ghostly-pale skeleton leaves. Through it, he could see her body. She seemed to be made of sticks and twigs, moss and lichen, all dried out and bleached. A band of thin twisted roots circled her head like a crown and her matted cobweb hair wafted in the breeze. William stared at her in horrified fascination. How could such a creature exist outside the darkest of nightmares?

The strange white eyes turned to stare at William. 'Human.' The single word was as soft as an exhaled breath.

William shivered and clutched the bag to his chest. He barely even noticed the cold that speared through his body from the bowl.

'Evil!' The dark gap of her mouth widened, showing teeth made of vicious black thorns. William had a sudden image of those teeth biting into flesh and tearing sinew from bone, and he took an unsteady step backwards.

'Stand your ground!' Shadlok whispered sharply.

The fay woman turned to Shadlok. 'You bring evil to the forest.'

'We mean no harm,' Shadlok said. 'We are on our way to find one who might be able to destroy it.'

The woman gazed at Shadlok. It was impossible to guess what she would do. William could see the tense set of Shadlok's shoulders and the tightness of his jaw as he waited for the woman to speak.

'The Great Spirit of the forest alone decides who is allowed to walk the hidden ways.'

'Then I would ask the Great Spirit to let us pass,' Shadlok said evenly. 'Let us continue our journey along the Old Way and finish what we have set out to do.'

William risked a quick glance around. *The Great Spirit?* What was that?

A breeze stirred through the trees. It sounded like many soft voices whispering all at once. William saw that the forest was alive with movement, quick darts of vivid colour against the muted browns and greens of the woodland. They flicked away too quickly for him to be able to see what they were. The breeze died and the movement ceased.

'Go on your way,' the woman said at last, 'but leave the forest before nightfall, or you will not leave at all.'

Shadlok inclined his head to her. The woman drifted away and seemed to melt into the sunlit air.

Shadlok breathed out a sigh of relief and stood for a moment with his head bowed and his hands on his hips. He turned to look around the faces of his companions. 'We need to be on our way now.'

'What was that . . . thing?' Brother Snail asked with a quaver in his voice.

'A forest fay,' Shadlok said. 'A guardian of the Old Way.'

'Is she dangerous?' William asked, thinking about the sharp thorn teeth.

'She can be, if she catches an unwary traveller alone in the woods after dusk. Just be thankful she did not try to stop us from using the Old Way,' Shadlok said, taking hold of Matilda's bridle and guiding her across the ditch. 'Bringing the bowl into the forest was not a wise thing to do. It could have gone very badly for us just now.'

The hob clung onto Brother Snail as the horse scrambled up the slope of the ditch onto the Old Way. 'She doesn't like humans,' he said breathlessly as he was bounced around behind the monk. 'She eats them.'

Shadlok's eyes narrowed as he looked back at William, and there was the shadow of a smile on his lips. 'But only if you do something to anger her.'

William met Brother Snail's startled gaze.

'What is the Great Spirit she talked of?' the monk asked. He peered into the shadows beneath the trees as if he was frightened something would be lurking there.

'It is the spirit of the Wildwood,' Shadlok said. William heard something in the fay's voice that he hadn't heard before, an awed respect. 'It existed long before mankind and faykind came into this world, and will be here long after we have gone.'

William looked up at the hob. 'Did you ever see it when you lived in Foxwist?'

'No!' The hob shook his head vehemently. 'Non*ono*! It keeps to the deepwoods, and fays never go there. The magic in that part of the forest is too strong for us.'

William was quiet for a while as he tried, and failed, to imagine what such a being could possibly look like. Brother Snail appeared to be having the same problem. He glanced down at Shadlok with a troubled expression.

'Can the demon harm the Great Spirit?'

Shadlok's expression hardened. 'I hope not, for all our sakes.'

They made their way along the Old Way quickly and in silence. William stayed just far enough behind the others not to upset Matilda. He thought of all the times he had walked through Foxwist, on his way to one of the villages, or to take the pigs out to forage in the autumn, never suspecting for even one moment that the forest was home to creatures like the guardian of the Old Way or the Great Spirit. It seemed the woodland revealed its secrets slowly, layer by layer, and each one was darker than the one before. He didn't think he would ever feel safe here again.

The Old Way led them as far as the edge of the hill overlooking Weforde, and then it just seemed to melt away into the long grass and dead bracken. They turned right along the shoulder of the hill, heading for the main track down to the village. William looked back for a last glimpse of the Old Way, but to his surprise, he could no longer see it. The ditches had vanished and trees grew across the gap where the old road had emerged from the forest.

'It's gone,' William said in astonishment.

'The Old Way stays hidden until one of the fay needs it,' Shadlok said.

'So, if I went looking for it, I wouldn't find it?' William asked.

'No, and you would be reckless to try. The guardian is there for a reason.'

The hob looked over his shoulder at William and pulled a face. 'She will crunch your bones and suck out your eyes . . .'

'Yes, thank you,' William said hurriedly, 'there's no need for details.'

'I never realised magic was so common in this world,' Brother Snail said, then added, 'or so dangerous.'

Shadlok shrugged. 'It is everywhere, if you know what you are looking for.'

They reached the track and followed it through the fields and into the village. Shadlok hid the hob from sight and told him to remain quiet. People stopped to watch them go by, the monk on horseback, the servant boy and the armed man with the white hair and strange eyes. The villagers whispered to each other, and William saw several people cross themselves. Word of what had happened at the abbey must have reached the village, he thought. The stonemasons' sudden return had probably caused a stir, and by now stories of ghosts and demons would be running like wildfire through Weforde and the surrounding farms.

The gates of the demesne farm stood open. Edmund Maudit, the bailiff, was talking to a group of villeins outside one of the manor's barns. He broke off when he saw the visitors from Crowfield and walked over to ask what it was that brought them to the village.

'We've come to talk to Sir Robert,' Brother Snail said, 'on abbey business.'

'And what might this business be?' the bailiff asked suspiciously.

'That is between the abbey and Sir Robert,' Brother Snail said firmly. 'Kindly let him know we are here on a matter of great urgency.'

Master Maudit's annoyance was plain but he knew he could hardly question the monk any further. 'Follow me, then,' he said gruffly, and stumped away towards the manor gatehouse.

The villeins drew into a huddle and watched uneasily as they passed by. One of them whispered something to his neighbour and William thought he caught the word *demon*.

'Anyone would think *we* were the demons, the way people are looking at us,' William muttered. He was feeling cold and uncomfortable; the chill from the bowl was eating its way into his bones and he had lost all feeling in the hand holding the bag.

'They can feel the evil,' Shadlok said, keeping his voice low. 'It is growing stronger with the passing hours.'

William rubbed his arm with his free hand, trying to get the blood moving again. He looked over his shoulder and saw a huddle of women peering at him from the doorway of the brew house. They quickly ducked back inside.

Master Maudit led them across the courtyard in front of the manor house and through the gateway into the inner yard. Several of the stonemasons were going about their work and the sound of chisels and hammers ringing on stone came from the new wing of the manor house. William recognised a couple of the men and nodded to them. Glancing at each other, they turned their backs on him. One of them hurried away, presumably to tell Master Guillaume of the new and not very welcome arrivals.

The bailiff watched while Shadlok helped Brother Snail down from the saddle. William felt the hob climb onto his shoulder and wrap his arms around his neck. The hob kept very still and all William could hear was soft breathing against his ear.

'Wait here,' Master Maudit said. He walked over to the door of the manor house and went inside.

'I don't think the stonemasons were best pleased to see us,' Brother Snail said, rubbing his knees and bending his legs as he tried to ease his aching body after the long ride. 'Nor the villagers.'

The hob patted William's cheek. 'I want to get down now. The bowl is making my skin scrittle.' He dug his fingers into William's hair and scrabbled at his scalp. '*Scrittle scrittle*, like this. Not good.'

'No,' William jerked his head aside, 'not good, so stop it.' He helped the hob down onto the cobbles.

'It is not safe to make you visible yet,' Shadlok said, 'so you must stay close to us at all times.'

'I will,' the hob said from somewhere over near Brother Snail's feet.

'And don't touch anything,' William added with a meaningful stare at the empty cobbles.

Master Maudit appeared in the doorway. 'Sir Robert will see you. Leave your horse over by the stable and follow me.'

Shadlok led Matilda over to the stable on the far side of the yard and tied her reins to an iron hook in the wall. Brother Snail and William waited for him by the manor door, and together they went up the stairs to Sir Robert's private quarters.

Brother Snail paused outside the door for a moment and turned to look from Shadlok to William. He smiled, but there was no disguising his apprehension at what they were about to do. William nodded and forced a smile in return. There was no need for words.

Chapter Twenty-Six

S ir Robert sat at a table with his back to one of the two-light windows set into the thick walls. Beside him stood a short bald man, well dressed and fond of his food, to judge by the heavy jowls and rounded belly beneath his fine blue woollen tunic.

'This is Master Henry Woodcote, my steward,' Sir Robert said, with a nod in the plump man's direction.

The steward glanced at Shadlok. Shadlok might have lived as a guest in the manor house for a few weeks last winter, but it was plain there was no friendship wasted between these two. Master Woodcote smiled at Brother Snail. The fleshy cheeks dimpled but the smile didn't reach his eyes. They were cold and calculating as he took the measure of the crippled monk.

Sir Robert glanced at William. 'Fetch a chair for Brother Snail, boy.'

William looked around and spotted a carved and gilded chair to one side of the huge stone fireplace. He carried it over to the table and set it down for the grateful monk.

'You have matters you wish to discuss with me?' Sir Robert asked. He leant his elbows on the table and linked his fingers together. His sharp grey eyes were alight with curiosity.

'Of grave importance,' Brother Snail said. 'To do with the recent . . . events at the abbey.'

Sir Robert nodded. 'Master Guillaume told me a little of what has been happening there.' He gestured to his steward with a flick of his hand. 'You can speak freely in front of Master Woodcote.'

The two men listened as Brother Snail explained why they had come to Weforde. The monk took the leather bag from William and unwrapped the bowl. He stood it on the table. Sir Robert reached for the bowl but before his fingers touched it, he hesitated and withdrew his hand.

When Brother Snail had finished, Sir Robert sat in silence, one finger tapping the table absently. William glanced at Master Woodcote. The steward was staring at the bowl nervously. It had grown noticeably colder in the room, but in spite of this there was a sheen of sweat on the man's face.

'Did you bring Abbot Bartolomeo's letter with you?' Sir Robert asked at last.

'Yes,' Brother Snail said, pulling the folded parchment from his cloak pocket. He handed it to Sir Robert and waited while the lord of the manor read it through.

'You are hoping I might be able to trap the demon in the bowl, just as my ancestor did a hundred years ago?' Sir Robert said.

Brother Snail nodded. 'It is a lot to ask, but we are desperate.'

Sir Robert looked up at Shadlok, who was standing silent and still beside the monk's chair. 'It was you, I assume, who told the prior and Brother Snail here that I practise alchemy?'

Shadlok nodded. 'I had little choice. They cannot fight the demon alone.'

'I asked for *your* help last winter,' Sir Robert said, quietly angry, 'but you refused. Now you come here to ask for *my* help. That is hardly fair, I think.'

Shadlok gave Sir Robert a look that would have made most people think twice about pushing the matter further. William felt a grudging admiration for the lord of Weforde when he merely stared back at the fay, a determined gleam in his eyes.

'If I do this, then I expect you to help me in return.' Sir Robert spoke directly to Shadlok. Whatever was happening here, William realised, was between these two and nobody else. Brother Snail was forgotten for the time being.

'And if I refuse?'

'Then . . .' Sir Robert sighed and spread his hands in a gesture of apparent regret, '. . . the fate of the monks will be on your conscience.'

Shadlok closed his eyes for a moment. The fay had been backed into a corner, just as William had feared he would be.

'Please,' Brother Snail sat forward in the chair and rested one thin hand on the table, 'can you not find it in your heart to help us without asking Shadlok to pay the price for that aid? I don't know what it is you want from him, but it is clear to me that he doesn't wish you to have it.'

Sir Robert turned to the monk but his expression didn't soften. 'Ridding you of a demon isn't just a matter of snapping my fingers, Brother. It will be difficult and dangerous, and it might not even succeed. All I want is fair payment for my trouble, and the fay has the one thing I want.'

'But what *is* it?' Brother Snail looked from Sir Robert to Shadlok, baffled and anxious. 'What can Shadlok possibly possess that is worth more than the abbey and all those who live there?'

'He can tell me how to find the Unseelie Court. I want him to open the gateway between his world and this one.' He paused for a moment. 'I want to meet King Comnath.'

Brother Snail stared at Sir Robert as if he hadn't quite understood what the man had just said. Shadlok turned away. He folded his arms and stared out of the window. The thick panes of glass distorted the view. The village and the fields and woodland beyond it wavered and twisted into a landscape from a dream. There was a look of defeat in his eyes that William had never seen before, and he felt an overwhelming pity for him.

'The Dark King?' Brother Snail asked uncertainly. 'Why in God's name would you want anything to do with that . . . *creature?*'

'When Jacobus Bone came here last winter, he told me he had been cursed with immortality by a king of the Unseelie Court,' Sir Robert said. 'I have studied and practised alchemy since I was a boy no older than your servant here. I have searched for that one secret without success, but now, at last, with the help of this fay, the gift of eternal life could be within my grasp.'

'Such a thing is against God,' Brother Snail said, appalled. 'It is blasphemy! You will forfeit your soul.'

Sir Robert sat forward and smiled. 'Don't you understand, Brother? None of that will matter because I will never die.'

'May God forgive you,' the monk whispered. He twisted his body in the chair to look up at Shadlok. 'Do you intend to show him how to reach your world?'

'If I do not, he will not help us.' He glanced at William. 'And the demon will come after the boy. What choice do I have?'

William cleared his throat and stepped out from behind Brother Snail's chair. 'Begging your pardon, my lord, but what makes you think the Unseelie king will help you?'

Sir Robert stared at William in thoughtful silence for a few moments. He seemed to consider the question. 'What makes you think he won't?'

William glanced anxiously at Shadlok. *How much should I say?* he wondered, and then decided the time for keeping secrets had long since gone.

'I've met him,' William said. He had Sir Robert's full attention now. 'He's cunning and cruel and he hates humans. He won't help you.'

Sir Robert sat back in his chair. 'Perhaps I can offer him something of value in return for the gift of immortality. Everyone has their price.'

William felt a stirring of foreboding. It seemed Brother Snail shared his feelings.

'What have you got that he could want?' the monk asked.

Sir Robert's face became carefully expressionless. 'I am sure I will find something.' His gaze flickered to William. The grey eyes were as hard as stone. There was a sick feeling in William's belly as he realised what Sir Robert was hinting at. Beside him, he heard Brother Snail gasp.

'You would offer the *boy* to the Dark King to get your own way? May God forgive you for even *thinking* such a thing.'

Shadlok leant his hands on the table and put his face close to Sir Robert's. 'Harm the boy and I swear I will kill you.'

Sir Robert looked startled and sat back in his chair, but his gaze was steady. 'His life is in your hands, fay. The choice is yours.'

Shadlok straightened up. 'I will give you what you want. Bind the demon again.'

Chapter Twenty-Seven

Sir Robert drew aside a wall hanging and unlocked the small door hidden behind it. He instructed Master Woodcote to go about his duties and make sure nobody disturbed them, and then asked Brother Snail for help searching through his books and papers to find the ritual his ancestor had used to trap the demon in the bowl.

William stood in the doorway of the small and windowless room and looked around curiously. The walls were lined with shelves and a table stood in the middle of the floor. Every surface was crammed with strange implements and vessels whose use he couldn't even begin to guess at. Iron tripods and candlesticks and small bronze dishes covered the table top. Amongst them were flasks and thin tubes of glass, the like of which he had never seen before. There were glass jars of coloured powders and stones and bundles of leaves, and an array of large earthenware pots lined up on the floor. The whitewashed walls between the shelves were covered with words and numbers and strange ciphers, scrawled in charcoal. The air had an unpleasant smell, as if someone had cracked open eggs that had begun to rot. William held his nose.

Sir Robert took a spindly iron key out of the purse hanging from his belt, and unlocked a large cupboard. It was full of books and rolls of parchment. He selected a thick leather-bound book and handed it to the monk.

'Begin with this one, Brother. It is *Ars Notoria*, a grimoire of ancient magical knowledge told to King Solomon by an angel many centuries ago. It's very fragile, so please be careful with it.'

'What am I searching for?' Brother Snail asked, taking the book with a barely concealed look of distaste.

'Look for the name of the demon, and it should tell us the sigils by which it may be summoned and controlled.' Sir Robert took two more books from the cupboard. He held one up. 'This is *Ars Goetia*, the book Abbot Bartolomeo gave to my ancestor. It contains the names of many demons and angels. There's a good chance that Raum may be amongst them.' He patted the cover of the second book. 'This is a copy of the *Ghayat al-Hakim*. It is a book of magic written in the Arab tongue. We should find what we need in at least one of these.'

'What are sigils?' William asked.

'Symbols and signs, like the ones carved into the bowl. They have immense power and if we can find the right ones, we can trap the demon in the bowl again.'

Brother Snail frowned. 'Surely the sigils on the bowl *are* the ones we are looking for?'

'They are binding sigils, but first, we have to find the correct summoning sigils,' Sir Robert said briskly. 'Make yourself useful, William, and start rolling up the carpets.' He saw William's blank look and added, 'The floor coverings. Then push the furniture up against the walls.'

Shadlok helped William to clear the middle of the room. Sir Robert and Brother Snail sat at the table by the window to begin their search through the books.

'This may take some time,' Sir Robert said, frowning down at a page crammed full of writing, numbers and ciphers. 'William, find Master Woodcote and tell him to bring Brother Snail and myself some food and drink. You can eat with the servants in the kitchen.'

He glanced up from the book and stared at Shadlok for a moment. 'You, as I recall, don't need to eat at all.'

As William walked down the staircase, he heard the scrabble of the hob's feet on the wooden steps behind him.

'Wait for me!' the hob said breathlessly. William felt a paw grab the hem of his tunic and cling on tightly.

Shadlok caught up with them in the cross-passage between the old house and the new wing.

'What will happen to you for allowing Sir Robert to go through to your world?' William asked.

Shadlok smiled bitterly. 'I am sure my people will find a suitable punishment for me, something even worse than exiling me here in your world.'

'Will they kill you?' William asked hesitantly.

'Sometimes death is not a punishment, but a blessing.'

William thought of Jacobus Bone, craving death after centuries of suffering as a leper, and realised that Shadlok was right.

A cold draught whipped along the cross-passage. William shivered and rubbed his arms to warm himself.

'But *will* they kill you?' William repeated. He was racked with guilt. Shadlok had agreed to Sir Robert's demands partly to save William's life.

'Eventually, perhaps. If I am lucky,' Shadlok said. He left the house and the door closed quietly behind him.

William was pleasantly surprised to find that the manor kitchen was as different from the abbey kitchen as it was possible to be. It was a large stone building set apart from the manor house on the far side of a stone-paved yard. A bread oven was built up against a gable wall, and storerooms and a brew house were ranged around the yard. In the middle of the yard there was a well with a thatched roof. Inside the kitchen it was warm, bustling with people and full of wonderful smells. The servants were cheerful and friendly, and William was welcomed with an easy acceptance.

'I was told to find Master Woodcote, to ask for some food to be sent up to Sir Robert and Brother Snail,' William explained to the man who seemed to be in charge.

'We don't need to trouble Master Woodcote, lad. Best let him go and annoy someone else. Make yourself useful and stir this sauce, and don't let it burn. Sir Robert's dinner will be ready soon enough.'

A little while later, a serving boy carried a tray of food up to Sir Robert's chamber. William sat on one of the benches at the kitchen table with Master Brice the cook and the other servants, eating a meal of pottage, thick and tasty with barley and vegetables, and freshly baked bread. The hob sat under the table, and William managed to slip him bits of food without anybody noticing. By the time he had cleared his bowl for a second time, William's stomach felt as if it was about to burst and he surprised himself by regretfully turning down a third helping.

'You need fattening up, lad. The holy brothers don't feed you properly, by the looks of it,' Master Brice said, inspecting him with a frown.

'It's Lent,' William said, not wanting to try to explain Brother Martin to the people in the manor kitchen. 'The monks are fasting.'

'Aye, well, we all are, but there's a line to draw between fasting and starving.' The cook chewed a mouthful of bread and gazed at William with open curiosity. 'So what brings you here with the monk and the leper's manservant?'

William glanced at the ring of interested faces around the table and felt awkward. 'Brother Snail has abbey matters to discuss with Sir Robert.'

'We heard the church fell down,' one of the other servants said, leaning forward to look along the table at him, 'and that the abbey's haunted by a demon that can conjure up a storm.' A murmur went around the table at this. The stonemasons had wasted no time in spreading the word of what had happened at Crowfield, it seemed.

'The tower collapsed,' William said, 'not the whole church. The monks have gone to one of their granges for now.'

'But what about the *demon?*' the servant asked, clearly relishing the tales being told around the village and manor.

'*I* heard it ate one of the monks,' another man said. 'Chewed him right up and spat out the bones.'

'It didn't . . .' William began, but the man wasn't listening. He clearly preferred his own version of events, regardless of whether or not it was true.

'And that the stones of the abbey are burnt black from the demon's fiery breath,' the man continued with horrified glee, 'and that it carried off a whole field full of sheep.'

'No,' William tried to get a word in sideways, but gave up under the storm of wild rumours and stories flying around the table.

'We heard they found the Holy Grail in the church,' Master Brice said, mopping up the last of his pottage with a piece of bread.

'It's just a wooden bowl,' William said, half expecting to be shouted down again. 'It's not the Grail.'

But nobody was listening to him now. He sighed and folded his arms on the table and sat quietly until the meal was finished and the servants went back to their work. With great reluctance, William decided he ought to return to Sir Robert's private chambers. He took a last, longing look around the busy kitchen. He wished with all his heart that Father Edric, the priest in Iwele, had thought to find a home for him somewhere like this, and not in the abbey.

'Thank you for the food,' William said, nodding to Master Brice. He couldn't imagine the cook beating someone because they broke a jug.

Master Brice smiled back. 'You're welcome, lad.'

William felt the hob brush past him as he left the kitchen.

'The food here is much, *much* better than the brother man's cooking,' the hob whispered as they crossed the yard to the manor house. 'There were no burny bits or fish heads, and it did not smell like the inside of the goat pen.'

'Well, don't get too used to it. We'll be suffering Brother Martin's food again soon enough.'

William stood by the manor-house door for a moment. He knew he should go back up and see if Brother Snail and Sir Robert had found anything of use in the books, but the lure of spending a few minutes in the mild spring sunshine was too great. He glanced around the yard to make sure nobody was watching, and then walked quickly over to the gateway of Sir Robert's garden. Behind him, he heard the hob's claws tapping on the cobbles.

Gravel paths between low turf walls led to the centre of the garden, where an old mulberry tree grew. The garden was bare and dressed in winter browns and greys, but small green buds on the twisting stems of the rose bushes were flushed with red and ready to unfurl. There was a feeling of peace here which William liked. In summer, when the roses were in flower and the turf walls had greened up, the garden would be hidden from the courtyard. He sat on a bench and closed his eyes. The hob climbed up to sit beside him. They sat in companionable silence and William felt a rare contentment. His belly was full of good food and the sun warm on his face. For those few minutes it was easy to forget about the demon and what lay ahead.

He jumped and opened his eyes when a shadow fell across his face. It was Shadlok. He hadn't heard the fay approach.

'Brother Snail and Sir Robert have found what they were looking for,' Shadlok said. 'Sir Robert is ready to begin the summoning.'

William stood up. The enormity of what they were about to do hit him and he suddenly felt very afraid. 'Is it going to work?' he asked.

'We will find out soon enough.' Shadlok waved a hand and the hob reappeared, sitting on the bench. Shadlok crouched down in front of him. 'You will be safer in the stable. Wait there until this is all over.'

'But I want to stay with you,' the hob said anxiously, looking from the fay to William.

'No,' Shadlok said firmly. 'We will come and fetch you later, but for now you must stay hidden in the stable. It is for your own good,' he added gently.

Reluctantly, the hob nodded. He reached out and patted Shadlok's cheek. The fay looked startled and quickly got to his feet, clearly thrown by the tender gesture. William had the feeling there had been precious little softness of any kind in the fay's long life, and he felt an odd stir of pity.

'Look after Matilda,' William said, leaning down to put a hand on the hob's shoulder.

The hob nodded again and climbed down from the bench. The air around him shimmered briefly and he was gone. William heard him patter away, his feet crunching on the gravel.

'You can go with him,' Shadlok said. 'You do not need to be here for what is to come.'

William took a few deep breaths to try and steady the wild beating of his heart. He had never felt fear like this before, but he shook his head. 'No, we're all in this together.'

William clenched his fists and jaw to stop them trembling and followed Shadlok back through the garden. *God help us all*, he thought, *because we are going to need it.*

Chapter Twenty-Eight

Sir Robert had closed the window shutters. Lanterns and candles placed around the chamber formed a circle of light. Shadlok closed and barred the door. William stood beside Brother Snail near the fireplace.

'Something has been troubling me,' Sir Robert began.

'What is it?' Brother Snail said.

'From what you have told me, the demon has almost severed the ties binding it to the bowl. It is, to all intents and purposes, already free.'

'So it would seem,' the monk agreed.

'Then where is it? Why hasn't it tried to stop us?' Sir Robert said. 'It is almost as if it is *letting* us summon it.'

'I fear you may be right.' Brother Snail sounded worried. 'The demon followed us through the forest but it made no attempt to stop us from bringing the bowl to you. Perhaps we should abandon the summoning.'

'If we do that, we are letting go of our only chance to imprison it again,' Sir Robert said.

'What if it doesn't work?' William asked.

Sir Robert said nothing.

'We have no choice but to continue,' Shadlok said.

Sir Robert nodded. 'I agree. Brother Snail? Are you with us on this?'

The monk put a hand on the wall to steady himself and shook his head. 'No,' he whispered. 'In all conscience, I cannot say I am.'

'William?' Sir Robert said. 'What do you think?'

With an apologetic glance at Brother Snail, William nodded. 'We have to try.'

'I'm sorry, Brother,' Sir Robert said gently, 'it's three against one.'

'Very well,' Brother Snail whispered. 'Do what you have to do.'

They watched from beside the fireplace as Sir Robert carefully drew two circles on the floorboards, one inside the other, with a lump of chalk. He murmured words that sounded strange to William's ears. Brother Snail lowered himself awkwardly to his knees. He closed his eyes and clasped his hands so tightly that the knuckles and joints were white, and he started to pray.

Sir Robert placed the bowl on the floor between the two circles. He straightened up and turned to the others. His face was pale and tense. A muscle twitched below one eye, so it seemed as if he was winking at them. William might have found it funny if he wasn't feeling sick with fear.

'I will cast a circle of protection around me when I am ready to begin the summoning. You are welcome to stand inside it with me,' Sir Robert said.

'Will we be safe if we stay outside?' Shadlok asked.

Sir Robert nodded to the circle he had already cast. 'The demon will be imprisoned in there, so yes, I believe you should be. But you must remain still and silent throughout, not a word or so much as a movement of the head. Is that understood?'

William wondered if shaking with terror counted, but he just nodded.

Sir Robert hesitated for several moments. He appeared calm and in control, but William saw the apprehension in his eyes. 'I would have preferred it if I'd had time to prepare for this properly. There are certain rituals and observances that should be made before a summoning of this nature. And it would have been better to wait until the full of the moon. As it is, the moon is waning, and that is not a good time to attempt work such as this.'

'Even so, we must do this *now*,' Shadlok insisted.

Sir Robert nodded. 'I know. But there is one other thing . . .'

Shadlok folded his arms and regarded the man coldly. 'What?'

Sir Robert glanced down at the bowl, then looked at William. 'To complete the ritual, I need the blood of an innocent. It is what the creature craves to make it strong, and will draw the demon to us more surely than anything else.'

Brother Snail recoiled in horror and struggled to his feet. He understood immediately what the man was saying. 'No! *No!* You will not touch the boy!'

'I need only a few drops,' Sir Robert said quickly. 'His blood is necessary for the summoning to work.'

William put a hand to the scratches on his face. 'Dame Alys took some of my blood yesterday.'

'I take it you didn't give it to her of your own free will?' Sir Robert asked sharply.

William shook his head.

'That's something, at least. If she means to summon

the demon, then your blood will be of limited use to her if it wasn't given freely.'

'If you do this, then you are no better than Dame Alys and her ancestors,' Brother Snail said softly, a look of disgust on his face.

'*You* came to *me* for help,' Sir Robert reminded him shortly. 'You can take it or leave it, the choice is yours.'

'Is there no other way to do the ritual?' William asked.

'We can do it without the blood offering, but I can't be certain it will work.'

William glanced at Brother Snail. 'The blood is mine, so the choice is mine too.' He held his arm out to Sir Robert. 'Do it.'

'Will!' Brother Snail sounded shocked. 'Think what you are doing!'

'I have,' William said.

Without a word, Shadlok stepped forward and took his knife from its sheath. He held William's wrist and drew the point of the blade across his palm. There was a sting of pain and blood welled from the cut. Sir Robert picked up the cursed bowl and hurried forward. Shadlok turned William's hand to allow drops of blood to fall into the bowl, where they gleamed wetly against the dark wood. Shadlok sheathed his knife and let go of William's arm. Sir Robert returned the bowl to the edge of the chalk circle. Brother Snail knelt again, his eyes gleaming with tears.

William squeezed his hand into a fist. He could feel the blood in his palm. He ignored the ache from the cut and watched as the ritual began.

Sir Robert took one of the books from the table. He opened it at a particular page and put the book on the floor in front of him. He squatted down and began to draw around himself with the lump of chalk.

With infinite care, he copied the drawing of a circle from the book onto the floorboards. He quartered it with straight lines, and then quartered it again. He drew complicated sigils around the inner curve of the circle and between the lines, and then added words, until at last it was complete. He picked up the book and got to his feet. Taking several deep breaths, he squared his shoulders and slowly began to read the words of magic out loud.

To William, the words were just sounds without any meaning, but he felt their power humming in the air around the chamber. He glanced down at Brother Snail. The monk's lips moved in silent, desperate prayer. Beside him, Shadlok looked as if he had been carved from stone.

Sir Robert's voice rose as the words gathered strength. The chalk markings around him started to glimmer with a pale, eerie glow. The demon's circles scorched the floorboards, and the air within them wavered like a heat haze. There was an acrid smell of burnt wood, mingled with the sickly-sweet stench of decay, which caught in the back of William's throat and made him gag. A dark red form glimmered into view and gradually took shape.

William could barely breathe and his body was rigid with fear. He grabbed Shadlok's arm and held tightly. At first, all he could see of the demon were crimson-feathered wings, which wrapped its body from head to foot. Sir Robert's face shone with sweat. His voice took on a husky tremble but he didn't falter, even when the wings slowly started to unfurl. They spread to the very edge of the inner circle and for the first time, William saw the demon clearly. Forgetting Sir Robert's instruction not to move, he sank to his knees beside Brother Snail.

Raum, the fallen angel and demon, was surrounded by a deep red glow. *Like the light of hell*, William thought. The demon had the head of a crow, though the feathers were crimson rather than black, and it wore a long dark-red robe. As far as William could see, it had the body and limbs of a human, and its skin was a dusky red.

Sir Robert pointed to the bloodstained bowl. His voice rose and it held an unmistakable note of command. Brilliant white sparks of light crackled inside his protective circle. Several touched his skin and he flinched as they burned him. The demon turned its head to look at him with one dark, unblinking eye.

William jumped when Brother Snail clutched his arm. 'It isn't working!' the monk whispered, panic-stricken.

William fought to stay calm. Sir Robert's voice rose to a shout as he tried to force the demon to obey him. His skin had taken on a grey tinge now, and his eyes were wide and bulging with terror. William realised Brother Snail was right; the ancient words were not working. Their magic was strong, but not nearly strong enough, not by a long way.

And then the demon spread its wings wide so that they crossed the barrier of the circle as if it simply wasn't there. William fell back against the wall and stared in revulsion as the demon reached down and dipped its fingertips in the blood in the bottom of the bowl. It opened its beak and wiped its fingers on its tongue, tasting the blood. It held a hand over the bowl and white light speared out from its palm. A moment later all that was left of the bowl was a small pile of ash.

The demon was free. The words of power died on Sir Robert's lips and he cowered as the demon stepped out of the circle. The chalk circle around Sir Robert no longer glowed. The demon put out a foot and, slowly and deliberately, rubbed out one of the protective sigils. Sir Robert moaned softly and hid his face in his hands. The demon stretched out a finger and leant down to touch the man on the forehead. Sir Robert fell forward with a gurgling sound in his throat and lay there, half in and half out of the circle.

The demon turned its head and looked at William and the others.

'Run!' Shadlok yelled, hauling William and Brother Snail to their feet and shoving them towards the door. 'Go! As fast as you can! I will cover you.'

William grabbed the monk and dragged him to the doorway. He was beyond coherent thought, beyond fear. His desperation to escape gave his body the strength it needed to get Brother Snail out of the room, down the stairs and out into the yard, where they collapsed into a heap on the cobbles. William rolled onto his back, barely noticing the puddles and mud soaking into his clothes and hair. Tears slid down his cheeks and he closed his eyes tightly.

'Where's Sir Robert?' someone demanded sharply. William recognised Master Woodcote's voice and he winced as the steward kicked his leg. 'Answer me, boy! Where is he?'

'It didn't work,' William rasped. 'We failed. I think Sir Robert is dead.'

Chapter Twenty-Nine

William sat up. He wiped his face with his sleeve and looked around for Brother Snail. The monk was lying in a puddle nearby. William leant over and shook his shoulder. 'Brother Snail? Are you all right?'

The monk murmured. William knelt over him anxiously.

'What have we done, Will?' Brother Snail whispered. Mud streaked his face and his habit was wet with puddle water. William stood up and, as gently as he could, helped Brother Snail to his feet. The monk held tightly to William's arm for support.

By now, a small crowd of manor servants had gathered around them. William recognised several of them from his hour spent in the kitchen. They whispered and muttered between themselves as they wondered what was going on. Master Brice took charge of Brother Snail.

'Come with me back to the kitchen now, Brother, and let's get you cleaned up,' the cook said soothingly, as if he was speaking to a small child. He led the monk towards the open door of the cross-passage. 'The rest of you, get back to work.'

William noticed a group of stonemasons watching the commotion from the far end of the courtyard. Master Guillaume and Reynaud were amongst them. They stood silently, glancing up at the shuttered windows of Sir Robert's private chambers and staring with open hostility at William.

'What happened?' one of the kitchen servants asked, peering curiously at William. Finding two of the abbey visitors lying in puddles was not something that happened every day. William ducked his head and pushed past him.

William stood in the manor doorway and tried to find the courage to go up the stairs after Master Woodcote. He felt guilty that he hadn't tried to warn the steward what was waiting for him up there. But more than that, he was worried about Shadlok. Had the demon attacked him too? Was he dead? William had just put a foot on the bottom step when he heard voices. To his enormous relief, he realised one of them was Shadlok's, and the other was Master Woodcote's. He hurried up the staircase and into Sir Robert's chambers.

The demon had gone. William was surprised to see that Sir Robert wasn't dead after all. He was lying on the floor by one of the windows, moaning softly. The shutter had been pulled open, allowing a little daylight into the room. Master Woodcote was leaning over Sir Robert, his plump face white with shock. Shadlok was kneeling nearby and rubbing away the chalk marks on the floor with a cloth. The demon's circle, however, had been burned deeply into the floorboards. The ash from the bowl stirred in the draught from the open door and lifted in a fine grey cloud. It mingled with the chalk dust swirling slowly in the light from the window.

'Where did the demon go?' William asked.

Shadlok sat back on his heels and glanced at William. 'I do not know, but it has not gone very far. I can still feel it close by. How is the monk?'

'He's very shaken. Master Brice has taken him to the kitchen.' William thought of the cook's good-humoured face. 'He's in safe hands.' He nodded to Sir Robert. 'Will he be all right?'

Shadlok shrugged. 'Who knows?'

'Help me to get Sir Robert to his bed. I can't carry him on my own,' Master Woodcote said to Shadlok. He glanced at William. 'Open the bedchamber door, boy, it's behind the hanging on the end wall. And pull back the bed coverings.'

William hauled the heavy coverings to the foot of the bed and stood back as Shadlok and the steward lowered the barely conscious man onto the bed. William saw an angry red burn on Sir Robert's forehead where the demon had touched him.

'Fetch Brother Snail. He may be able to help Sir Robert,' Master Woodcote said. 'Put the carpets and furniture back as quickly as you can, before anyone sees something they shouldn't.' He frowned over his shoulder at them. 'I am sure I don't need to tell either of you not to talk about what has happened here today with anyone. All they need to know is that Sir Robert was taken ill.'

'Nobody will believe that,' William said.

'They will believe what they are told,' the steward said grimly.

Between them, William and Shadlok laid the carpets and dragged the furniture back into place. When they had finished, William asked, 'What will happen now that the demon is free?'

'Nothing good, I am sure.' Shadlok opened the rest of the shutters. The late afternoon sunlight splashed gold on the floor and lit up the colours in the carpets. Everything looked much as it had before, but there was a subtle change, as if in spite of the light coming through the windows, a shadow had settled over the chamber. The expensive luxury of the room had dimmed and there was an atmosphere within the walls that left William feeling on edge. Traces of the demon seemed to linger on the dusty air.

William was glad to escape from the chamber. He ran all the way to the kitchen, ignoring angry mutters from the stonemasons when he passed them in the kitchen yard. He found Brother Snail sitting by the hearth, a cup of warmed and spiced small beer in his hands. The colour had returned to his cheeks. His damp habit had been wiped clean of mud and was drying in the heat from the fire.

'Master Woodcote wants you to come and see if there's anything you can do for Sir Robert.'

'What's wrong with him?' Master Brice asked, sounding surprised.

'I don't know,' William said truthfully, 'but he's unconscious.'

Brother Snail set the cup down on the hearthstones and pushed himself up out of the chair, gripping the back for support. 'I will come immediately.'

The cook looked worried. 'I'll send for Dame Alys, Brother, she's skilled at healing people and can help you.'

'I don't think that is necessary,' the monk said, with a quick glance at William. 'Thank you for your hospitality, Master Brice.'

'You're sure?' the cook said doubtfully. 'People here at the manor usually send for the dame when they're ill. Young Wat can run and fetch her. He has a nimble pair of legs and will be back with her in no time.'

Brother Snail didn't look happy at the prospect of the wise woman coming to the manor, but he said nothing. Perhaps he realised that Master Brice was likely to send for her anyway.

William accompanied Brother Snail as far as the door to the manor house. 'I'll go to find the hob and tell him what's happened,' he said.

The monk nodded and said, 'We will have to take word of our failure to the prior at Bethlehem. It's too late to set out today, but you and Shadlok must go first thing tomorrow.'

'We can't leave you here by yourself,' William protested, 'especially if Dame Alys comes to the manor, not now that her demon is free.'

'It doesn't matter, Will. Nowhere is safe now. I might just as well be here tending to Master Robert as hidden away at Bethlehem.' Brother Snail sounded weary. He bowed his head and closed his eyes for a moment. His next words seemed to cost him dearly and there was deep sadness in his voice when he spoke again. 'And when you have delivered the message to the prior, you and Shadlok should leave Crowfield. He will take care of you. Find somewhere far from here and begin your life again.'

William stared at him, too shocked to speak for a moment. 'You want me to *leave?* But what about you and the hob?'

The monk patted his arm. 'We will take our chances, but I will rest easy knowing you are safe.'

William shook his head. 'No, I won't go. I'm staying and so is Shadlok.'

The monk opened his mouth to argue but William turned and walked away without giving him a chance to get a word out. He knew Brother Snail meant well, but the monk didn't know him at all if he thought William could live with himself after abandoning the two people he loved most in the world. He knew the hob wasn't a *person* as such, but the hob and Brother Snail were his family now. He had already lost one family, he wasn't about to lose a second.

Chapter Thirty

The hob was delighted to see William safe and unharmed, but his happy mood quickly faded when William told him that the attempt to bind the demon had failed.

'Maybe it will go away now that it's free,' the hob said hopefully. He was still invisible but William could see the hollow in the straw where he was sitting.

'It might,' William said, stroking Matilda's face. But somehow he didn't think it would.

The hob was silent for a while. The straw rustled, and something long and dark moved through the air apparently of its own accord. To his surprise he saw that it was a bone whistle.

'I found this and thought you could play it until Shadlok makes you a new flute,' the hob said.

William took it from him and turned it over to inspect it. The bone was dark and shiny from years of use. He put it to his lips and softly blew a wavery note. He felt for the holes and blew again. The whistle was a crude instrument and had fewer holes than his flute had, but after a few attempts, he managed to play a recognisable tune.

'Where did you get it from?' William asked.

'It was in a wooden box in a shed,' the hob said, sounding very pleased with himself. 'There were spiders' webs all over the box, and dust. I don't think anyone wants it, so you can have it now.'

'Hmm, I'm not sure that's such a good idea,' William said. Stealing from Sir Robert, even if it was only a long-forgotten whistle, was not a wise thing to do, but perhaps he could borrow it for a while.

'Play the summer song,' the hob said.

William rolled his eyes but he smiled. 'Very well, but just the once.'

'Or maybe twice,' the hob said.

William leant against the wooden partition and began to play.

At dusk, Shadlok came to find him.

'I have been looking for you,' the fay said. Matilda whickered with pleasure at the sound of his voice. He stood beside her and stroked her neck.

'I'm keeping out of the way,' William said. The hob was curled up beside him, still safely invisible, sleeping off a meal of hazelnuts and apples he had found in one of Sir Robert's well-stocked storerooms, and a great deal of *cuckooing*.

'That is probably for the best,' Shadlok said. 'Rumours of what has been going on here today are rife, and word is out that Sir Robert is ill. It is fair to say we are not popular,' he added wryly.

William pulled a face. He had no doubt about *that*. 'How is Sir Robert?'

'There is nothing wrong with Sir Robert's body,' Shadlok said. 'But the demon has blighted his mind. He is conscious now, but he mumbles and mutters and does not know who or where he is. I think there is very little the monk can do for him, and whether or not he will recover remains to be seen.'

'Is Dame Alys here?'

'Why would she be?' Shadlok asked sharply.

'Master Brice was going to send for her.'

'Well, if he did, she did not come.'

'Is the demon still close by?' William asked.

'No, it seems to have gone, but I am sure we have not seen the last of it.'

There were a couple of apples in the straw, left over

from the hob's meal. Shadlok picked one up and held it on his flat palm for Matilda. Her soft lips scooped it up and she munched it contentedly, her eyes half closed. A small smile touched the fay's mouth as he watched her.

William glanced down at the patch of straw where the hob was snoring softly. 'We'll stay here in the stable tonight.'

'Very well.' Shadlok gave Matilda a last pat. 'We will set out for Bethlehem at dawn. Be ready.'

William nodded and settled himself deeply in the straw. For now, he felt reasonably safe. The demon had gone for the time being and, apart from Sir Robert's illness and the burnt circle in the floor, had done no damage. It was not how William had feared the summoning would go. Nevertheless, as he felt sleep creep over him, he pushed away the frightening thought that the demon was simply biding its time. Sooner or later, it would be back.

Chapter Thirty-One

The sound of shouting and yells woke William from a deep sleep at dawn the following morning. Matilda was stamping and skittering around the stall, whinnying in panic. Her hooves narrowly missed William as he lay in the straw. He rolled out of the way and stood up.

And then he smelled it. Smoke. Fear tightened his chest. He glimpsed flickering yellow light through chinks in the timber walls of the stables. This was no dream. Something was on fire.

'Brother Walter?' William called, reaching down to feel for the hob in the straw, but the hob was not there. The smoke was getting thicker. William grabbed Matilda's halter and, covering his mouth and nose with his sleeve, he led her to the stable door. He lifted the heavy wooden bar and shoved the door, but it didn't move. Someone was pounding on it from outside, but the door was stuck fast.

William tried to calm the frightened mare, but Matilda wasn't listening. She kicked out wildly, and William had to throw himself out of the way to avoid being hurt. The mare thrashed around and turned to charge madly through the stables. Answering whinnies came from the other stalls.

William looked around for something to force the door open with, and saw several hay forks and rakes hanging from pegs on the wall. He grabbed the heaviest-looking one and swung it with all his might, battering at the door. The heavy timbers held and as the smoke caught in his throat and stung his eyes, he knew he was wasting his time, but he couldn't leave the animals trapped inside to burn to death. He ran as fast as he could from stall to stall, releasing each horse in turn. They jostled and pushed each other in terror. There was no sign of the stable boys, but whether they had somehow managed to escape or had been overcome by the smoke, William didn't know. Then a gash of light in the gable wall cut through the smoke and William waved his arms to drive the horses towards it. The light grew and above the screams of the terrified horses, William heard the sound of axes splitting wood and saw hands reach through the gap to haul the timbers away. The horses started to push through.

Smoke-blinded and barely able to breathe, William stumbled to the last stall. The horse inside was stamping and snorting, desperate to escape. As William pulled open the door, the horse baulked and kicked out and a rear hoof caught William on the side of his head. Bright light shattered into splinters behind his eyes, and the world went dark.

William opened his eyes. His head was fogged with pain and shapes swam in and out of his vision. He groaned and tried to sit up.

'No, do not move.' It was Shadlok's voice. Gentle fingers felt his head. 'There is nothing broken but you have a cut on your scalp.'

William tried to remember what had happened, but all he could see was a confusing muddle of smoke and terrified horses. None of it made any sense. He pushed Shadlok's hand away and struggled to his knees. Shadlok held his arm to steady him and William peered blearily around.

The courtyard was a nightmarish scene of flames and panic. For a moment, he wondered if this was hell. Was he dead and damned for letting his blood be used to summon the demon? He remembered *that* all too clearly. But if he was in hell, then so were Shadlok and most of the people from Weforde manor.

William slumped against the nearest wall. The storerooms, barn and the stonemasons' shed were all on fire. Trails of smoke threaded up between the tiles on the roof of Sir Robert's new hall, which probably meant the roof timbers had caught fire. Only the old manor house at his back remained untouched.

'There were two stable boys in there,' William wheezed, pointing to the stable.

'They broke out through the roof thatch,' Shadlok said. William heard the derision in the fay's voice. 'They made sure their own skins were safe.'

William couldn't blame them from escaping any way they could. As he stared at the blazing buildings and felt the heat sear his skin, he began to shake. Memories of the night his family died in the burning mill in Iwele came flooding back. The smells and the sounds around him were bitterly familiar and the sense of hopelessness he'd felt that night overwhelmed him again. He closed his eyes tightly against the hot tears. He had rescued the horses today, but he hadn't been able to save his family. Life sometimes made very little sense at all.

With a wild leap of panic, he remembered who else had been in the stable.

'Where's the hob?' he said.

'Do not worry, he is safe,' Shadlok said. 'He was foraging for food in a storeroom when the fire started. I sent him to the barn in the demesne farm and told him to wait there for now.'

William felt as if a weight had been lifted from him, and he nodded.

'You saved those horses,' Shadlok said. 'You should be proud of yourself.'

'Ha!' William said bitterly. That was the *only* thing he felt proud of. He closed his eyes and leant his head against the wall. 'If we hadn't set the demon free in the first place, I wouldn't have needed to save them at all.'

Brother Snail washed the cut on William's head and gave him a cup of water.

'You were very fortunate this wasn't a great deal worse, Will,' the monk said. 'A kick from a hoof could have killed you.'

The water soothed William's raw throat. He was feeling much better and the world around him had come back into focus. He stood up and his legs were steady.

The buildings around the yard were just smouldering heaps of charred timber and blackened thatch. The horses were being taken to the demesne farm to be stabled in a barn. William saw Shadlok leading Matilda and a small brown mare out of the yard. The fire in the roof of the new hall had been put out by the stonemasons. They had used long ladders and a lot of courage to climb up and douse it with pails of water, passed along a line of villeins and manor servants from the well in the kitchen yard.

Word reached the manor that fires had broken out all over the village around dawn that day. Several houses had burned to the ground, and six people were dead. It didn't take long for rumours to spread that the visitors from the abbey had brought something evil with them, rumours fuelled by Master Guillaume and his stonemasons. Master Brice sent the kitchen boy to Dame Alys's house for a second time. In the aftermath of the fire, there were burns and cuts to be tended. Brother Snail offered to help but people were now wary of him and kept their distance.

William tried to help with the clearing-up, but he was met with a sullen suspicion that quickly grew into simmering resentment. Even Master Brice was offhand with him when they met in the kitchen yard.

William was washing his face and hands in a bucket of water, and trying to rinse the blood and ash from his hair.

'Still here?' the cook said, hands on hips. There was no invitation to sit at the table in the warm kitchen today.

'We're leaving for Bethlehem shortly,' William said awkwardly. 'Brother Snail is staying here, to tend to Sir Robert.'

The look on Master Brice's face left William in no doubt that the cook wasn't happy about the monk staying behind, but it wasn't up to him who stayed and who left. And until Dame Alys could be found, Brother Snail was needed at Sir Robert's bedside. Even so, Master Brice disappeared into the kitchen and returned a few minutes later with a plate of bread and cheese and a cup of small beer. 'Bring the plate and cup back when you've finished with them,' he said gruffly. He nodded to a bench beside the door. 'You can leave them there.'

William carried his meal into Sir Robert's garden and sat beneath an arbour of rose bushes to eat it. The chilly breeze carried the smell of burnt timber and the turf seat was dusted with ash. Bits of charred thatch lay scattered over the gravel path and flowerbeds. His throat was still sore from the smoke and ash he'd breathed in, and he ate the bread and cheese slowly, without tasting it. His thoughts were lost in memories of his home and family and he was filled with an aching loneliness.

Noticing something tucked into his belt, William remembered the whistle the hob had found. He stared at it for a moment, then lifted it to his lips and blew a couple of notes, but his heart wasn't in it. For the first time in months, he felt as if the music had gone from inside him. He put the flute on the turf seat and gazed off into the distance without seeing anything. The future seemed more than usually bleak this morning. The stonemasons were right to blame the people from the abbey for what had happened here, he thought dejectedly. Six villagers had died because they had brought the cursed bowl and the demon to the village.

William closed his eyes and breathed deeply. There was nothing to be gained from feeling sorry for himself, he decided. He rarely did, and he didn't mean to start now. What was done was done and they would just have to try and put things right – somehow.

He got to his feet and wandered slowly along the gravel path to the middle of the garden. He stood by the mulberry tree, shivering in the cold breeze and rubbing his arms to try and warm himself. He stared up at the sky and thought about the angel he had helped Shadlok and Jacobus Bone dig out of its grave in the Whistling Hollow last winter. He remembered the look of compassion in its dark eyes. Surely it wouldn't just stand by while so many innocent people were made to suffer?

'You came to fight the demon once before,' William whispered in desperation, 'can't you do so again? We need you. We can't defeat it by ourselves, it's just too strong.'

William held his breath and looked around the silent garden. He had the strangest feeling that there was somebody there, listening to him. 'Please help us,' he added softly.

Something small and white floated down on the breeze and settled on the gravel by William's foot. He leant down and picked it up. It was a feather, no longer than his finger, with a perfect, milky sheen. He looked around but there were no birds in the garden, and nowhere a feather could have come from. Was this a sign that the angel had heard him, he wondered, hardly daring to believe it. Hope sparked into life. The angel hadn't turned its back on them after all, he was sure of it. With great care, he tucked the feather into his belt. He looked up at the sky and smiled. 'Thank you,' he whispered.

Chapter Thirty-Two

William took his empty cup and plate back to the kitchen and left it on the bench as Master Brice had told him to. Brother Snail was by the well, struggling to haul up a bucket of water. William hurried to help him.

'How is your head now, Will?' the monk asked.

'Sore, but I'll live,' William said with a quick smile. He emptied the water into a smaller pail. 'I'll carry this up to Sir Robert's chambers.'

'That's very good of you,' the monk said with a smile.

William stood the pail on the floor by the door of Sir Robert's bedchamber. The lord of the manor lay among the heaped bed covers in the darkened room, so still and pale he might have been dead.

'Will he recover?' William asked.

'Sir Robert is in God's hands now,' the monk said

gently. William left the house and made his way to the demesne farm to find Shadlok. Yesterday's fine spring weather had gone and there was a spit of rain in the breeze. They needed to set out for Bethlehem before it settled in for the day. Unfriendly eyes watched as he passed by. Someone threw a stone at him. It caught him on the back and he turned quickly, just in time to see two people dart out of sight behind a shed.

William stood by the farm gate for a few moments and stared out across the village. He was shocked by the extent of the destruction. Apart from the burnt-out houses, other buildings had lost their thatch and some of the crofts looked as if a herd of cows had trampled through them. It was Wednesday, but there was no market on the green today. Weforde was unnaturally quiet and people stood around in groups, taking stock of the damage to their homes and their tofts and crofts. Even the children were subdued and kept close to their parents.

The demon had been busy, William thought in dismay. But where had it gone now?

He caught sight of Dame Alys as she walked along the lane towards the green. Her white crow flew ahead of her. She looked over her shoulder, then stopped and half-turned towards him. He saw that she was carrying a sack. Something inside it wriggled and thrashed furiously. William was filled with cold loathing. The sack, he was sure, held some unfortunate animal whose blood was about to be spilled as another offering to the demon. But there was nothing he could do about it, and he, the hob and Shadlok needed to be on their way. Even if he went after her and somehow managed to free the animal, there would be others. He couldn't be there to free them all.

Dame Alys turned and continued on her way, walking quickly and with a sense of purpose.

William trudged back through the muddy farmyard. He saw Shadlok leading the last of the horses from Sir Robert's stables towards a barn and broke into a run to catch up with the fay by the barn door.

'Where's the hob?' William asked.

Shadlok nodded towards the far end of the barn. 'With Matilda.'

'I'll fetch him and we can be on our way to the grange farm.'

The barn was full of restless horses and ponies, their halters tied to whatever was available. Matilda was in the farthest corner of the building, beneath the hayloft. She smelled the smoke on William and rolled her eyes uneasily.

'There, Tildy, you're safe now,' he murmured, reaching out to stroke her neck. She shied away from him and scraped at the floor with a hoof. He stepped back and looked around for the hob.

'Brother Walter, we're leaving for Bethlehem now.'

There was no reply.

'Brother Walter?'

Matilda whickered and jerked at the rope halter. William knew he was upsetting her, and it was clear the hob wasn't there. He hurried back to Shadlok.

'The hob's gone,' he said.

Shadlok frowned at him. 'I told him to wait with the mare.'

'Well, he's not there now.' A sudden, appalling thought occurred to him.

'Oh, no! Oh, please, no,' he breathed. He looked at the fay in horror. 'I think I know where he is. '

'Where?'

'With Dame Alys. I saw her a few minutes ago, carrying a sack. There was something alive inside it.'

Shadlok stared at him for a few moments, eyes narrowed, and then he nodded. 'Follow me.'

Shadlok sprinted away and William had to run as fast as he could to keep up with him. They were heading for Dame Alys's hut.

People stared at them as they raced through the village, but William barely noticed. His breath came in great harsh gasps and his legs felt as if they would collapse beneath him, but he forced himself to keep going, running along the grassy lanes and muddy pathways between the crofts after Shadlok. The fay ran swiftly, his white hair streaming out like a banner behind him. He was standing by the open doorway of the hut when William, breathless and sweating, reached Dame Alys's croft several minutes later.

'They are not here,' Shadlok said.

William pushed past him and went into the hut. It was dark and silent, and the hearth was cold. He ran his hands through his hair in despair. Where had she taken the hob? What did she mean to do to him? He shied away from the answer that slid into his mind.

The creak of floorboards made William start. The sound had come from the loft.

'Who's there?' he called, leaning on the ladder and peering up at the dark square opening. There was a soft shuffling overhead and a face appeared.

At first glance he thought it was the hob. Then he saw the straggling red fur and greying muzzle. It was Dame Alys's stub-tailed hob, the Old Red Man.

'Where is she?' William demanded. 'Where has she taken my hob?'

There was a soft footfall behind him and William glanced around. Shadlok came to stand beside him.

'Answer him,' the fay said, 'and make sure it is the truth.'

The Old Red Man crept slowly down the ladder and stood in front of them, his dull gold eyes watching them warily.

'Old Woman has taken him to the forest,' he said in a voice dusty with disuse.

William and Shadlok glanced at each other.

'What does she want with him?' William asked.

The Old Red Man didn't answer. Shadlok leant forward. The hob cowered under his icy-blue stare.

'Whereabouts in the forest has she taken him?'

'I will take you to her,' the Old Red Man said. He glanced away and licked his lips. He looked, William thought suspiciously, like a creature with secrets to keep.

Shadlok stood aside. He glanced meaningfully at the door and the hob took the hint. He scuttled past them and out of the hut.

The Old Red Man led them past the mill and along a path to the West Field. The path kept to the drier ground along the ridges of the field headlands until it reached the track to Foxwist.

William was growing more uneasy with each passing minute. They only had the Old Red Man's word for it that Dame Alys was in the forest. For all they knew, the creature could be leading them into a trap. He had been suspiciously quick to offer to show them where the woman had gone, but if there was even the faintest chance that he could help them to find the hob, then they had to take it. William felt sick with worry when he thought of what the woman might have done to Brother Walter. Had she harmed him? Was he already dead?

When they reached the edge of the forest, Shadlok reached down and grabbed the hob's arm.

'If you try to escape from us, you will regret it. No tricks. Just take us to the woman. Do you understand?'

The creature's eyes bulged in fright and he nodded so hard his teeth rattled. Shadlok let go of him.

'Good. Now, move.'

The Old Red Man slipped and stumbled along the track. His large hairy feet soon became heavy with mud and he stopped every now and then to try to clean some of it off. Shadlok watched him with growing impatience.

'If you stop one more time, I will pick you up and carry you,' he snapped.

The hob looked alarmed. 'I cannot *help* it. The mud . . . my feet . . .'

'Then stay on the grass.'

The Old Red Man tried his best to keep to the grassy edge of the track, but branches tangled in his long fur and his feet kept slipping. He murmured and muttered to himself, and every so often gave a small, pained yelp as another tuft of fur was ripped out by a bramble whip. William found a sturdy stick and handed it to him.

'Keep the branches back with that,' he said. The hob took it with a grateful nod and, after that, managed to pick up a little speed.

Much to William's surprise, the hob kept to the main track. He had thought Dame Alys would have taken Brother Walter deep into the forest, to some hidden place of her own, but the Old Red Man trudged doggedly onwards, swinging his stick at brambles and branches in his way.

'We're heading towards the abbey,' William said nervously, glancing at Shadlok.

'So it would seem,' the fay said. There was something in his voice that told William he was not happy about this.

They continued their journey in tense and watchful silence. Around them, the forest was eerily quiet. It seemed that all the woodland creatures, fay and animal alike, were staying hidden.

The Old Red Man slowed down when they reached the rag-hung bush near the Whistling Hollow. The fur along his spine bristled and he held the stick tightly in his paws. His eyes were white-rimmed with fear as he stared into the undergrowth. 'This is an evil place,' he whispered.

'You'll be safe as long as you keep to the trackway,' William said. 'Keep going.'

The hob hunched his shoulders and scurried away. William and Shadlok had to run to keep up with him. When they reached the turning to Crowfield, the Old Red Man stopped again.

'Old Woman is there,' he said, pointing towards the abbey.

'I thought you said she was in the forest. Why has she brought the hob here?' William asked suspiciously. The demon was no longer trapped in the side chapel, so why would the old woman come to the abbey?

The Old Red Man's hairy face crumpled miserably

and he shook his head. Tears welled up in his eyes. 'I cannot tell you that.'

'Because you do not know? Or because you do not want to?' Shadlok asked.

The creature covered his face with his paws and hunched forward as if he was in pain. 'Old Woman told me not to speak of it.'

'I think you should try.' Shadlok's voice was hard.

'I *cannot* disobey her,' the hob said unhappily. 'Please . . .'

Shadlok made an impatient gesture with his hand. 'Then we will just have to find her and ask her for ourselves.'

Shadlok led the way down the slope towards the causeway. The Old Red Man followed, with William close behind him in case the hob took it into his head to bolt. William looked across the rooftops of the abbey buildings, towards the huge hole in the church roof. Beyond the orchard, he glimpsed the wreckage of Brother Snail's workshop. An air of desolation hung over everything. For the first time ever, he couldn't hear the cawing of the crows in Two Penny Copse. Even the sheep were silent today. He could see them in the distance, crowding close together beneath the trees.

'Ent none of the monks left there,' someone called from the trackway behind them. William turned quickly and saw Edgar the carpenter and two freemen from Yagleah at the top of the slope. In an instant, the Old Red Man vanished from sight. 'They're all at Beth'lem,' Edgar said, stopping to lean on the long stick he was carrying. His two companions also carried hefty sticks. 'Though they might be regrettin' that now.'

'Why?' Shadlok asked with a quick frown.

'There's been trouble in Yagleah, and a mite o' bother in Beth'lem too,' Edgar said. 'Hal Brunleggin's house and barn burnt down in the night, and the small barn and brew house up at Beth'lem caught fire. And if that weren't enough, Mag the bee-woman's house in Yagleah, and all her beehives, were caught up by a gret wild wind and blown away.' Edgar shook his head. His cheeks above his stubbly jaw were grey with tiredness and worry. The two men beside him didn't look much better. 'There's summat bad on the loose, and no mistake. We're on our way to see Sir Robert at Weforde. We're hopin' he might be able do summat to help us, though I ent sure *anyone* can help us against whatever's back there.' He jerked his head in the direction of his village.

William and Shadlok glanced at each other in dismay. This was the worst possible news.

'There were fires in Weforde last night too,' William said. 'Most of the manor and several of the village houses were destroyed. And Sir Robert has been taken ill.'

Edgar stared at him, appalled. 'What happened? Did he get *burned?*'

'No, he's just . . . sick,' William said. No doubt Edgar would hear the rumours flying around Weforde soon enough.

'Well, that ent good.' Edgar shook his head and looked at his two friends. The news from Weforde had clearly shaken them.

'My sister's married to a Weforde man, Thomas Caudyle. Don't s'pose you know if his were one of the houses that got burned?' one of the Yagleah men asked anxiously.

William shook his head. 'No, I'm sorry, I don't.'

'I'd best get over there and find out for meself,' the man said with a worried glance at his companions.

Edgar nodded to Shadlok and William and the three Yagleah men set off along the track.

The Old Red Man reappeared as soon as the men were out of sight.

'It is as we feared. Nowhere is safe from the demon now,' Shadlok said grimly. He turned to stare at the gatehouse. The wicket gate was open. It seemed Dame Alys was already inside.

Shadlok set off along the causeway, splashing through the floodwater and onto the bridge. William and the Old Red Man caught up with him in the passageway beneath the gatehouse. He held up a hand, warning them to keep quiet.

The yard was deserted. The buildings were silent and dark.

'The woman is waiting for us,' Shadlok said softly. 'I can feel her dark heart.' He looked down at the Old Red Man. 'That is why she left you behind, isn't it? To lead us here to her.'

William had suspected as much. 'She meant for us to follow her, didn't she?' he said. The Old Red Man was huddled against the wall of the passageway as if he was trying to melt into the stones. Reluctantly, he nodded.

'You led us into a trap,' William said angrily. 'I knew we shouldn't have trusted you.' But the truth was, trap or no trap, they had no choice but to be here, not as long as Dame Alys was holding Brother Walter prisoner.

'You search the barns,' Shadlok said. 'I will look in the garden and graveyard, but do nothing rash if you find her. Do not get close enough to let her take your blood again.'

William snorted. 'Oh, don't worry, I won't.'

Shadlok slipped away around the corner of the gatehouse.

'You are coming with me,' William said grimly, glancing down at the Old Red Man. He wanted to keep the hob close, so he could keep an eye on him.

The creature pattered across the cobbles to William's side. The wind ruffled his fur and he rubbed his skinny arms briskly to warm them. William was taken aback by the look of wretchedness on his face, but he hardened his heart: the Old Red Man had betrayed Brother Walter, who was supposed to be his friend, and to William that was unforgivable.

William searched the two barns, the woodshed and the stables. There was no sign of Dame Alys or the hob. They reached the pasture behind the open-fronted shed, but that was empty too. Perhaps Shadlok had found her, he thought hopefully.

'There!' the Old Red Man said suddenly, pointing to the west door of the church. It stood ajar and in front of it stood Fionn, the white crow. The bird watched them with its head on one side, then with a flap of its wings, it hopped inside the building.

William ran across the yard. Behind him, he heard the Old Red Man scurrying through puddles, the long claws on his toes clacking against the cobbles. He took the steps two at a time and followed the crow into the church. He saw Fionn lift into the air and glide along the nave. The bird landed on a large chunk of fallen masonry and gave a long, triumphant *caw*.

William walked slowly along the nave until he reached the crossing. The Old Red Man was close behind him. The church was silent and there was an oddly heavy feel to the air. He wished with all his heart that Shadlok was here with him.

Fionn watched them beadily but made no move to fly away. There was no sign of Dame Alys, but William knew she was here somewhere. His shaking fingers brushed against the holey stone, still tucked safely inside his tunic. What would he see if he looked through it now? Would it help him? He hesitated for a couple of moments, then pulled it free and raised it to his eye.

The grey clouds above the church roof faded away and William found himself looking up at a moonlit sky through bare branches. Moving the stone, he saw that he was standing inside a ring of oak trees. An ancient oak, its massive trunk hollowed out with age and its branches twisted like witches' fingers, grew in the middle of the grove. There were streaks of blood down its gnarled bark, and the ground underfoot was soft and oozing with something dark and sticky. William stared at the tree in revulsion. This surely had to be the Hunter's Oak, he thought, which meant this was the demon's sacred place, the seat of its power. Things hung from the branches, indistinct shapes in the moonlight. William walked forward slowly, then recoiled in horror when he realised that the tree was covered with corpses of animals and birds. Some were fresh, but others were just scarecrow scraps of fur and feathers. And then he saw a human head, hanging by its hair from a branch high up in the tree. Sickened, William forced himself to keep looking. There was something at the top of the tree. He could make out a huge creature silhouetted against the night sky. Moonlight gleamed on its spread wings as it lunged forward and swooped down towards him. William gasped and staggered backwards. He jerked the holey stone away from his eye and gripped it tightly against his chest. In an instant, the vision of the grove and the demon disappeared.

William glanced around. This was where the demon's grove of trees had once stood. The abbey church had taken the place of the trees, but the ground beneath the building was still sacred to Raum. He could feel an unnatural chill striking up through his body, and knew that the demon's power still beat like a huge heart in the earth below the abbey walls.

There was a movement over by the side chapel and Dame Alys walked out of the shadows, dragging the sack behind her. The coarse fabric was patched with old bloodstains and William's stomach turned in disgust.

'So, you have a holey stone,' she said coldly. 'And what did it show you?'

'I saw the Hunter's Oak,' William said, tucking the stone back inside his clothing. 'It's no wonder the monks cut the tree down.'

She pointed to the gaping hole where the tower had been. 'But they are paying for it now. And this is just the beginning.'

William glanced down at the sack, which had begun to jiggle around at the sound of his voice. 'Let the hob go,' he said. To his surprise, his voice was steady and didn't betray the apprehension he felt. A glance around the church showed nothing out of the ordinary. No tell-tale glimpse of crimson warned him that the demon was here.

Dame Alys's odd-coloured eyes gleamed with satisfaction and her small mouth twitched into a wrinkled smile. 'You care what happens to him. That's good. You'll do as I tell you, then.' She turned to the Old Red Man and pointed to the sack. 'You can let him out now, Heremon. But don't untie him just yet.'

William looked from the woman to her hob in astonishment. 'You know his name?'

'Of course I do,' she said with the hint of impatience. 'Don't I, Heremon, eh?' She prodded the hob with her stick.

The creature gave the old woman a look that held a lifetime of resentment, then his gaze slid away from her and he shuffled over to the sack. He squatted beside it and fiddled with the knotted rope tying the neck.

'I should thank you,' Dame Alys said, looking back at William. 'You and your friends have finally released Belinus from the sorcery holding him prisoner in that bowl. Generations of my family have tried and failed to do just that.'

William scowled at her. 'That wasn't what we were trying to do.'

The woman's expression hardened. 'Even so, Belinus is free and he will now resume his rightful place as lord of this land, of the forest and the villages.'

'It's not a god,' William said angrily, 'it's a demon. And its name is Raum. It will destroy everyone and everything in its path. It has already burnt down part of the manor and several houses in Weforde – *your* village. People died there last night.'

'A god must punish those who sin against him.'

'I don't think the villagers who died had sinned against anyone,' William said.

'Their deaths were . . . unfortunate.'

William thought he heard a note of doubt in her voice.

'And what about me?' he asked. 'I'm not a sinner either. Do I deserve to die?'

This time the regret in the woman's eyes was unmistakable. 'Belinus has chosen you, boy. It is not for me to question. I merely serve him.'

Heremon finally managed to untie the sack and the hob struggled out. He was tied hand and foot and a grubby bit of linen had been stuffed into his mouth to gag him. His eyes blazed with fury and the fur around his neck bristled. He saw William and began to wriggle across the floor towards him. William knelt to untie his ropes, but Dame Alys brought her stick down smartly across his knuckles.

He gave a yelp of surprise. 'Ow!'

'Leave him!'

William stood up, rubbing his sore hands, and scowled at the woman. 'There was no need for that,' he said angrily.

'I'll let him go when I am ready,' she said. She tensed suddenly and glanced around the church. The crow cawed and flapped its wings. It had grown colder in the last few minutes and a chilly breeze chased through the ruined building. Dame Alys jabbed at William with the stick. 'Kneel down,' she said urgently. 'Down! Now!'

William didn't move. His heart was racing. If he was going to rescue the hob and make his escape, he had to do it *now*. He looked at Heremon. 'Are you going to let her do this?' He nodded to the trussed-up hob. 'I thought he was your friend?'

Heremon's body was hunched with misery. 'Old Woman will not harm *him*,' he whispered. 'Only you.'

'That's enough!' Dame Alys snapped, swinging her stick at Heremon. It missed him by a whisker. 'Keep silent, you wretched creature!'

Heremon closed his eyes, as if that would make

everything go away.

'And you,' Dame Alys reached out and prodded William in the ribs. 'Leave Heremon alone. He's none of your concern. I'm losing patience with you, boy. This is Belinus's time; kneel down or I promise you, I will kill your hob. Do it *now*.'

William stared defiantly at her. Dame Alys's lips drew back in an angry grimace. She lifted her stick and held it with both hands above the hob. Another moment and she would bring it down on his head. The hob banged his heels on the ground and grunted furiously.

'Don't!' William said sharply. He quickly fell to his knees beside the hob, keeping a wary eye on the stick.

Dame Alys took several deep, harsh breaths that shook through her body. She leant the stick against a pile of stones and then raised her skinny arms skywards. She began to speak in a language William didn't recognise, intoning the words in a low voice that made the hairs on the back of his neck stand on end. He glanced down at the hob and silently mouthed, 'Roll out of the way.'

The hob managed a nod. William turned his attention back to Dame Alys. Her voice rose as she chanted words which pulsed with power. The breeze strengthened and yowled through the gaps in the wall and roof, whipping William's hair across his face. Shadows flitted between the nave pillars. William struggled not to look at them. He needed to keep his nerve if he was to escape before the woman succeeded in summoning the demon. He clenched his fists and braced himself.

Dame Alys raised her face to the sky beyond the shattered roof. 'Great Belinus! I have brought the boy to you! Return to your sacred grove and accept this offering!'

We have to get away from here now, William thought desperately. He saw his chance and lunged at Dame Alys. She shrieked in fright as he brought her crashing to the floor. In the same moment, the dark shapes in the nave dispersed and the breeze dropped.

'Heremon! *Heremon!*' Dame Alys screeched furiously as she struggled to push William away. 'Help me!'

William bundled the woman tightly in her cloak and held her down. Heremon watched what was happening, but made no move to help his mistress.

'Untie the hob,' William called to him as Fionn landed on his back and began to stab viciously at him with his beak. William batted the bird away with his arm and it flapped into the air with a hoarse cry.

With a wary glance at Dame Alys, Heremon crouched down beside the hob and began to pick at the knotted ropes.

'Get away from him! Do as I tell you, you worthless wretch!' the woman shrieked. Her thin body wriggled and bucked beneath William as she fought to push him away. She was surprisingly strong and it was an effort to stop her from getting free. William was at a loss to know what to do with her now. He had broken whatever spell her words were weaving, but the demon could still appear at any moment, and then they would all be lost. Fionn circled overhead, darting down in a fury of white feathers to attack him at every opportunity. Between the woman and the crow, he had his hands full and couldn't hope to escape from the church.

A figure stepped into view. Shadlok had found them. William closed his eyes for a moment and felt his body go weak with relief. 'Quickly! I can't hold her for much longer.'

'Move aside,' Shadlok said. 'I will deal with her now.'

As William scrambled to his feet, the fay pointed towards Fionn. The bird screeched with pain and tumbled away through the gap in the chancel wall. Shadlok quickly took the linen rag out of the hob's mouth and knelt by Dame Alys to gag her. His expression was grim and he looked down at the woman with deep loathing. She struggled and howled and tried to bite his fingers, but Shadlok was too strong and her curses were quickly muffled. He grabbed the rope which had been used to tie the sack and wrapped it around her body. With a few murmured words, the rope tightened and wove itself into knots. Dame Alys could barely move. Hatred twisted her face as she stared up at him.

William helped Heremon to unravel the last loops of rope from around Brother Walter's legs.

The hob spat bits of linen thread from his mouth. 'I think she used that cloth to wipe her nose. *Very, very bad woman,*' he said in disgust.

William helped him to his feet. The hob's fur bristled with indignation and his eyes were bright with anger as he scowled down at the trussed-up woman.

'Someone should put *her* in a sack and drag her through the forest, and see how *she* likes it!'

'We should leave this place,' Shadlok said. 'We do not want to be here when the demon appears, as it undoubtedly will.'

'What do we do with her?' William asked, nodding to Dame Alys.

'I will carry her up to the track through the forest.' Shadlok smiled thinly at the woman. 'The rope will loosen in a day or so. But if you come after the boy again, old woman, I *will* kill you.'

Dame Alys stopped struggling and William saw the fear in her eyes. She knew Shadlok meant what he said.

'What about her hob?' William asked. He felt sorry for the creature. Heremon might have done the woman's bidding, but he hadn't done it willingly.

'She used his name to make him do what she told him to,' Brother Walter said quickly. He patted his friend's bony shoulder in sympathy. 'He had no choice in the matter.'

Shadlok walked over to Heremon. He looked down at the trembling hob for a moment. 'Is that true? You did not act with free will?'

Heremon nodded miserably, then shook his head. 'Old Woman had power over me. I could not fight it.'

Shadlok crouched down in front of him. 'Then we will give you a new name and break the power of your old one. This time, keep it secret.'

Hope burned in Heremon's eyes. 'You can do that?' he asked uncertainly.

Shadlok leant forward and whispered something in

the hob's ear. A shudder went through the creature's body and he closed his eyes tightly. Shadlok touched Heremon's head and then stood up. 'You have your freedom, hob.'

Heremon opened his eyes slowly. Tears spilled down his wrinkled face and dripped onto his fur. He sniffled loudly and wiped his nose with a shaking paw. 'Thank you,' he whispered. 'Thank you, *thank you*. I will not forget this.'

'What will you do now?' William asked.

'I shall go home to the forest,' Heremon said, his voice full of longing. He walked over to Dame Alys and stared down at her in silence. Years of bitterness and misery darkened his eyes. Without a word, he crossed to the gap in the wall and slipped like a shadow back to the wild world where he belonged.

Chapter Thirty-Three

'P'erhaps we should make sure all the animals are safe before we leave for Bethlehem,' William suggested. 'We can feed and water them, and save Brother Stephen a journey.'

Shadlok nodded. 'Very well, but be quick.' He leant down and lifted the old woman onto his shoulder. She didn't struggle. She probably knew she would be wasting her time. 'I will wait for you on the track.'

They left the church by the west door. None of them said so, but there was a reluctance to take the shorter route through the cloister and kitchen. There was a peculiar stillness over the abbey, a feeling that they were being watched which made William deeply uneasy. Shadlok took his leave of William and the hob outside the small barn and carried the old woman towards the gatehouse.

'The hens first,' William said to the hob. 'Brother

Stephen keeps their food in the small barn.'

The hob stayed close to William as they fetched the food and carried it in a pail to the hen house. He seemed none the worse for his rough treatment at Dame Alys's hands, but he was unusually subdued. The late afternoon shadows gathered in corners and the feeling of being watched grew steadily. William glanced around nervously and caught fleeting movements on the edge of his vision, but each time he turned to look, there was nothing there.

The hens were huddled together at the far end of their hut when William went in to feed them. They clucked nervously and flapped their wings in agitation at the sight of him, sending feathers and straw up in a dusty cloud that made William sneeze. He bolted the door securely behind him when he left the hut. It wasn't right to keep the hens locked up like this, but with nobody at the abbey to keep an eye on them if they were allowed out, they would probably be taken by a fox. They were safer where they were.

William let himself into Mary Magdalene's pen. The hob climbed up to sit on a fence post. The old pig was sitting against the back wall of her shelter, grunting softly, her eyes white-rimmed and frightened.

'It's all right, it's only us,' William said soothingly.

'The pig does not want to be left alone,' the hob said. 'She thinks the demon will come back and hurt her.'

William crouched down beside Mary Magdalene. He rubbed her ears and spoke softly to her but she was too agitated to be comforted by his company. *The animals can sense danger*, William thought. He could feel it too, that warning itch between his shoulder blades. He stood up and gazed around at the empty yard and buildings. He could almost taste the evil in the air. 'Stay with her. If there's any . . . trouble, open the pen and set her free.' He saw that her trough was empty and licked clean. 'In the meantime, I'll see if I can find her some food.'

The hob nodded and climbed down from the fence. William heard him murmuring to Mary Magdalene, whispering words of reassurance, and the pig grunting in reply.

William fetched more water from the well and went to tend to the goats. They were restless and ran from him when he opened the gate of their pen. Usually they were friendly animals who liked to have their heads scratched, but not today. He herded them out to the orchard to forage on the new growth of grass beneath the trees. They kept as close to William as they could, jostling him and each other.

'Go on,' he said in exasperation, trying to push them away, 'go and eat.' But the goats wouldn't leave him alone and he had no choice but to lead them back to their pen. He filled a basket with grass and leaves for them; that would have to do for now.

William picked some cabbage leaves for the pig, and added a few apples from the store in the small barn. He leant over the fence and dropped them into her trough.

'The pig wants to hide in the forest,' the hob said anxiously.

'I can't blame her,' William said, 'but I don't think she'll be much safer out there.' He touched the feather tucked into his belt. 'Tell her . . . tell her help is on its way.'

'Someone is coming to help us?' the hob said hopefully, his face brightening.

William hesitated. 'I asked the angel to come back to the abbey and I think it heard me.' He took the feather from his belt and held it out to the hob. 'I think it sent me this as a sign.'

The hob took the feather and turned it slowly to look at it. 'This is a nangel's feather?' he asked dubiously. 'Is it a very *small* nangel?'

'No,' William said, 'it's huge. The feather is just a sign. Its size isn't important.'

The hob sniffed it. 'It smells of pigeon.'

William felt a little foolish. 'Maybe the angel couldn't spare one of its own feathers, so it used a pigeon's, I don't know. But that doesn't matter, it's still a sign that it heard me and is going to help us.'

The hob handed the feather back to William without a word. A little of William's certainty ebbed away. Was he just fooling himself, he wondered? Clinging to a slim hope when in reality there was none? He tucked the feather back into his belt. Sometimes you had to believe what you knew in your heart to be true, he told himself, even if it made no sense to anyone else. Sometimes you just had to trust. *The angel* will *come*, he thought fiercely, *I* know *it will*.

As he turned away from the pigpen, William saw that the door to the kitchen was open wide. He was sure it had been closed when he had passed by earlier. Had Shadlok returned to the abbey for some reason? What was he doing in the kitchen?

'Wait here for me,' he said to the hob. 'I'll be back in a few minutes.'

William ran over to the doorway and looked inside. The kitchen was empty, but the door to the cloister stood open. William took a couple of hesitant steps into the kitchen and then stopped. Why hadn't Shadlok come to find him when he returned?

'Shadlok? Are you there?'

Keeping quite still, William listened. At first all he could hear was the blood pulsing through his body, but then he heard something else. It was someone calling his name. It was faint, as if it was coming from some distant corner of the abbey. William held his breath. Was that Shadlok's voice? He wasn't sure, but it didn't sound quite right . . .

Then he caught it again: '*William.*'

'Shadlok?' he called uncertainly. 'Is that you?'

There was no reply. William still hesitated. It *had* to be the fay calling to him. Who else could it be? William crossed the kitchen and walked cautiously along the west alley until he reached the archway at the bottom of the abbot's staircase. It was too dark to see if anyone was on the small landing at the top of the steps.

'Shadlok?' he called again, his voice sounding small as it echoed around the shadowy cloister.

'*William . . . I am here.*'

William turned sharply on his heel, his heart pounding. The voice was coming from behind him.

He caught a brief glimpse of a dark figure by the kitchen doorway. In a moment it was gone, passing out of sight behind a pillar in the south alley. It was too tall to be Shadlok. Had one of the monks returned to the abbey, perhaps?

'Who's there?' he called.

The silence in the cloister was absolute. William watched the space between the pillars but the figure did not reappear. If it had been one of the monks, he would have shown himself by now. So who was it? The feeling of being watched that had haunted him since reaching the abbey deepened, and he felt a shiver of fear. He looked at the kitchen door, some idea of escaping back to the yard forming in his mind, but he knew nothing would persuade him to walk back along the alley, towards the watcher hiding in the shadows. The only other way out of the abbey was through the church.

William ran as fast as he could to the south door of the church, weaving his way between the statues in the north alley. When he reached it, he looked around nervously, half expecting to see the dark figure following him, but there was nobody there.

He let himself into the church. The hollow drip-drip of rainwater echoed in the nave. The ropes with which the hob had been tied up were scattered across the floor, and the sack lay in a puddle. The rain was a grey mist in the roofless crossing. An air of hopelessness seeped through the walls of the ruined building, as if God had turned His back on this place. And that, William thought bleakly, probably wasn't so far from the truth.

As William picked his way across the rubble-strewn floor, the softest sound, a mere breath, whispered just behind him. He turned quickly and stared in horror.

There stood the demon, almost close enough to touch. Its crimson wings were folded around its body, the feathers gleaming like blood. Its crow head was turned to one side. A single black eye, cruel and unblinking, regarded him coldly.

'I have been waiting for you,' the demon said. Its voice was beautiful, rich and deep.

William realised suddenly that it had been the demon's voice he had heard in the cloister. It had lured him here deliberately, just as Dame Alys had, to the dark heart of its power. And like a fool he had come straight to it. Why hadn't he just stayed out of the church when he knew how dangerous it was to be here? He felt sick at his own stupidity.

His shaking fingers brushed against the feather in his belt. He pulled it free and held it tightly, crumpling it in his fist. *Where are you? I need you now*, he silently implored the angel.

'Step back slowly,' someone said softly behind him. 'Stand here beside me.'

William could have cried with relief at the sound of Shadlok's voice. He edged backwards and stood with his arm just touching Shadlok's. The fay had drawn his sword and the blade gleamed like ice in the half-light. The demon's wings opened and swept back from its shoulders in a soft *whoosh* of air. It raised its hands and clawed at the back of its head. William watched in horror as it ripped at its scalp. The heavy beak clattered to the floor in a shower of small red feathers.

The demon shook its head, freeing long crimson hair and showing its true face at last. It was terrifyingly beautiful, with pale red skin and wide black eyes that were so like the eyes of the angel in the Hollow that William gasped. But what was most shocking of all was that the demon did not *look* evil. Its expression was serene and a smile touched its full-lipped mouth.

Shadlok held the point of his sword blade towards the demon's chest. His hand was steady and his fierce gaze never wavered. If he felt the same numbing fear as William did, he hid it well.

The demon calmly pushed the blade aside. 'That will not help you now, fay.'

The demon turned its dark gaze to William. 'Your blood is mine, Human. You gave it freely. I would have your soul too. Kneel to me.'

William recoiled. 'N . . . no,' he stammered. He turned to Shadlok in terror. Did he *really* belong to the demon now that it had tasted his blood?

'He will not kneel before you,' Shadlok said, a dangerous edge to his voice. He lifted his sword to the demon's long neck. If the demon moved, the deadly edge would cut into its skin. 'Neither of us will.'

'It is not *you* I want, fay,' the demon said. 'This one carries the light within him. It is *his* soul I want.'

'No,' William said. He gripped the feather more tightly in his shaking hand and straightened his back. 'I won't kneel to you, now or ever.'

'You have your answer,' Shadlok said.

In one quick movement, the demon pushed Shadlok's sword aside and stepped forward to put its mouth next to William's ear. 'Kneel to me and I will let the fay live,' he whispered.

William jerked his head away. The demon's breath

was icily cold against his cheek and it made the bones of his skull ache. *Any moment now*, he thought desperately, *the angel will be here*. He just needed to stay strong.

Shadlok took hold of William's arm and drew him back from the demon. He stepped between them, shielding William with his body. 'Go! Get as far from here as you can.'

'I'm not leaving you by yourself,' William said.

'Do as I tell you!' Shadlok said angrily.

If they were going to die, they would die side by side. William stepped out from behind Shadlok. The fay glanced at him with an angry frown, and then turned his attention back to Raum.

Like a dart of light Shadlok's sword blade cut through the air, but in the same instant, the demon lifted its wings and soared upwards and out of sight. William peered up at the roof but couldn't see it. Where had it gone?

'You must leave here now,' Shadlok said, turning to face him. 'I will stay and hold the demon back for as long as I can.'

'The demon will kill you and catch me before I'm halfway across the yard,' William said.

'Perhaps you are right, but we cannot give up

without a fight.'

'I don't intend to,' William said, hoping he sounded braver than he felt. Where was the angel? Why hadn't it come to help them? Doubt began to gnaw at him; perhaps it hadn't really heard him after all.

Shadlok walked out into the nave and stood there, sword at the ready, circling slowly as he looked up at the roof, as if daring the demon to swoop down on him. It was a defiant gesture that made William catch his breath in fearful admiration. He wanted to shout at him to come back, not to risk himself like this, but he didn't. He knew the fay wouldn't have listened.

'Show yourself!' Shadlok called scornfully. 'What are you waiting for?'

William followed cautiously, picking his way between fallen stones to stand beside Shadlok. He peered up at the roof and wondered where the demon was.

He didn't have to wait long to find out. With a sudden rush of wind that almost knocked William off his feet, the demon swooped down and landed lightly in front of them. It raised its arms. Instinctively William crouched forward and crossed his arms over his head. He heard Shadlok gasp and squinted up to see what was happening. Stones whipped through the air and battered the fay unmercifully. The demon stood in the middle of the whirlwind, its face twisted into a mask of cruelty. Shadlok slumped to the floor and lay there unmoving.

The demon lowered its arms and the stones suddenly clattered to the ground in a painful shower, splashing into puddles and raining down on William's arms and shoulders.

In the silence that followed, William slowly straightened up. There were several deep cuts on his hands and his already sore head smarted with fresh pain. None of that mattered. All he could think of was seeing if Shadlok was still alive. Keeping a wary eye on the motionless figure of the demon, William knelt beside the fay.

Shadlok lay in a large puddle, half-buried beneath a layer of stones, his white hair streaked with blood. William rolled him onto his back. There was an ugly bruise on the fay's temple. He held a hand close to Shadlok's mouth and was relieved to find that he was still breathing.

'Shadlok, wake up,' he said, shaking the fay by the shoulder. 'Please, wake up *now*.'

A dark reflection moved across the puddle. The demon had glided silently into the air above them, its wings spread wide. It held a large ashlar block in its hands.

In panic, William grabbed Shadlok's arm and hauled him aside. The block crashed onto the nave floor and splintered into deadly shards.

'You have to get up,' William said urgently, pulling at Shadlok's arm. He darted a quick look upwards. The demon still hovered overhead, watching them with a look of such malevolence that William's blood ran cold. In that moment he knew that they were on their own. There was no angel coming to rescue them. He threw the crumpled feather aside. It landed in a puddle and floated in slow circles on the grey water.

Shadlok stirred and opened his eyes. He looked dazed and put a hand to his forehead. With William's help, he struggled to his feet. Together, they stumbled towards the shelter of the south aisle. Shadlok leant against the wall and closed his eyes for a few moments. He was in pain and William watched him anxiously.

'Thank you,' Shadlok whispered at last, putting a hand on William's shoulder and gripping it tightly. 'Where is the demon now?'

'It's high above the nave,' William said. He wondered why it hadn't come after them but then thought that it was probably in no hurry. They couldn't escape from it. Sooner or later it would kill Shadlok and there would be nothing to stop it from taking William's soul.

'And my sword?' Shadlok asked.

William nodded to the nave floor. 'Over there.'

Shadlok pushed himself away from the wall. 'This is the end, but I will not die hiding in a corner.' He walked over to his sword and picked it up, then glanced back at William and smiled briefly. 'Stay alive, human.'

William wrapped his arms tightly around his body and blinked away the hot tears that were filling his eyes. He thought of the angel and bitterness welled up inside him. He put his head back and yelled in rage and frustration, 'Why didn't you come back?'

Chapter Thirty-Four

The demon glided down to land in front of Shadlok. It towered above him, its wings spread wide. William wanted to look away but couldn't. Shadlok faced the demon with his head held high and a sneer on his lips, a warrior to his final breath.

At first, William thought the light coming down through the hole in the crossing roof was sunlight breaking through the rain clouds. It grew steadily brighter until it lit up the walls of the church with a searing brilliance that half blinded him. William's heart began to race. *I've seen that light before!* he thought. Bright spots danced in front of his eyes and it was several moments before his vision cleared and he saw that there were now three figures in the nave. Shadlok was standing his ground but the demon had fallen back. Between the demon and the fay stood a warrior angel, a creature of white and silver, surrounded by a shimmering aura of light. It wore a mail shirt and carried a longsword. Its wings were folded across its back and its blue-shadowed, silver hair hung over its broad shoulders. Against the luminous sheen of its skin, its black eyes were shockingly vivid.

William's legs started to tremble and he fell to his knees. He watched as the angel walked towards the demon, holding the longsword with both hands. The demon's face twisted with hatred. It drew back a hand and light speared from its fingertips. In one swift movement, the angel leapt into the air and landed lightly behind the demon. In the same instant, the demon whirled around and lunged towards the angel. William saw the flicker of surprise in the demon's eyes as the longsword slashed across its chest. But instead of blood, the wound bled light. William was shocked to realise that beneath its skin, the demon was not flesh and bone.

The demon flew up to hang in the air above the nave. Gouts of light trickled from its wound and fell onto the floor, hissing as they spattered into puddles. The angel streaked after it, moving with the speed of a lightning bolt. For a few bewildering moments, they were just a blur of crimson and silver, a whirling mass of brilliant light that sparked and crackled, and then the demon came hurtling to the ground right in front of William.

The angel was just a breath behind it. The demon was on its feet again in an instant. It lowered its head and lunged at the angel. They twisted together, wings thrashing until, with a snarl of fury, the demon sent the angel slamming back against a pillar.

'I told you this day would come, Sariel,' the demon hissed, gliding across the nave to stand in front of its adversary. 'I will destroy you and all those who come after you.'

The angel's face was impassive. It lowered its sword. 'The Creator will forgive you.'

This seemed to enrage the demon. It leant forward so its face was close to the angel's. 'I do not *want* His forgiveness!'

'Then what do you want?' The angel's gaze flickered to William and Shadlok. 'Their destruction? Is this what you have become, Raum? One who lurks in the shadows and feeds on death?'

'Your Creator tells you to serve these . . . abominations,' the demon said softly. 'I will never do that! I have lived amongst them and I have seen how worthless they are, less than nothing. I have seen how eager they are to sacrifice the living creatures of their world to me.'

'You are wrong, Raum,' the angel said. 'Some may turn from the light and worship you, but there are many more who stand straight and true, whose souls are pure.'

The demon's dark gaze flicked towards William. 'Like this one? You are too late, Sariel. His blood is already mine, and his soul will be mine too. I will take him down into the darkest pit of despair for eternity. It will not matter how brightly his light burns there, for neither you nor the Creator will be able to reach him.'

William stared into the demon's eyes in utter horror. What had he ever done to deserve such a fate? He heard Shadlok draw a sharp breath and felt the fay's hand on his arm.

The angel drew itself up to its full height and its eyes blazed down at the demon. 'You go too far! I will not allow you to harm this boy.' It turned to William. 'Your soul is your own. It is for you alone to choose whether it is to be given to the darkness or to the light.'

'He has already decided,' Raum sneered. 'He gave

his blood willingly to set me free.'

William's lips stuck to his teeth. He tried to swallow but his throat was as dry as dust. 'Only so we could bind you to the bowl again,' he managed to croak.

Sariel turned back to the demon. 'He has chosen the light, Raum. You have failed.'

With a snarl, the demon flung out a hand and raked blades of light across the angel's face. Sariel gasped and staggered backwards. William flinched and covered his eyes as light flared with painful brilliance from the angel's wounds. He heard Sariel's sword clatter away across the floor, followed moments later by the clap of wings and a cry of rage. He opened one eye just the merest crack. The angel and the demon had gone. William blinked to clear the dark shapes floating in front of his eyes. He peered around, and then looked up.

High above the church, Sariel and Raum whirled and twisted furiously as they fought each other with a savagery that shocked William. The beat of their wings was like thunder rolling across the sky. William watched them, feeling sick with fear. The angel trailed ribbons of light from its wounds, but he couldn't tell how seriously it was hurt. Slowly, slowly, Raum was weakening the angel, William was sure of it. What if Sariel wasn't strong enough to defeat the demon?

Sensing its advantage, the demon dived towards the angel once more, slashing at its body with deadly fury until, finally, the beautiful, shimmering creature came tumbling down onto the tiled floor of the abbey. Light pooled around its body and glistened in tiny bright droplets on its wings. William stared at it in anguish. Sariel was still alive, but for how much longer?

The demon lowered itself until it was standing over the angel, a look of triumph on its face.

'Where is the Creator now, Sariel?' Raum taunted. The demon leant forward to stare into the angel's black eyes. 'Join with me! We could be so powerful, you and I. You will no longer need to serve creatures such as these.' It gestured towards William and Shadlok with a look of utter disdain.

The angel lay still and silent. Its eyes were wide and unblinking. They gave nothing away.

'You would sacrifice yourself for *them?*' Raum asked in disbelief. A quiver of rage went through the demon's body and its lips drew back in a snarl. 'A mistake, Sariel, a bad mistake.'

The demon spread its fingers, pointing them directly at the angel's face.

'No!' William croaked. The angel had answered his plea for help. And now, because of him, it would be destroyed. He could *not* allow that to happen! If he did, then he would be as worthless as the demon believed all humans to be.

Without stopping to think, William snatched Shadlok's sword from his hand and, before the fay could stop him, he ran forward, the sword raised above his head. With a yell of fury, he threw himself at the demon and, using the full weight of his body, buried the sword blade up to the hilt in its chest.

A shower of light spilled out of Raum's body, drenching the angel beneath him in a radiant stream of blinding light. With a look of astonishment on its face, the demon fell slowly to its knees, then crumpled sideways and lay with its crimson wings crushed and broken beneath it. It opened its mouth and screamed, a horrifying noise of fury and anguish that left William cowering in terror. Even Shadlok gasped and hunched forward, his hands covering his ears. The scream tore at the air and echoed around the walls. William felt the floor beneath him shudder. He half expected the church to come thundering down on top of them.

The terrible sound trailed away and the demon lay

still, death already starting to dull its eyes, turning them from black to grey. The angel slowly got to its feet. It drew the sword from the demon's body, then laid it on the floor.

'It is over,' it said. William was surprised to hear grief in its voice.

William glanced at the feather, lying crumpled in the puddle, and felt guilty that he had ever doubted the angel would come back. Would it be angry with him for his lack of trust?

The angel gazed down at him, an expression of such compassion in its eyes that William felt a warm glow spread through his body. The fear and horror of the last few days melted away and he was filled with peace. Beside him, Shadlok bowed his head.

'We owe you our lives,' the fay said.

'You owe me nothing.' The angel turned to William. 'For the second time, it is *you* who has saved *me*. Thank you, William. You are indeed a child of the Light.'

William didn't know what to say. He felt his chest swell with such pride that he thought it would burst.

Shadlok looked up at the angel. 'Then forgive me, but there is one more thing I would ask of you.' He glanced briefly at William before continuing. 'You lifted the curse on Jacobus Bone and allowed him to die. I am asking you now to lift the curse binding me to this human.'

William was too surprised to say anything. He looked hopefully at the angel.

'You would still be exiled from your own world,' the angel said.

'I know, but the boy would be free.'

'Your fate is bound to the fate of this boy for a reason, far beyond the one which the fay king intended. He'll have seen what happened here and laid his plans accordingly,' the angel said gently. 'You face a time of darkness and you will be stronger together than apart. If I break the tie that binds you, I will be doing a great harm to you and the world you live in.'

'What do you mean?' William asked in dismay, staring up into the angel's serene face.

'That is something I cannot tell you.' The angel turned back to Shadlok. 'The boy needs you, fay, but you also need him. If you are to come through what lies ahead, you will need to be tied by strong bonds of trust and loyalty, the beginnings of which already exist between you. Your place is at this boy's side. Do not let him down.'

There was an unreadable expression on the fay's face at the angel's words. 'You ask a great deal of us,' he said, 'but it seems we have no choice.'

'There is always choice,' the angel said. The dark eyes were full of tenderness as it leant down and briefly touched William on the forehead. 'Walk always in the light.'

The angel laid a hand on Shadlok's shoulder. 'May you find what you are searching for, fay.'

The angel leant down and lifted the demon's body in its arms. There was a look of infinite sadness on its face as it gazed into the dead eyes of the demon.

'Will we ever see you again?' William asked. The thought that they might never cross paths again filled him with unexpected pain.

'We will meet again,' the angel said. It spread its wings wide and lifted into the air. White light shimmered over its wings like wildfire, and William shielded his eyes. The light faded and when he looked again, the angel and the demon had gone.

Chapter Thirty-Five

The March twilight settled around them in shades of violet and grey. The cloud of evil which had hung over the abbey for so long lifted and blew away on the breeze. William was surprised to see that the evening sky had cleared and the first stars were twinkling into life.

'That was bravely done, human,' Shadlok said, laying a hand on William's shoulder and nodding in approval. 'We owe you our lives. All of us.'

William felt his cheeks redden with delight at the fay's praise. He shrugged and said gruffly, 'I had to do something.'

'A good choice of weapon, too,' Shadlok added. 'A fay weapon in the hand of a human so pure in heart is a powerful combination. If I had struck the demon with my sword, I do not believe I would have destroyed it. You were the only one who could do that.'

William puzzled over this for a moment. 'Then why was the Dark King's arrow able to harm the angel?'

'The magic in the arrowhead was strong and for a hundred years, the angel was neither alive nor dead. But the king's heart is so filled with darkness that even he could not *kill* an angel, no matter what weapon he used.'

William was quiet for a while, then asked, 'What do you think the angel meant about us facing a time of darkness?'

Shadlok's mouth drew into a hard line. He picked up his sword and turned it slowly to examine it. A faint bluish glow played over the blade and it looked as if it had been newly forged. 'I am sure we will find out soon enough.'

William grimaced. 'Whatever it is, it can't be worse than facing the demon.'

'One thing I have learnt, human, is not to go looking for trouble before it comes to find you.'

'We're still bound together by the king's curse,' William said. 'Are you angry about that?'

Shadlok considered this for a moment. 'I am . . . disappointed.'

'If the angel *had* broken the curse, where would you have gone?'

There was an odd expression on the fay's face. 'Perhaps I would have stayed here.'

William snorted.

Shadlok looked sideways at him and smiled. 'Perhaps I have grown used to living in cold and poverty. Perhaps I actually *like* it.'

'Now I know you're lying,' William grinned.

'The truth is, I have nowhere else to go,' Shadlok said with a shrug. 'I have travelled this world many times over with Bone. I have no wish to do so again by myself.' He regarded William thoughtfully. 'But we are still bound together, so when I leave this place, it will be with you. Until then, I will content myself by turning you into a fine musician. That will be enough of a challenge to keep me occupied for years to come.'

William raised his eyebrows. 'I thought you said I was a quick learner?'

'Quick enough, for a human,' Shadlok said, but the hint of a smile softened his words. 'You will have your new flute in a few days' time, and then we will continue with your lessons. Be prepared to work hard.' The bruise on the fay's temple was already fading, along with the blood and dirt in his hair. The stains on his tunic were barely visible now, and somehow his clothes seemed to have dried out.

How does he do *that?* William thought in exasperation. *I look as if I've been dragged along a ditch twice and he looks as if he's been sitting quietly somewhere clean and dry the whole time.*

William spotted the feather in the puddle and went over to pick it up. Perhaps it was only a pigeon's feather, but to him it would always be the angel's feather. He wiped it on his tunic and carefully smoothed it out.

'What is that?' Shadlok asked, glancing at it curiously.

William held it up.

'A feather? What do you want with that?'

'The angel gave it to me,' William said, 'back in Sir Robert's garden, when I asked it to come and help us.'

'Oh, so it answered *your* prayers, but not the monks'?' Shadlok said, dryly. 'I would not mention that to Prior Ardo if I were you.'

William put the feather into his belt. 'I'm not that eager for another beating,' he said, smiling wryly, 'but we should let everyone at Bethlehem know that the demon has gone.'

'We will go there now,' Shadlok said. 'It will be dark soon, but I think there will be no danger for us in the forest tonight.'

'I'll go and find the hob,' William said, 'and tell him what's happened. I'll meet you by the gatehouse.'

The hob greeted William's news with joy. He capered about Mary Magdalene's pen, kicking up the straw and singing, 'Gone! Gone! Gone*gone*gone, all gone!'

The pig came over to let William give her ears a good scratch, then with a contented grunt, she flopped down in the straw and moments later began to snore.

'We're leaving for Bethlehem, to tell the monks that the demon is dead,' William said. 'I think they'll want to come back to the abbey and start rebuilding it as soon as possible.'

'Then I will wait here for you, with the pig,' the hob said. 'Bring *plenty* of food back with you and don't be gone too long.'

'It's good to see the demon didn't dull your appetite,' William said with a grin.

'Gonegonegone,' the hob sang softly as he settled down beside the pig.

As he turned to go, William caught the last whispery snatch of the hob's song, 'Gone, all gone. . .'

Daily timetable at Crowfield Abbey

2.00 am – **vigils,** then reading/praying.

Sunrise – **lauds.**

6.00 am – **prime**, followed by High Mass.

8.00 am – **tierce**, followed by Chapter Meeting.

9.45 am – 12.00pm – work.

12.00 pm – **sext** (if monks are away from abbey, in fields, they stop and pray where they are).

1.00 pm – **nones**, followed by dinner, then into church to give thanks for food and to sing Psalm 31.

2.45 pm – work and time spent in cloister or warming house.

Dusk – **vespers** followed by reading in cloisters, then **compline,** warm drink and to bed.

Glossary of terms

Ashlar – blocks of building stone with smooth faces and straight edges.

Book of Hours – a book of prayers, psalms and holy texts, hand-written and illuminated by monks.

Caudle – a medicinal hot drink for minor ailments, made with wine or ale, thickened with breadcrumbs, egg yolks or ground almonds.

Cellarer/cellarium – the cellarer is the monk in charge of the abbey's provisions and store room, or cellarium.

Cess-pit – a pit for rubbish and/or sewage.

Chancel screen – a decorated screen of wood or stone separating the chancel from the nave of a church.

Chapter house – a room off the cloister, close to the south door of the church. The monks met here each day to discuss abbey business and listen to a reading from the Rule of St. Benedict. This room was second only in importance to the abbey church and was often elaborately decorated.

Chilblains – red, itchy swellings on the feet, hands, nose or ears, caused by the cold and damp in the winter months.

Choir – at Crowfield Abbey, this is the area between the transepts and the east end of the church. Two rows of wooden stalls, or seat, face each other across the width of the choir. The monks sit here during the daily round of services.

Cloister – four covered alleys or corridors surrounding a central garden or garth, usually situated on the south side of the abbey church. The main rooms of the abbey can be reached from the cloister.

Couvre feu (French) – This means 'cover fire'. Many medieval houses were built of wood and wattle and daub, with thatched roofs and straw or rushes on the floor. Stray sparks from the fire –often in a pit or hearth in the centre of the main room – could set fire to the house. During the day the fire could be watched, but at night, it was covered with a clay dome with holes poked through for ventilation.

Croft and toft – the toft was the yard on which a peasant's house and outbuildings were built. The croft was an adjoining plot of land used by the family to grow vegetables and fruit and keep a few goats, chickens and a pig or two.

Crossing – the intersection where the nave and transepts meet. There is often a tower above the crossing, supported on large pillars, or piers.

Cross-passage – a passageway that leads from the front to the back of a building, or from inside a cloister to outside the abbey.

Demesne farm – land owned and used by a manorial lord or the king, as opposed to land rented out to tenants.

Dorter / dormitory – the open plan room on the first floor of the east range of the buildings surrounding the cloisters, where the monks slept.

Frater – a long room where the monks ate their meals. At Crowfield Abbey, the frater is in the west range, between the kitchens and the guest quarters.

Hurdy gurdy – a stringed musical instrument. The strings pass over a wheel which is turned by a crank handle. The wheel acts very much like a violin bow, producing musical notes from the strings. When played, the hurdy gurdy sounds like a bagpipe.

Lent – in the Christian church, the forty days leading up to Easter.

Maslin bread – made from a mixture of rye and wheat flour. After a poor harvest, dried and ground peas or beans could be added to the flour.

Midden – a rubbish tip.

Mummers – mummers and guisers were street performers in towns and villages, who dressed up and wore masks and entertained people, usually around Christmas. They cavorted around the streets, singing carols and playing music and sometimes begging for money from door to door. Later on, mummers performed plays which included such characters as St. George, Beelzebub and Robin Hood.

Nave – the long, main body of the church

Pannage – the practise of allowing pigs to forage in woodland for beech-mast and acorns during from September to early November.

Parchment/vellum – thin sheets of sheep, goat or calf skin used for pages of books or manuscripts. The skin is stretched, scraped and dried to prepare it. Better quality skins are called vellum.

Pinfold/pinder – in villages and towns, any animals found straying were rounded up and kept in a pinfold. To get them back, their owners had to pay a fine to the pinder, who was appointed by the lord of the manor to care for the animals until they were claimed.

Pottage – A cross between a soup and a stew, usually made with whatever vegetables were available. In winter, dried peas were a staple ingredient. Sometimes a little meat or fish would be added. Herbs such as wild garlic, thyme, rosemary, sage and parsley would be to add flavour, and salt would be added for seasoning.

Psalms – religious songs sung or recited as part of daily worship. A book of Psalms is a Psalter.

Reeve – a villager chosen annually to supervise workers on the farm and land of the lord of the manor.

Reredorter – the latrines or toilets, situated next to the dorter.

Rushlights – a type of candle, made from rushes. The inner pith of the rush is dipped in fat, grease or beeswax. The pith then acts as the wick when the rushlight is lit.

Sacristy / sacristan – the room where the abbey's more valuable possessions are kept locked away. The sacristan is the monk in charge of the sacristy. At Crowfield Abbey, this is one of Brother Snail's duties.

Shawm – a woodwind instrument, similar to a modern oboe.

Sigils – magical symbols created to summon and control spirits.

Tallow – rendered beef or sheep fat, used as a cheap alternative to wax in candle-making.

Transepts – the shorter cross-arms of the church, between the nave and the choir.

Triforium – an arched gallery running above the nave of a church.

Two-light window – a light is a pane of glass; a two-light window consists of two panes of glass divided by stone, wood or metal uprights called mullions or muntins, set within a single window frame.

Villein – medieval tenant farmer.

Window embrasure – an opening for a window set into a thick wall, often with the sides splayed so that the opening is larger on the inside than the outside.

Acknowledgements

My heartfelt thanks go to everyone at The Chicken House, for their endless support and encouragement. In particular I want to thank Imogen Cooper and Chrissie O'Brien, my wonderful, insightful editors.

And a big thank you to John, David and Kate, and to family and friends for their unfailing generosity and support.